DAUGHTER OF THE NIGHT

A NOVEL THE FRAY

TOBY NEIGHBORS

Daughter Of The Night: A Novel of The Fray

ISBN: 978-1-952260-80-3 print

978-1-952260-78-0 eBook

Mythic Adventure Publishing, LLC

Idaho, USA

The Warrior Ethos is not, at bottom, a manifestation only of male aggression or of the masculine will to dominance. Its foundation is society-wide. It rests on the will and resolve of mothers and wives and daughters—and, in no few instances, of female warriors as well—to defend their children, their home soil and the values of their culture.

PRESSFIELD, STEVEN. *THE WARRIOR ETHOS*

CHAPTER 1

I KNEW IT WAS COMING, but nothing really prepares you to have your father sell you off.

"Ain't good for much," he said, clearly resentful that I didn't have a marketable skill that would drive up the price. "Complains a lot. Can't keep house worth a fig, and her cookin's atrocious."

"She's ripe," the hunter said coldly. "Why not lease her to a pleasure house, or sell her as a concubine?"

"I would, but she's got a temper," my father complained. "They won't have her. She needs a stern hand, that one. But she'd make good bait."

"Fifty," the hunter grunted. "And say your goodbyes now."

My father was a sloppy man. His clothes were wrinkled and stained. His fingers were black from degreasing old parts salvaged from the shipyard. His belly stuck out and his chest sunk in.

The hunter was short and thin, but well-kempt. Everything, from his clothing to the weapons his apprentice carried in a satchel made of Vanj bones and hemp, was clean and organized. There was strength in the hunter, not just muscle and bone, but strength borne from facing danger again and again without turning away.

"Even as meat she's worth twice that," my father replied. But there was no conviction in his voice, no outrage at being lowballed on the price.

"Take it or leave it," the hunter said coolly, as if he couldn't care less.

"It's a crime."

"Nobody's holding a gun to your head. She's healthy. You want to keep her, nobody'd blame you. Might even find her a husband if you tried."

For half a second, hope flared bright inside me. I thought maybe he would change his mind, perhaps he would see me for who I was and love me the way a father should. But that hope was snuffed out just as quickly as it had kindled to life. My father sagged a little and stuck out his hand.

"Give it to me," he said.

I watched the hunter count out ten silver coins and hand them to my father, who turned and walked away without a single glance in my direction. I know about pain. I know how to inflict it so that a person would kill their own mother to make it stop. But watching my father walk away scared me more than any wound, and cut deeper than the tortures I've endured since.

"Stand over there with Griff," the hunter ordered. "Don't make trouble, and you won't have any."

I moved back beside the boy holding the bag. He was a couple of years older than I was and noticeably stronger. He also had the beginnings of gray skin. I could see it creeping up his neck and peeking out of the collar of the sleeveless jacket he wore. He looked at me with yellow eyes, another symptom of the genetic disorder.

"Don't expect no free ride," he said quietly under his breath. "You do what you're told."

I nodded. I hadn't expected things to be easy. I had been sold like an old garment. My father had left me behind with a total stranger for only fifty silver Pecks. It was more coin than I had ever seen in my life, but I was only fourteen years old. Yet, despite the pain and fear, there was also a sense of relief in my mind. At least I didn't have to listen to my father rail about how worthless I was, or worse still, dodge his clumsy blows when I pushed him too far.

I stood in silence for most of the afternoon, but I wasn't the only child being sold that day. A set of twin boys, slightly younger than me and with mischief in their eyes, were taken on as apprentices. The hunter paid eighty silver Pecks for the pair, which made me feel a little better about my own value. Another girl was bought, too. She was older, a round-faced mute who had clearly come from an incestuous mating. The man who sold her was very old, and could hardly get two words out without falling into a fit of ragged coughing. He did manage to convey that she could cook and clean. The hunter had only to promise the old man he wouldn't use the girl as bait, and she joined our little group.

"That's enough for now," the hunter said. "Griff, go get camp going in the usual spot. I'm taking this lot to the slaughterhouse."

My father's admonition that I was worth more as meat came back to me. But I had a good sense about people, and the hunter seemed like a decent sort of man. He didn't look at me with lustful stares or talk down to anyone. Even the beggars he passed on the street were treated with silence rather than cursing, the way my father usually responded.

The older girl—her name was Mana—was sent with Griff, while the twins and I followed the hunter. We hadn't gone far when the twins moved in on either side of me.

"I'm Tip'un," the one on my right side said. "He's Rip'un."

"Twins," Rip said.

"I figured that out on my own," I said softly.

"True bloods," Tip said. "No genetic mods. You?"

"I don't know," I replied honestly.

It wasn't my intent to make friends with the twins, but it was no good lying about the mods, either. We were a race borne of genetic engineering. The Maston overlords had dabbled in our DNA until we all looked the same and sounded the same. Then they abandoned us on Ferret and we set out trying to advance ourselves. I don't have to tell you what kind of disaster that was. To make matters worse, Ferret was a game world. Vanj hunted down people on the surface, which was why we had long ago built underground havens. I was born and raised in Gipid, a small village inside a big cavern.

"We do," Rip said. "Gonna be hunters, me and Tip."

"Been planning it for a while now," the twin to my right said.

"'Course, not everyone can do it," Rip said. "You know what the casualty rate for apprentice hunters is?"

I shook my head. I knew there were hunters who harvested game animals up top, but that's all I knew of the dangerous profession. Going up was suicide, that's what my mother always said. The gray skin had taken her when I was just eight years old. I watched her shrivel up and die with blood seeping from every pore in her puckered skin. Like I said, I know pain well.

"Eighty, or ninety percent, depending on who you ask," Tip said. "But we'll make it."

"Yeah, we will!" Rip chimed in, high-fiving his brother right in front of me.

I had to stop to keep from getting slapped in the head. The hunter turned and gave the twins a frown, but didn't say anything. He glanced at me, then turned back around. I did my best to keep up.

Gipid was not a big village. And keeping animals was difficult underground. Most of the butchery that was done was on game animals. The slaughterhouse was where hunters sold their kills. It was a small alcove, just a big crack in the side of the cavern, really. I had never been inside before, but I had smelled the blood and rancid fat that was scraped from the animal hides.

The hunter stopped just outside the crack in the wall.

"This is what happens when you die," he said coldly.

He waved his hand, and we stepped past him. The twins stiffened at the sight of the bodies hanging from hooks that were attached to the high walls of the alcove. There was an elk already gutted, but only halfway skinned. A small pig was hung by its rear legs, and a butcher was cutting the carcass into sections. Most shocking of all was a person. It was an old woman with her head removed. There was a big hook in her back, and a butcher was removing her entrails.

"This is what we do to the dead," the hunter said. "But it's also what the Vanj do to us if they catch us."

"No," Rip said softly.

I looked at the twins. They were pale and clearly frightened. Rip had big tears welling up in his eyes. Tip was about to be sick. I was shocked by what I saw, but it didn't seem as bad to me as seeing my own mother wither and die. There was something practical and organized about seeing the carcasses neatly butchered.

The workers wore long aprons made of animal skins that were spattered with blood and nothing else. Their hands and small, sharp knives made quick work of the carcasses, including the old woman.

"I'm gonna..." Tip groaned.

"Outside," the hunter snarled.

Both twins ran out. I heard them heaving and for a moment I felt my own stomach cramp. It was hard to stay and watch, but it wasn't the first time I had seen death up close. And even though the smell in the slaughterhouse was pungent, it wasn't as sickening as the smell of disease.

"You okay?" the hunter asked me.

I shrugged my shoulders and looked up at him.

"Hang on to that resiliency," he said in a voice that wasn't unkind. The hunter was a gruff man of few words, but that day he spoke encouragingly to a young girl who had lost everything. "It will serve you well all your life."

He turned and left the slaughterhouse. I followed him.

†††

The first night was the hardest. We made camp inside a little grotto about half an hour's walk from the village inside the main cavern. It was the first time I had been on the surface. We left at sunset, but even that seemed incredibly bright to me. For a while, I stood at the mouth of the cave system looking out across the grassy valley. There were low hills in the distance with trees. The air was soft, warm, and clean. I had never in my life smelled air that wasn't dank and tainted with mold spores. There were plenty of dangers on the surface of Ferret, but it was the open spaces that scared me most. As the sky turned dark purple and stars appeared, I felt like I would go spinning off into them at any moment.

"Keep up," the hunter told us.

The twins were still in shock from the slaughterhouse, and all their bravado was swept away when we reached the surface. They looked very young indeed, and while they didn't wrap their arms around one another, they stood shoulder to shoulder. We were all dealing with the changes. The hunter didn't seem to notice, or maybe he just didn't care that we were all stupefied. He led us along the base of the mountain until we reached the grotto.

I smelled it before I could see it. Smoke from something other than dried dung, and meat roasting over the flames. I smelled the sweet aroma of fat dripping into the flames, and it made my stomach growl. I could count on one hand the number of times I had eaten fresh meat. We lived on dried jerky, mushrooms, and whatever foraged vegetables my father could trade for. It wasn't much, and we rarely had enough. But as a child, I had no concept of anything different.

The grotto was a fine place to make camp. It was concealed by low bushes and only big enough for a few adults, but the hunter was the only grown-up among us. And he wasn't very big. That night we ate roasted jackrabbits that had been caught in the hunter's snares not far from the grotto. Griff had collected them just before sunset. By the time we arrived at the cave, they were turning on spits over a pit fire dug deep enough to hide the flames.

"We keep it dark," the older boy explained. "Can't do nothin' that attracts attention on the surface."

"Won't the animals come and eat us?" I asked.

He shook his head. "There are animals that will attack a human, but most of 'em are more scared of us than we are of them.

They stay away. But light attracts the Vanj, sure enough. They ain't got noses, though. They can't smell us or the smoke. We'll be safe enough in the grotto."

He gave each of us a pelt that was big enough to sleep in. Mine was pure white, a mountain ram's coat. It was worth more coin in Gipid than the hunter had paid for me. The leather side was soft, the fur clean. That night we ate roasted rabbit with wild potatoes and onions mixed into a stew. Griff had also collected a basket full of watercress greens and had a stash of blueberries. It was the best meal I had ever eaten, and there was enough for everyone to eat a full portion, too. I was in awe at the richness of the meal, but soon after, as I lay with my back to the wall of the grotto looking up at the stars in the distant sky, I realized that we could eat so well because we were risking so much. My father would never have allowed me to indulge in such rich fare. He would have said it was wasted on me and would have sold it instead. But money didn't mean much to someone who risked their life to provide the village with food. I knew there were other subterranean colonies and that hunters often provided for several different settlements. They also carried messages and sometimes even trade goods. But as I lay staring up at the stars, all I could really think of was dying all alone in the wide open spaces. If someone had given me a choice to go back into Gipid that night, even as a slave in a pleasure house, I would have gone. That first night I missed my mother so much I couldn't hold back tears. Staying quiet wasn't easy, but I managed it. And I was thankful that the darkness hid me.

Between the grief of being sold to a stranger and being terrified that a bear or wildcat would attack us in the dark, I didn't get much sleep, despite the fact that I was more comfortable and well-fed than at any other time in my short life. The floor of the grotto was lined with fresh-cut spruce boughs, and the ram fur was luxurious. Still, I couldn't help but wonder how many other girls had wrapped up in the fur before they were sacrificed so the hunters could get a kill.

The next morning, we rose early. Griff showed the mute girl how to check the snares, while the hunter made me and the twins exercise. We did pushups and sit-ups until my body ached, but it pushed the fear and grief out of my mind. The twins were not so cocky in the bright light of day. I was grateful to have been roused early enough that the light increased gradually. Still, we were in no shape to do much outside the grotto.

Griff returned with a bundle of thistle grass that was as long as my leg from hip to heel. He showed us how to strip off the layers and twist them into cordage. It was simple work. I sat on my ram hide and created a long strand from the twisted grass, which Griff then braided into a thicker cord.

"You can snare all sorts of animals with this," he proclaimed, holding it up and demonstrating how the snare worked with his hand. "A critter goes through and the snare tightens. It's in their nature to tug against it, which only makes it tighter. Most animals break their own neck trying to get out."

Tip was looking hard at Griff. The older boy's gray skin was more noticeable in the light of day. It was all along his neck and on both of his hands.

"You know you've got the flake?" Tip told him.

Griff erupted in a fury that neither Tip nor Rip expected. He grabbed Tip's shirt and jerked him close.

"Shut your mouth," he snarled, before shoving the smaller boy to the ground.

"Hey!" Rip shouted. "Lay off him."

Griff backhanded Rip so hard that he spun around and hit his head on the roof of the grotto where it sloped down toward the ground. The twin dropped to his knees and started bawling.

"And keep it down, you buffoon!" Griff said. "Put a stopper in it, or I'll shut you up permanently."

"Don't worry," Tip'un said to his weeping brother. "He'll be dead soon."

"Don't count on it," Griff said savagely. "I suspect I'll outlive either of you."

For the next three days we made cordage and feasted on rabbit, grouse, and other small animals. Griff showed the mute girl how to skin the animals. If she had a name, we didn't know it and she couldn't tell us. Griff called her Til'da. On the second night, they started sleeping together. There wasn't much privacy, and Griff's disease, what most people called gray skin but what some called the flake, was too advanced for him to be intimate with her. But Til'da didn't seem to mind Griff holding onto her through the night. At least she didn't resist.

Every day the hunter left after making us do our exercises. He rarely returned before dark. On the third evening, he came back with a deer. Its organs had already been removed. That night we ate venison heart and tongue. The rest of the meat was taken back to Gipid and sold.

The following morning, after our usual round of exercises, we were told to pack up.

"Where are we going?" I asked Griff.

"Ain't much big game 'round here," he said. "Probably trek out to the hill country."

That meant nothing to me, and yet I felt better knowing it. We wrapped the grass cordage we had made around a stick that had been cut for that purpose. It had two prongs on each end. I wrapped my braided cord around it and guessed I had about a hundred paces worth of twine. I also had a shorter cord, which I used to tie up my ram hide after I had the skin rolled tight.

We walked all day. By nightfall, we were well into the hill country. We ate apples from a tree we passed in the afternoon and made camp near a river. There was no fire that night, and we all took turns staying awake. I was keeping watch in the dark an hour before sunrise when I saw my first spaceship. It was too far away to make out the details, but I saw the lights on the sides blinking as it descended toward a distant hill. I woke the hunter, who stayed awake and watched it land. Then he rolled back up in his bearskin robe and went back to sleep.

Over the next few weeks, I learned to hunt and trap game. It wasn't easy. Our weapons were primitive on Ferret. Maybe we could have had guns of some sort, but firearms make noise that draws unwanted attention. Instead, we used simple weapons like throwing sticks and stone slings. Every day was busy from sunlight to darkness, but the work was fun. I enjoyed learning to tie snares and set them. After a few days of watching Griff, I was permitted to set my own snares. I can still remember the thrill of catching my first rabbit. I learned to make fish traps too, weaving bull rushes into funnels that river trout swam into and couldn't find their way out.

The twins didn't have the patience to tie snares. They thought that kind of hunting was beneath them and wanted to go with the hunter after big game. They were pretty good with throwing sticks, but the only success they had hunting was a sick rabbit that was so full of parasites it couldn't be eaten. They weren't quiet enough to get close to anything, and they had to get within a dozen paces to be effective with their throwing sticks. Worse yet, they didn't have the patience to close the distance. Most of the time they threw their weapons at something as soon as they saw it. I learned a lot by watching them fail. At the end of the third week, it was pretty clear that I was much more suited to the life of a hunter than either of the twins.

"Tomorrow, I'm taking Tip and Azree'el with me," the hunter told Griff. "You keep Rip here."

Griff nodded. I couldn't keep the smile off my face, but Tip wasn't as thrilled. The truth was that the twins were still frightened on the surface of the world. And they didn't like being separated from one another. But I wasn't thinking about them; I was looking forward to the hunt. I had discovered a genuine satisfaction from being able to provide, and I enjoyed stalking prey. I had hunted small land animals and taken down a variety of game birds. The hunter had even allowed me to use his spear stick. It was a simple rod with a small nodule on the end that fit neatly into the butt of a lightweight, flexible javelin. It was nearly as tall as I was, with feathers at the rear and a cross-shaped, metal arrowhead. After an hour's practice, I became quite proficient with it. The spear stick gave me a much greater range than a throwing stick, and it increased my accuracy, too. I had spent several fun-filled days alone stalking game. Twice I had seen larger animals, a small group of deer with slender faces and one bull elk, though it had been nearly a hundred meters away. It came out of a copse of trees and stopped on the hilltop, where it turned its head full of majestic antlers and looked at me before continuing on its way.

The night before my expedition with the hunter, I could hardly sleep. We were camped near a spring under the shade of a huge oak tree. It was possible to climb the tree if necessary to escape a predator's reach, but it wasn't much protection. Still, I had come to love the sense of freedom in my new life. The thought of going back to the dark, gloomy cave dwellings didn't interest me at all. I wanted to be free and enjoy what the surface world had to offer, but I still didn't really comprehend the danger that cast its long shadow over us.

We left camp at dawn and walked for nearly two hours before arriving at the edge of a long, flat plain. The hills were behind us, and beyond them the mountains that hid the people of Ferret. But it wasn't the plain that caught my attention. It was the starship.

"What is that?" Tip'un asked.

"That's a star boat," the hunter replied in a coarse whisper. "That's what the Vanj travel in."

"Why's it just sitting there?" Tip asked, his voice trembling slightly.

"Why do you think?" the hunter replied.

Tip had no answer, but it was obvious to me. "It's bait to draw us out," I said.

The hunter nodded, his eyes still on the ship.

"The Vanj are lazy hunters. There's one out there on the plain just waiting for us. It's probably watching us right now."

"We should leave," Tip said, his voice breaking into a squeak.

"That's what we're here for," the hunter explained in a patient whisper. "That ship has tech on it that we need. Water filters, power generators, right down to the wiring connecting everything. It's worth more than your entire village ten times over."

"But the Vanj..."

The hunter nodded. "The Vanj indeed, boy. If we want the ship, then we have to kill the alien who flew it down here."

"Impossible," Tip said.

"No, it isn't," I replied.

"But you can't even see it," Tip argued. "How can you kill something you can't see?"

"They're invisible when they're still. They can blend right in and you'll never see 'em," the hunter explained. "But when they move..."

Movement was the enemy of concealment. Even in camouflage that is so good a figure is invisible, it can't mask movement. It was the same with the Vanj. They could hide themselves, but they couldn't conceal their movements. It made the air around them almost ripple. It was like looking at a reflection in water, only to have the image distorted by the movement of the liquid.

"H- how do we do it?" Tip asked.

"With these," the hunter said. He had been carrying a pair of stout-looking spears. They were on well-shaped dowels of sturdy wood. The head was all metal, about as long as the hunter's hand. Both sides of the thin, metal blade were sharpened. And small barbs curled back at the edges of the triangular spearhead.

"They've got armor," Tip said. "Their skin is impenetrable."

"It's plenty tough, but not unbreakable," the hunter whispered. "And you can find a gap with these."

"Run it in hard," I said. "Fast and deep."

Another nod of agreement. The hunter was staring at me, not just glancing over because I said something. And not simply agreeing, either. He was staring hard, studying me.

"What makes it move?" Tip asked.

That was the big question, and my father's words came back to me in a rush as I returned the hunter's stare: *She'd make good bait.*

"Bait?" I tried to say, but my voice betrayed me.

Still, the hunter read my lips and gave a curt nod. When he

spoke, his voice was stern. He wasn't angry at me, he was conveying how dangerous the task was, and how important.

"Azree'el goes out first. She goes alone," the hunter said. "Tip and I spot the Vanj and kill it."

I had some problems with that plan, but I knew arguing wouldn't change the hunter's mind. And I had illusions that Tip'un would be useful in killing the alien. That's when it crossed my mind that there might be more than one.

"If we can't see them, how do we know there's just one out there?" I asked.

"That's a single-person ship," the hunter said. "The Vanj consider killing us a rite of passage."

"A what?" Tip asked.

"Sort of a way to prove their valor."

"They show off by murdering people?" Tip asked with undisguised shock.

The hunter nodded and looked back toward the ship. "More than the meat and the forage we provide the villages, that ship is what keeps us alive."

"But the Vanj are monsters," Tip said. "What if we can't kill it?"

"Then it kills us, or worse."

"Worse?" Tip asked.

The hunter just nodded but didn't bother explaining. I think he wanted us to fear the alien. He certainly wanted us to understand how serious the situation was.

"Azree'el, go straight for the ship. Don't run, no matter what you hear."

"Okay," I said, half numb from fear.

I couldn't even argue at that point. For the first time in my life,

I was actually happy. I didn't feel loved by my companions, but my father never loved me, either. And the hunter didn't hit me, or rage until I was left quaking in a corner. Griff was careful not to get too friendly with me, probably because he knew I would be killed. And Til'da wasn't capable of bonding with anyone. The twins were simultaneously arrogant and jealous. They were all talk and yet never really accomplished much. Their grass cordage was of poor quality, their trap lines unsuccessful, and their hunts a disappointment. They thought of themselves as being above me and yet they were jealous of what I could do that they couldn't.

But unlike many people, I didn't need companionship. I didn't need to be respected or loved. All I ever really wanted was the freedom that I had found on the surface of Ferret. To be alone and to feel capable was empowering to me in a way that nothing else was. I didn't want to lose it. I didn't want to give up the new life I had discovered, but I didn't have a choice in the matter, either. The hunter had weapons and knew how to use them. Killing was his profession, and he wouldn't hesitate to cut my throat or beat me senseless if I refused. And, if I was honest, the truth was I didn't want him to think of me as a coward.

"Just walk toward the ship," I said. "Fast or slow?"

There was light in his eyes when he looked at me. I like to think it was recognition, perhaps even admiration. I don't know for sure, but I liked what I saw.

"Slow at first. Keep it steady as long as you can."

I nodded, hoping that he meant I should walk at the same speed until I was too frightened not to speed up, rather than becoming incapable of walking at all because the alien had killed me.

"Don't miss," I told him just before I got to my feet.

The hunter and Tip weren't exactly hiding. They were stretched out on a low mound. Maybe they blended into the bushes and surrounding hills. I had no idea how good the alien's eyesight was. Or if the tech that made it invisible impaired its vision at all. But I didn't look back as I got to my feet and started walking. The last thing I wanted was to draw attention to the two people who were supposed to kill the thing that was going to try to kill me.

The only weapon I had was a short flake of stone. I had seen people in Gipid use them like tools. Mine wouldn't be good in a fight. It was really only useful to cut cordage or do a little whittling on dry sticks. But I took it out of my pocket anyway and held it tight. Just having a weapon in hand, no matter how feeble it was, made me feel better.

My legs felt weak as I walked down the hill. I felt more alone and exposed than I ever had in my entire life. It took all my willpower not to look around for the alien. The hunter had said it was there, and I believed him. Instead, I focused on the ship. My skin tingled as if the monster was right behind me. Maybe it was the bright sunlight shining on me, but I just couldn't believe that I might die on such a brilliant, beautiful day.

But it didn't take long before I heard something moving. I was halfway to the starship. It seemed unreal all by itself. Sure, I knew we had come from the stars. The Maston had stolen our genetic code, but no one knew where we came from. They called us Heterrids. They mixed and mingled our DNA, always selecting the best physical and mental attributes until our entire race collapsed like a failed experiment. Left on Ferret, we had fought to survive the Vanj, but that was only the beginning of our troubles. Forced underground, the gray skin affliction set in, killing over half our numbers. Those who survived interbred, but our DNA was so similar that most babies died in utero, and many of those who survived had defects. Til'da, moon-faced, mute, and simple-minded, was a prime example. It wasn't her fault, or even her parents' fault. They were just people, doing what people did. The Mastons were the real culprits, tinkering with our genetics and then leaving us stranded in a dangerous world, as if we had no inherent value as a species at all.

The starship represented all that, and while my knowledge of such things was limited, I was both awed and disgusted by the spaceship at the same time. I hadn't even seen stars until I was sold to the hunter, much less imagined that I might one day travel from system to system. Yet, the means for such travel was right in front of me as I walked across the grassy plain.

Behind me, something was shuffling through the grass. My hearing was keen. I could make out the sound of the long blades of grass brushing across a rough exterior. The sounds came from behind and to my right. Without even realizing it, I sped up my walk. Terror was setting in, and I could hear my heart pounding as the blood rushed through my ears. My breathing came in short little puffs. I was nearly to the vessel when a shadow loomed over me.

I can tell you what the hunter did because I survived that hunt, and afterward saw him do it, and even helped him do it. The alien couldn't be seen at first. But when it moved, the creature's camouflage created a refraction of light, like the waver over an open flame. And of course, the grass, which was nearly knee-high, bent under the alien's weight.

The hunter watched for that movement. Once he spotted it, he leaped into action. To his credit, Tip followed the hunter. They both ran toward us, their spears held ready. The alien was almost on top of me. Had it simply attacked me, it could have killed me in the time it took the hunter to intervene, but the Vanj prefer to stalk their prey. They love the thrill of moving in close before they kill.

The alien had come around behind me and was sneaking closer and closer. It was so fixated on me that it didn't take notice of the hunter or Tip until they were almost on top of it. Then it whirled around, disabling its cloaking technology. The creature was twice as tall as I was, with a curved back and massive head. Its arms and legs were skeletal, its skin dark and thick.

The hunter pulled to a stop just a few paces from the alien and held his spear out in a threatening gesture. Tip did the same, only he got a little too close. The alien swiped at the hunter. Its hand was shaped more like an eagle's talon, with long, curved claws. The hunter stepped back, avoiding the blow, but Tip was too close. He valiantly tried to stab the monstrous creature. His spear blade hit the alien's body but didn't penetrate. Looking back, I doubt Tip was strong enough to have any real chance of damaging the creature. If I was bait, Tip was a distraction that allowed the hunter to move in for the kill. It may sound cruel and heartless to you, but that was the way my people had survived on Ferret. It was the hunter who was valuable, not the children he had bought. The people in the underground caverns depended on hunters to bring in food and gear. They were celebrated and rewarded for their work, but their apprentices didn't fare so well. Everyone knew it and accepted it. Children were a drain on scant resources. The loss of one was rarely seen as a tragedy.

The alien's swiping attack missed the hunter, who had anticipated it. It didn't miss Tip, though. The spear hit the alien, bounced off, and left Tip exposed. The claws, three of them, sank deep. One tore a bloody gash across his cheek. Another carved a rivulet along his collarbone. But it was the third claw that did him in; it sank into his neck and tore open his throat and ripped his jugular vein. He couldn't even scream in agony or fear. Blood fountained into the air as the young boy fell to his knees. I saw the terror in his eyes, but he died quickly. It was the only merciful thing about his death.

I had turned, seen the alien, and seen Tip's death in the span of a single breath. Just a few seconds of mind-numbing terror, and I was completely paralyzed with fear. Fortunately, the hunter knew how to attack the alien and exactly what its weaknesses were. He charged in and rammed his spear up under its wide, arching skull plate. Then it was the alien's turn to feel fear and pain. It screeched, the sound was loud enough to hurt my ears and so strange it made my blood run cold. I staggered backward as the hunter released his spear and jumped away from the alien, who suddenly twisted around in a thrashing manner. The hunter circled wide, recovered Tip's spear, and when the alien's back was turned, struck again.

The Vanj are big creatures. Their bodies exude a caustic, transparent liquid. It's so viscous, I've heard people call it slime. It's more like engine grease that allows their hard exoskeletal sections to rub without abrading. All their vital organs are held in a fleshy sack at the back of their heads, which is covered with a thick, curving plate that hangs halfway down their back. The body is all dense muscle, bone, and tendons. They're almost like strange stick figures. The only way to bring them down is to get in under the head plate, which is more like a helmet of bone. The hunter rammed the second spear up under the alien's skull plate and dodged away again. I had never seen him move so quickly.

By that point, the damage was done.

"Stay back!" the hunter shouted at me.

It was a pointless command. I wasn't going anywhere near the alien and had already begun moving to the side so that I wouldn't get caught between it and the ship. The spacecraft was clearly the alien's destination after being mortally wounded. Perhaps it hoped that it could escape and survive somehow, or maybe it knew it was dying and didn't want us to get the ship. It staggered toward the craft, reaching out with a long arm. Its talons were flexing on the end of delicate-looking fingers, and I sensed that the alien was trying to reach the controls that opened the ship. Only before it could reach the vessel, its legs gave out and it fell face down onto the ground.

The hunter rushed forward, grabbed one of the spears, and shoved it in again. The alien began to shake hard, its arms and legs drumming on the ground. The hunter twisted the spear, pulled it back, and shoved it in again with a grunt of effort.

The alien's death seemed sudden. It went limp, and the hunter stepped back, breathing hard. I was panting, too, as if I had run hard for several minutes. Then I looked over at Tip'un, but he was already dead.

"He's gone," the hunter said. "We need to work fast before another one of those nasty beasts shows up to finish what this one started."

"You killed it," I managed to say.

The hunter nodded. "We killed it. The three of us."

It was a shocking statement, partly because I had never been included in an adult's work, much less credited with anything. I had been successful hunting and trapping small game, of which there was an abundance on Ferret. But that only served to feed our group and contributed very little to the overall welfare of either the hunter or our people.

The hunter walked over and pulled out the spears. Then he turned and looked at the ship. He didn't look happy.

"What?" I asked.

"I was counting on the alien to open it up," he said.

I turned and examined the ship's hatch. It was thick metal with a tiny seam. The controls the alien had been reaching for were well over my ability to reach.

"Can you lift me up?" I asked.

The hunter gave me a strange look, then walked over to the ship and cupped his hands together. I put my hand on his shoulder and stepped into his hand. He lifted me, grunting a little as he pushed my feet up.

"Stand on my shoulders," he said.

I was holding onto the spaceship to steady myself and stepped onto his shoulders. He put his hands around my ankles, and I could just reach the controls. It was a recessed dial with three holes that were too wide for me. I had to use both hands, grunting with the effort, but the dial turned and the hatch popped open with a hiss. Hot, humid air shot out, and the hatch lowered from the top down, forming a ramp.

"Ha!" the hunter shouted. "You did it!"

He lowered me carefully and then put his hand on my shoulder. He was only slightly taller than I was.

"You're something, girl. Your father was a damned fool."

I tried not to cry, but I couldn't stop the flood of emotions that poured through me. It was the first time anyone had ever spoken such powerful affirmation into my life.

"You've got spunk, and you're smart," he continued. "You stick with me and I'll make a damn fine hunter out of you."

"Yes," I said. It was all I could get out, to be honest. My chin was trembling, and my vision was blurry from tears. I could feel them cutting a swath through the dirt on my face. But that one word, *Yes,* was also a proclamation. I accepted his praise and his offer all at once. I let the affirmation sink into my heart and take root.

"Call me Elaa'zar," he said. "Let's see what we can carry out of here."

I honestly don't remember what we salvaged from the alien's ship. Everything was wondrously new to me. The ship wasn't very big. It was a shuttle, not an interstellar ship, but it was loaded with gear. We took everything we could carry, tucking small things into our clothing, slinging items onto our backs, and filling up a large crate that we had to both take hold of to carry. Then we fled the ship. There were lights blinking inside, and chirping noises were sounding from the strange vessel's controls. Back then I didn't know what any of it was, or what it meant. But the ship had detected us. The security system marked us as intruders and sent an automatic warning that was picked up by other Vanj vessels. We were a few kilometers away when the sound of an approaching ship was heard.

"Quick, get down," Elaa'zar ordered.

There wasn't much cover, but the grass was tall, and there were shrubs between the rolling hills. Elaa'zar cut some of the branches off the shrubs with the sharp knife he carried and tossed them onto the crate of gear while I crawled under a bush with thick leaves. I didn't see the vessel, but I heard it pass. We stayed put until just before dark, then set out again for our little camp.

When we reached it, Rip'un was frantic. "Where's Tip?" he asked.

"Didn't make it," the hunter replied.

"What? What are you saying?"

"He's dead," Griff replied. He wasn't taunting, but there was no compassion in his statement.

"No, no, no, no," Rip said, before bursting into tears.

The hunter and Griff ignored him. I felt awkward and guilty. I had been the bait, yet it was Tip who had been killed. It was surprising to me how bad I felt that he died and I survived. Yet there was elation, too.

Griff and Elaa'zar went through the goods we had taken from the ship. And the next morning when we went back, the ship was gone, as was Tip's body. So, we settled for harvesting the Vanj's bones. Elaa'zar showed me how to slice through the joints, and we carried the parts back to our camp, which was in a thick grove of trees. It was a camp Elaa'zar had used before, with a deep pit already dug out and lined with stones. Once night fell, we kindled a fire and boiled the alien's bones inside the Vanj's own skull, which was by far the largest part of the creature.

Once the tight, leathery skin and viscous fluids were boiled away, Griff set to work creating utensils and tools out of the bones. I had used an old knife that had been sharpened so many times, the short blade wasn't even as wide as my pinky. When I tried to give it back, the hunter surprised me.

"You keep it," Elaa'zar said. "You earned it."

That got me a nasty look from Griff, who didn't like the idea of anyone other than him being in the hunter's good graces. But the truth was, his cough was getting worse, and the streaks of gray skin were climbing up his face.

Rip'un was inconsolable. He lay curled up, weeping. We all did our best to ignore him, but the boy's cries wore on my nerves. It took all my mental fortitude to not give in to the despair I felt. My elation was teetering on the edge of stark terror. I knew that sooner or later we would hunt the hunters again, and the next time I might not be so lucky.

The following day we took our haul to the nearest settlement, an underground city called Mynar Tep'ee. I went down into the darkness with Elaa'zar, and the excursion helped to divert my mind from the terror and guilt I felt. But it was depressing down in the dark, gloomy caverns. We traded all the goods we had harvested from the alien ship, and some of the creature's bones, too. Elaa'zar got silver coins, a whole bag of them, and I got good clothing that a tanner had fashioned out of animal hides. We also picked up another boy. He was big-boned, but painfully thin, with one eye that seemed untethered. It drifted around, sometimes even rolling back into his head so that only the white part showed. His name was Kurse, and there was nothing good about him.

The next day we set out from Mynar Tep'ee and began the hunting process all over again. That was my life, and it was good. Long, warm days spent in the sunshine. We worked our way down the mountain range. Elaa'zar began to teach me to shoot a bow, which was what he used to bring down big game animals. Kurse was given charge of the heavy bone-bag as Griff grew weaker. Tip'un never quite recovered from the loss of his brother. He rarely spoke and had none of the arrogant energy or flamboyance he had shown before. It was difficult even getting him to eat at times.

A week after the alien hunt, Griff said his goodbyes and set out on his own with only a stone knife. It wasn't enough to protect him, or even to use as a tool. The only use it had was to open his veins, which was a sad prospect, but better than letting his disease eat away at him. I remembered my mother's open sores, the way the gray patches of skin just sloughed off, and her screams when the disease ate into her body. Griff wasn't a friendly person—at times he could seem cruel—but I still felt sorry for him as he left our little camp and set out on his final trek into the wild.

That same night Kurse tried to worm his way into my bed. I slept, as I had from the first day Elaa'zar purchased me, in the ram's hide. It was big enough that it wrapped around my body and offered both warmth and comfort at night. We were camped in a very narrow valley between two towering mountains, and there was no need to keep a night watch. Clouds covered the moon and stars, so it was pitch black when Kurse started fumbling with my furs.

"What are you doing?" I asked in a whisper.

"Quiet," he hissed.

His hands were frantic, and the horror of what he intended to do was obvious. But I still had the thin, steel-bladed knife that Elaa'zar had given me.

"Stop!" I said, no longer trying to be quiet.

"Shhhh," he hissed.

His hand came up to cover my mouth but found the razor edge of the thin knife instead. It laid open his hand, cutting across his fingers and down into the meat of his palm. I felt the hot blood spatter on my face as he jumped back, suddenly cursing so loud everyone woke up.

"What the hell is going on?" Elaa'zar demanded.

"She...she *cut* me!"

"Why aren't you sleeping?" the hunter asked.

It was an open question. If Kurse had half a brain he would have kept his mouth shut. Instead, he trotted out an obvious lie.

"She was having a nightmare," he sputtered. "I was trying to help."

"Don't be a fool," the hunter said. "Stay in your place."

"She cut my hand!" he said in outrage.

"Be glad it wasn't your bloody throat," Elaa'zar snarled. "Wrap it and shut your hole. We're trying to sleep here."

I reached up and wiped the blood from my face. I knew it was smearing and would leave a stain on the beautiful ram skin. Yet it felt like a badge of honor. Kurse wouldn't come after me again if he knew what was good for him. And he wouldn't forget it whenever he saw my blood-stained fur.

It only took Kurse a few days to switch his attention from me to Til'da. It was impossible to know what she thought, or if she had any intelligent thoughts in her mind regarding Kurse. Griff had taught her to skin the small game we caught. She was skillful with her hands. He had given her his small stash of tools before going off on his own to die. Til'da was smart enough to learn her tasks. Each day she gathered wood, washed whatever needed it, and got their fire started once the sky was dark enough to hide the smoke. She was even strong enough to dig the pit if we camped somewhere without one. Every night she tended to the food we gathered, be it animals or wild greens and roots. But despite her skills and work ethic, it was clear she was simple-minded. In many ways, I could appreciate that she understood her role in the group and was happy to be able to contribute. Perhaps that was why I took such offense when I saw Kurse eyeing her like a piece of meat.

"He'll go after her," I told Elaa'zar.

He grunted but didn't otherwise respond. We were field

dressing a young goat we had harvested. It hung from the branch of a tree by its forepaws. Elaa'zar was dressing it with speed earned from experience.

"Don't tell me you're okay with that," I said. "She isn't smart enough to give consent."

"What does that matter?" the hunter said with a sigh, turning to me. "This is a hard world, Azree'el. A man takes comfort wherever he can find it."

"And what about Til'da? It won't be comfort to her."

"We need him. He's strong."

"Rip will be strong enough to carry the bag of bones."

"Will be, but he ain't yet. Might never be. Losing his brother has changed him."

"If you don't do something, I will."

He looked at me with his keen eyes and for a moment didn't say anything at all. Then he nodded. "You do what you have to, but keep in mind that if you kill Kurse, you'll be left carrying the bag."

I pondered his words, and that night I slept close to Til'da. Kurse noticed where I laid down and didn't try anything that night. But the next day, while Elaa'zar and I were away hunting, Kurse made his move.

I can't say exactly what happened, only that when I got back from checking my traps early in the afternoon, Rip was dead and Kurse was missing. Til'da's clothing was torn and dirty. She had Rip's blood all over her. She was still holding him when I got to the camp. There were tears on her face, too, and I didn't think they were just for Rip'un.

"What happened?" I asked, knowing she couldn't answer.

The answer seemed obvious, though. The Vanj bone-bag was

missing, although half of its contents were emptied out on the ground. Elaa'zar had been teaching me to track game and read trail signs. It didn't take much effort to see where Kurse had stomped off into the wilderness with our belongings. I wanted to go after him, but I needed to wait for Elaa'zar first.

That evening when the hunter returned, I told him my version of the events. He wasn't happy.

"We're going after him, right?"

"Can't let someone take your property," he said in a quiet voice. "First light."

"Yeah, okay," I said, wishing we could have tracked him through the dark. There was a good chance something else would kill Kurse, and I wanted it to be me.

That evening was the first time that Til'da didn't gather wood, start a fire, or cook our dinner. I had already moved Rip'un's body out of camp nearly a full kilometer so that now scavenger animals would be drawn to where we were sleeping. In the villages underground every resource had to be used, including the dead. But on the surface, we didn't eat our own. Rip'un was left to feed the animals that we would hunt, although mostly we harvested herbivores rather than scavenger animals. I felt bad for the twins, but my survivor's guilt was spent. I was learning the way of the world, the give and the take. All living creatures were either predators or prey, and none were exempt. Even the large apex predators were susceptible to others when they were young. If they were lucky enough to survive the first few years, they had less to worry about, but eventually, even they would become prey again as they got older and slower and food was harder to come by.

Til'da cried off and on. She sat wrapped in her furs. Silent sobs made her shoulders shake. All I could do was put an arm around her and assure her that Kurse wouldn't ever hurt her again. Every once in a while Elaa'zar glanced over at her with a shamed expression on his face, but he didn't speak. The next morning, I promised Til'da we would come back, then left her there in the remains of our camp to hunt down the traitor who had betrayed us.

It was early afternoon when we caught up to him. Kurse was in no hurry. We found him beside a stream, eating the last of the smoked meat we had stored up for when game was hard to come by.

"He had it coming," Kurse said when we were close enough to hear him. "The little bastard attacked me."

"Or maybe he tried to stop you from putting your hands on Til'da," I said.

He ignored me and looked at Elaa'zar. "So what? You here to kill me now? I ain't done nothing wrong and you know it."

"Murder ain't—" I started in, but Elaa'zar cut me off. He raised his hand and I fell silent.

"Knew you'd be mad, so I got some distance," Kurse went on. "Had to give you some time to cool down. Ain't no sense in us killing each other over a stupid kid."

"That why you stole our gear?" the hunter asked.

"Didn't steal it," Kurse replied. "I just took what I needed to get through the night till you found me. I can carry the bag and keep camp. We both know I can do it. I'm strong as you are. That's why you paid for me, remember? You need me. I'm sorry about the kid, but he didn't know his place. You need to slap me around a little to make yourself feel better, then have at it."

"Be more than a beatdown," Elaa'zar said.

Kurse made a frown, but he didn't seem surprised. He stood

up and brushed his hands on his filthy pants. "If that's the way you want it."

Elaa'zar hadn't moved. He stood stock-still beside me while Kurse pulled the long blade we used for butchering big animals out of the back of his pants.

"Well? What'cha waitin' for?" he asked, waving the knife in a beaconing fashion. "Come on and get what you've got coming. I've had about enough of being bossed around by the scrawny likes of you."

I'll admit I didn't see Elaa'zar move. He made a small motion with one hand, otherwise he was perfectly still. But a knife suddenly thumped into Kurse's chest. It was a well-shaped, double-edged blade with no guard and no attached handle, just the metal tang. It didn't kill Kurse, but he screamed and stumbled backward until he tripped over the boulder he had been sitting on.

"Know you want to finish it," Elaa'zar said. "But you better watch him. He ain't helpless."

I walked forward, my heart beating fast. I had killed animals plenty of times. The first few had been difficult, but it got easier with practice. By the time I reached the boulder where Kurse lay with one leg still up on the big stone, he had tears in his eyes and was begging for his life.

"Please...please," he gasped. "I'm sorry, OK? I didn't mean to do it. You have to believe me. I don't want to die. I don't..."

Keeping my mentor's warning in mind, I stepped on Kurse's right arm, pinning it to the ground. Then I bent over quickly and pulled the knife out of his chest. It had pierced his pectoral muscle and lodged between two of his ribs. When I pulled it free the motion pulled him up off the ground a little, and he used his momentum to roll into my legs. I staggered sideways, and he scrambled in an effort to get away from me. He was crawling on his hands and knees. I regained my balance and kicked him hard in the ribs. He grunted in pain but kept moving toward the stream. There were some stones there big enough to do some damage if he reached them. I kicked again, lashing out with my foot against his left arm. It flew out from under him, and his wounded chest wasn't strong enough to hold him up with just one hand. His face went down into the mud beside the stream bed, and I dove on top of him.

My knees landed in the middle of his back with all my weight. I was tall and had become thin after weeks of hunting. My muscles had hardened, but I was still half his size. But that was enough to knock the wind from his lungs. He wheezed, spitting mud, and lifted his head to try to catch a breath. I snatched a handful of his greasy hair and pulled his head even farther back. Then I bent down and whispered in his ear, "This is for what you did to Til'da, you pig."

"No!" he managed to say before I slashed the throwing knife across his throat.

It was honed to a razor's edge and cut the soft flesh easily, ripping through veins, tendons, and his windpipe. I released his hair and stood up as tears flooded my eyes. Kurse grunted and gurgled. His death took only a few seconds, and I was left wishing it had taken longer.

"You done?" Elaa'zar asked.

"He is," I said. "Bastard got off easy."

"Maybe, maybe not," he replied. "Gather the bag. Better get used to carrying it."

I picked up the bag of bones. It was constructed of three alien skulls. Elaa'zar had drilled holes in the hard edges of the skull and laced them together with twine made from twisted grass braids. I looked inside and saw that it was lined with some type of leather sack. Inside were more blades, a few furs, and a bag of coins that was larger than both of my hands put together. The sack that had held strips of smoked meat was empty. I took out the water skin, emptied it on the ground, and filled it from the stream. Then I took a long pull and handed it to Elaa'zar. He took a drink, too. I looked back at Kurse. He was still wearing his filthy clothes. After wiping his blood from the throwing knife, I picked up the big butcher blade and put it in the bag.

"We should go," I said.

Elaa'zar handed me the water skin, and I handed him the throwing knife. He nodded and led the way back. We arrived just after dark. There was no food that night, but Til'da had dug a firepit. We sat and watched the fire burn down, sipping water and glancing up at the sky. No one spoke, and that was fine by me. I realized then that I wasn't bothered by having killed Kurse. My hands didn't shake. I had no remorse. The execution felt like justice to me, even though I knew it didn't make Til'da feel any better about what had happened to her. And it certainly didn't bring Rip back. Not that the boy's death was a great loss to us. But still, I realized that I had waited too long to deal with a known threat. Rip was dead and Til'da was scarred because of my inaction. I vowed to myself as I lay in the darkness staring up at the night sky, that no matter what else happened in my life, I wouldn't put off what I knew to be right again. I wouldn't wait and give someone a chance to hurt me or the people I cared about.

The old women in the village where I grew up told stories about the sons and daughters of the night. They were believed to be avengers who moved in the shadows. Some of the stories were cautionary tales meant to scare children into doing what they were told. But others were myths about our ancestors, those who had ventured out into the unknown and sought adventure. I felt like I was one of them that night. I had faced Kurse and did what was necessary. His blood was on my hands, and I didn't mind that in the slightest. I was a daughter of the night, and that was just fine with me.

CHAPTER 2

WE SPOTTED an alien ship three days after dealing with Kurse. We made the trek toward it, but the distance took us some days to travel. The bone-bag was heavy. Elaa'zar kept several good pelts inside, along with all the cooking gear, extra weapons, and supplies. I carried it every day. Even when the hunter offered to help, I declined. I wasn't built for that sort of hard labor the way Griff and Kurse had been, but I was eating well and felt my body growing stronger.

Two days into the journey we saw signs that another hunter was in the area. Elaa'zar made camp in the hollow of a hillside that was nicely hidden by thick shrubs and a few trees. I set snares, happy to have the bag off my back, while Til'da dug a firepit and Elaa'zar collected stones to line it. The next day we left Til'da in the camp and set off to see what we could learn.

"I don't like leaving her alone," Elaa'zar said.

"She doesn't seem to mind," I pointed out.

"She don't know what might happen to us," he said.

I felt the weight of his words and was reminded that we weren't just hunting a dangerous quarry, but that we were actively being hunted ourselves. That fact was driven home to me not long afterward. We moved cautiously, spread out nearly forty paces just in case we wandered into a trap or got attacked without warning, at least one of us would have the chance to survive. Sometimes Elaa'zar led the way. He was a much better tracker than I was, but he was teaching me and allowed me to take the lead at times. That was how I came around a low hill and saw the alien.

It was big, just like the other had been, with a huge skull that curved down its back. The alien hunched forward when it moved, but had long arms and legs. The way it moved was odd, as if walking on a flat surface was foreign to it. The alien staggered around and used its arms on the trees whenever it could. I froze where I was and made a hand signal to Elaa'zar. The hunter caught up to me without making a sound.

"Hasn't been here long," Elaa'zar whispered. "See how it's moving?"

"Looks drunk," I said, thinking of my father, who had come back to our hovel many nights staggering from strong drink.

"They hunt all over the planet," Elaa'zar said. "Some have been at it longer than others. The new ones stagger around that way."

We watched the alien, who wasn't alone. He had already made a kill. Two hunters were strung up by their feet on sturdy branches in the nearby trees. Both already had their vital organs removed and most of their blood drained. The alien was using a pair of sharp knives to skin the humans. It had an odd-looking box that floated in the air nearby.

"What's it doing?" I asked.

"Butchering," Elaa'zar said.

The alien's process was much different from our own. It cut the meat from the bones with quick, skillful motions. After the skin was removed in one big piece, like peeling off a tight glove, it was rolled up and put in the floating box.

"What's that thing?" I whispered.

"A device that keeps things cold," the hunter told me. "Preserves everything so that the meat and skins don't spoil."

"Shouldn't we stop it?" I asked. "Avenge the hunters?"

"We could try," Elaa'zar said. "But they have security machines that would take us down before we got close enough."

"I could hit it with the spear stick."said

"You know that won't stop it, even if the spear penetrates, which it won't."

"So, we do nothing?"

"Nothing we do now will matter to those poor souls," Elaa'zar said.

We kept watching, and if not for a single misstep we would have been killed, too. The alien wasn't alone. Its companion had come around the hill, moving slowly in full camouflage. I heard the distinct sound of a leaf being stepped on. It was a familiar sound, and one that I worked to avoid making when stalking animals I was hunting. My heart began to pound and the hair on the back of my neck stood out. I turned slowly, wide-eyed. I had a spear in hand but had never used one to fight the aliens. Fortunately, Elaa'zar had heard the sound too, and unlike me, he sprang into action.

He whirled around, thrusting his spear out in front of him. The alien was still several paces behind us. Elaa'zar dashed forward, holding the spear at the tail end to give the weapon the maximum distance. The alien slapped it to the side to avoid the metal tip, but Elaa'zar jumped into the air and kicked with both of his feet.

The drop kick landed, sending the alien staggering backward, its camouflage failing. It barked in surprise, then, regaining its balance, rushed toward Elaa'zar. The wily hunter had expected the move and brought his spear around, planting the butt of the weapon into the ground. The alien practically fell onto it, the metal blade stabbing up along its neck and into its long skull cap. The alien stiffened, and Elaa'zar had just enough time to roll out of the way as it toppled over. He immediately grabbed his spear and began twisting and thrusting it to complete the kill.

I didn't see what he was doing exactly, but I heard him grunting with the effort. My hands were sweating, and I felt sick to my stomach. Not from the killing or the gore that flowed from the alien's wounds, but because the other alien was racing toward us. The first must have called for help in its surprised bark. The other alien was rushing forward, but in an unsteady fashion, often using its hands to steady itself.

There was only one thing I could do. Running wouldn't help, and even shouting to Elaa'zar wouldn't be enough to save me, though he would probably die trying. But I realized it was entirely possible that the second alien, the one who had been skinning the other hunters, hadn't noticed me. Elaa'zar was making a production of killing its companion. I heard him cursing as he finished off the alien.

That left a small chance that I might be able to hinder the onrushing creature. The plan wasn't without danger. I was still kneeling on the ground behind a clump of ferns, my spear held out of sight. Clenching my teeth and summoning all my courage, I sprang into action. There was no chance of landing a killing blow. The alien was moving too fast, and I wasn't practiced enough with the spear. Instead, I thrust it out into the alien's path between the two hills. If it had been trying to kill me, it could have pounced and sank its talons into my soft flesh, ripping my body to pieces. Instead, it was focused on Elaa'zar—my intuition had been right. My spear hit the alien's leg that was farthest from me, the metal tip lodging into the bony ankle just long enough that when the other foot came forward, it tripped. The spear was jerked from my hands, and the alien made a high pitch wail of surprise as it fell. The big creature went down hard and flipped completely onto its back.

I jumped away, scrambling up the hill to avoid the monstrous creature. It was scrambling back to its feet and turning toward me. Elaa'zar gave a cry of savage rage as he rushed to attack the alien. And that's when the tables turned.

The alien backhanded the hunter's spear and in the process sent him flying. Elaa'zar hit a tree, his spear snapped in half, and he dropped to the ground unconscious. I had no weapons, but managed to get to the top of the hill. The alien pursued, but staggered even more than before. I can't say if my spear had injured its foot or if moving uphill threw off its already impaired sense of balance, but it struggled. I had just enough time to sprint down the far side. At that point, I had to decide between running for my life or taking a stand. With hardly a thought I glanced up, hesitating long enough for the alien to commit to following me down the hill. Once it did, the creature was nearly out of control. It stumbled, its long arms acting almost like crutches. I didn't stay to watch, but ran as fast as I could make myself go back around the hill.

The alien pursued. I heard it crashing through the underbrush behind me. I ran so fast I could hardly breathe. My legs hurt and my mind was numb with fear, but somehow I made it back around to where my spear lay. I snatched it up and turned, feigning an attack then pulling back, just as I had seen Elaa'zar do to the alien he fought with Tip'un. My foe swung hard at my spear, expecting to bat it aside, only I pulled it back before he could make contact. The alien, perhaps hurt, perhaps just unsteady on its feet, staggered off balance. In that moment time seemed to slow down. I saw the creature's skull, and even the narrow gap between its skull and its long neck. My spear went up almost involuntarily. I certainly wasn't thinking about what I was doing. The target had barely registered in my mind before I was striking toward it.

I wish I could say that I slayed the alien then and there, but I simply wasn't skilled enough with my spear to do that. Perhaps it was fear, or just unfamiliarity with the weapon, but while my aim was true, I was too far away to do real damage. Only an inch or so of the spear's tip penetrated under the skull. The alien wailed so loudly that it hurt my ears. It also leaped away from me. I saw dark fluid, maybe blood of some kind, pour out onto the alien's shoulder. It hissed at me and then fled. My legs were shaking so badly by that point that I just dropped to my knees and tried to catch my breath.

The alien had run away from the camp area. Behind me the two bodies still hung from the tree, although one had both legs removed and the muscles along his spine had been cut off. I used the spear to steady myself as I got to my feet and went to where Elaa'zar lay. He was still unconscious, with one leg clearly broken and twisted in an unnatural fashion. I took advantage of the moment and straightened his leg. It made a sickening grinding sound, but then popped into the right shape. The pain was enough to make him scream, even though he was unconscious. The broken leg immediately began to swell. I had a small knife with a thin blade that I used for all sorts of tasks. But Elaa'zar had a larger knife, its blade was longer than my hand, with a curved point. From the spine to the blade edge it was three fingers wide, and it was much heavier than my only little knife. I took it and stripped two tree branches. The entire time I was working I felt an intense fear, almost panic, knowing that the alien I had fought could return at any moment to finish me off.

I had been afraid many times in my life. I was afraid of my father's bad moods, afraid that my mother would die, afraid when I was sold to the hunter, and afraid when Kurse had tried to force himself on me. But none of those times did the fear feel so debilitating and all-consuming. My hands shook as I cut off Elaa'zar's pants leg and ripped it down the seams to make a twin set of ties. After finding the right branch, I split it in half to make two long, stiff, but slightly flexible splints. I tied them onto either side of Elaa'zar's broken leg, getting them snugged in as tightly as I could. Then I tried to move him, but it was no good. I could drag him, but that would be torture to us both, especially the injured hunter. Plus, I was several hours away from our camp, and it would take me days to drag Elaa'zar that far. I needed another solution and began casting around for one.

That was when I saw the floating box in the alien's camp. I had no idea what it was or how it worked, but I thought that if I could get the hunter on top of it, maybe I could push the floating box back to our camp. With my spear in one hand, I retrieved Elaa'zar's broken weapon. I put his big knife in my belt, too. If the aliens came back for me I didn't want to face them empty-handed. Going into the aliens' camp felt wrong, and it was extremely dangerous....but I was desperate. I made straight for the floating box, moving slowly, looking all around me for any sign of the enemy. Fortunately, the alien didn't return while I was there. And while I was moving toward the floating box I saw something else.

The dead hunters hanging from the tree were an adult and what looked like an older boy. It was honestly hard to tell for sure with all the blood and missing body parts. But on the far side of the trees was a metal cage. Inside was a girl about my own age, maybe younger. Her skin was dark from exposure to the sun, and maybe dirt, too. Her hair was blond, but filthy, and all she wore was a tiny little dress that looked like it was completely worn out. She sat with her knees pulled up to her chest and her head down, but as I approached the camp, she lifted her head and looked at me.

"Help," she whispered.

I looked around, turning in a full circle. There was no time for distractions, and I didn't want to go any deeper into the enemy camp than I had to, but I couldn't ignore the girl.

"Please," she whispered, a little louder. "Don't let them take me."

I had reached the floating box. It seemed heavy, yet somehow it floated. The top was as high as my chest. Giving it a nudge, I was relieved to see it moved easily. I pushed down on the box, but it didn't fall, even with my entire weight on it. Getting Elaa'zar on the box would be difficult, but if I could manage that, getting him safely back to our camp would be much easier.

"Please," the girl in the cage said again, no longer whispering. "Help me!"

"Shhhh!" I replied, holding up my hand with the broken spear in it. "Quiet."

"I don't want to die," the girl whined.

Neither did I, and it felt like the girl was taking a terrible chance by talking out loud. But after looking around, I felt certain we were alone. I hurried to her cage and looked at the lock. It was thick, an almost solid block of metal that was built into the door of the cage. Opening it wouldn't be easy, and I didn't have time to waste trying.

The girl's skinny arm reached through the bars of the cage, and I handed her the half spear.

"That's all I can do," I said.

She took the spear and turned it onto the lock. I went back to the floating box. It was cold to the touch, and hummed slightly. I pushed it back the way I had come, and it glided easily. Even with the butchered body parts of the hunters the alien had killed inside, I couldn't help but marvel at how easily it glided.

When I reached Elaa'zar he was awake, but his skin was pale and his face was covered with sweat.

"Thought you left me," he said in a weak, tremulous voice.

"Would you have left me?" I asked.

I thought the question was rhetorical, but the hunter nodded.

"Yes," he said, his voice barely a whisper.

"Nice," I replied. "I guess I'm just a better person than you."

"Are they both dead?"

I looked over and saw only one alien body nearby. Part of me wanted to think I had done enough damage to kill the other creature, but I knew it wasn't true. I shook my head.

"Where is it?"

"I don't know," I said softly. "It ran off. All I managed to do was wound it. I don't think it's hurt bad enough to die."

"Bad enough to stay away?"

I felt like a fool. Why hadn't I pursued the creature and

finished it off? Because I was terrified, that's why. The truth was, I'd been incredibly lucky not to be killed myself. So why did I feel like such a failure that the alien was still alive?

I shook my head.said "No."

"It'll be back," he said. "Leave me and go. Get Til'da and escape to a village."

"No," I said. It came out a little more sternly than I meant it to. "We're both getting out of here."

"It's going to track you down, Azree'el," he said. "And I can't move."

"Why not?" I asked. "I splinted your leg."

"Ain't my leg," he said. "It's my hip. Might be broken. My back is wrenched, too. Leave me your little knife and I'll open a vein."

"No, I will not," I replied. "Look. I got the alien's box. If I can get you on that, I can get us both out of here. Now, come on. You have to stand up on your good leg."

He took my hand, and I slowly pulled him into a sitting position. He then leaned over and vomited. It was foul and violent. Afterward he slumped back down in exhaustion, but I pulled him upright again.

"We have to move," I told him.

"Can't," he said in a shaky voice. "Hurts too bad."

"You never let that stop us when we complained," I pointed out.

"You should leave me," he said, but we both fell silent at the sound of footsteps. I whirled around with my spear held ready in both hands, but even before I saw who it was, my mind registered the fact that the footsteps weren't alien. They were human.

"I got out," a soft, frightened voice said.

My heart was still pounding, but I felt relieved to see that it was just the girl from the cage.

"Good," I said. "Help me get him up."

She hurried over. I could see the surprise in Elaa'zar's eyes, but also the dread on his face. He was breathing hard as we both took an arm and helped him up. He groaned in pain and swayed on one foot but managed to grab onto the box.

"Don't...don't touch the broken leg," he said.

I grabbed the other leg, and the girl in the threadbare dress held the box to keep it steady. Heaving Elaa'zar up, I was grateful that he wasn't big like my father, who had a thick chest, heavy haunches, and a round gut that hung over the front of his pants. Elaa'zar was strong, but his body was compact, his muscles wiry. I managed to lift his back end as he pulled himself forward across the top of the floating box. It wasn't as long as he was tall, but with his head at one corner, only the foot of his broken leg hung off. He bent his good leg at the knee so that it didn't hang and put pressure on his lower back.

"Hold on," I told him.

He put both his hands on the sides of the box lid, which had a narrow groove where the parts met.

"Got it," he said, his voice pitched high with pain.

I started pushing. The box, with Elaa'zar on top of it, was just as easy to move as it had been without him. The girl still clutched the broken spear as she fell in beside me.

"Thanks," she said softly. "I'm Zerel'da."

"Azree'el," I replied. "Were you with the hunter?"

She nodded.

"How long?" I asked.

"A year almost," she said.

"What happened?"

"We were setting up camp in a little valley not far from here," she said, still keeping her voice down. "They hit us just after sundown."

"They?"

"Both of 'em," the girl said. "Bar'tus held the first one off, but we didn't see the other till it was too late."

"Bar'tus," Elaa'zar said. "You were with Bar'tus?"

The girl nodded. "He bought me."

"Where are you from?" I asked.

"Holedown," she said. "It isn't far, just a few days' walk from here."

"They got a doctor in Holedown?" I asked.

The girl nodded, and that was how we made the decision to go there.

†††

We didn't see or hear from the alien that afternoon. We reached the camp where Til'da was waiting just before dark. I went immediately and checked the traps. We had caught two prairie chickens and one jackrabbit. By the time I plucked the birds and gutted them, Til'da had a fire going. She had filled the day collecting greens and berries. We roasted the birds over the little fire and ate our fill, including Elaa'zar, who managed to get a few bites down. But my concern was the alien. It was still out there somewhere, and the hunter's warning was ringing in my ears.

"Pack it up," I ordered.

"Now?" Zerel'da asked.

"The alien is still out there," I said. "And you said yourself that they attacked your camp at night."

"So maybe we should hunker down and defend this place."

"It's not defensible," I said. "Not with just the two of us. Besides, by morning we'll be exhausted and no closer to safety."

"We could be attacked in the dark and never see it coming."

"Not if we stay ahead of it."

"You really think it can't catch up?"

"I think that time is against us. Til'da and I are heading back to the mountains. Elaa'zar needs a doctor, and there's no telling how long that box will keep floating, so if you want to go with us, you can. If you want to stay here, I'll leave the rabbit with you."

She shook her head. It only took a few minutes to load everything into the bone bag, which I slung onto my back. The moon, although not full, was bright enough that we could make our way through the hills. At dawn, we took a break near a spring and refilled our water skins. To her credit, Zerel'da offered to carry the bone-bag. My back was killing me and both my shoulders felt raw from the straps, but instead, I used the bag to prop up Elaa'zar on the floating box and kept us moving.

It would only be a matter of time before the alien caught up to us. They were hunters, and while they did things differently from the way we did, I was certain of their ability to follow our trail. We were three tired people moving through valleys that were full of wild grasses, shrubs, and trees. I hoped that walking through the night would buy us some time, but I couldn't count on it.

"I'm exhausted," Zerel'da said.

"We can sleep for a week once we reach the mountains," I said.

"And then what? We could be leading that alien right to the hidden caverns. Have you thought about that?"

"We'll have to fight, then," I said. "But I wouldn't say no to some help."

"We could split up," she suggested.

"That only makes us more vulnerable," I said. "Besides, I won't leave Til'da or Elaa'zar alone."

"You don't think they would leave us?" Zerel'da asked. "I know Bar'tus would have. He was a cold man."

"Good hunter," Elaa'zar grunted.

"You knew him?" I asked.

Elaa'zar was in a lot of pain, but he was conscious. He hadn't complained and had managed to sleep most of the night on the floating box. I didn't think it was comfortable, but it didn't shake or jolt over the terrain, which made it ideal for moving the injured man.

"We were apprentices together," he said.

"The man was a pig," Zerel'da said. "He bought me from my mother, who was desperate, and promised to look after me. That first night he...he..."

"You don't have to say it," I told her. "Just take comfort in knowing he's dead."

"He used me, and when he grew tired of that sport, he made me bait for the traps he set. He wouldn't have raised his pinky to save me, I know that for a fact."

"Well, he's not here," I said. "And I ain't leaving no one behind."

It wasn't long before a little red light began to blink. I knew our time with the floating box was almost up. Fortunately, I found a hill where something had been mined. I couldn't say what, or when, or even by who. It was just a hill that had a big area unearthed to create a hole. Weeds had sprouted up between the rocks, and animals had used the mine as a den, but it was unoccupied.

"This looks good," I said.

"Good for what?" Zerel'da asked.

"For a fight," I told her.

There was no need to hide the fact that we had stopped. Zerel'da slumped down on the ground and closed her eyes. I couldn't blame her for that. I wanted to do the exact same thing. Only there were preparations to be made.

"Til'da, can you check to see how deep that hole goes?"

The moon-faced girl nodded. I knew she was tired, too, but hadn't resisted or complained. She moved into the mine, and I turned to Elaa'zar. He was awake, but still looked weak.

"I don't suppose you could shoot your bow," I said.

"I can shoot it," he said. "Not sure I could hit anything, though."

"Maybe you don't have to," I said, as an idea came into my mind. "This time you can be the bait."

†††

It was almost dark when the alien came. In the dim light it was hard to see the creature, but we had a good position at the mine. The rocky overhang wasn't very tall, but it was deep enough that Til'da and Zerel'da could hide inside the shaft. The floating box had run out of power and was on the ground. Elaa'zar was sitting on a bed of cut spruce boughs with his back against the box. His quiver of arrows—he had half a dozen good shafts with metal points—was next to him so he could reach them easily. His bow was in his hand, resting across his thighs, with an arrow on the string. He didn't look formidable, but that was part of my plan. He needed to draw the alien in.

I was hidden in bushes at the far side of the mining area. There were tall weeds and tough grass around the clump of bushes. It was ideal cover for someone of my size. I held my spear low and fought sleep as I waited for the alien to arrive. When it did, I thought my eyes were playing tricks on me. I literally saw nothing, but an area back along the way we had come when approaching the mine seemed to waver. I rubbed my eyes and looked again. It was getting dark, the gloom growing around us, the first stars just appearing in the night sky. I watched, and it happened again. My vision seemed to waver like the area just above a fire. Only it wasn't everything I could see, but a specific place.

My entire body tensed. This was it. I couldn't see the alien, but I could see it moving. And I wasn't the only one. Even with a broken leg and his body covered in bruises, Elaa'zar spotted the alien. He raised his bow and fired an arrow straight at the creature. Its camouflage flickered as it tried to get away. The arrow hit the alien's exoskeleton and bounced off, but the impact was enough to cause it to screech. Elaa'zar nocked another arrow to his bowstring and raised the weapon just as the alien charged.

Perhaps the camouflage technology didn't work when the aliens move fast, or maybe the creature wanted Elaa'zar to see it coming. A lion will roar just before it springs to frighten its prey into a paralysis of terror. I certainly felt every muscle in my body tense as the creature attacked.

There were times when Elaa'zar seemed cold or uncaring, but

he was also fearless. The alien moved fast but was clearly suffering from its wounds. It limped, and one side was covered in a dark, sticky substance that had dripped from under its curving skull. How Elaa'zar took aim, or if he even did I couldn't say, but the second arrow he fired hit the alien square in its narrow chest and with enough force to punch through the exoskeleton that covered its body.

The alien actually fell backward. Its feet flew forward and it crashed hard on its back. I immediately launched into action. My legs churned hard as I rushed the creature, and other than my feet on the ground I made no noise. The alien was down, but far from dead. It screeched a high-pitched wail and then rolled onto its hands and knees. It was looking at Elaa'zar, who was trying to get another arrow on the string of his bow. I had just enough time to see the alien pull its legs under it. We both jumped at the same time. It jumped forward, clawed talons outstretched for Elaa'zar, but I jumped straight into the alien's side, knocking it off course. We came down hard, but I was on top, my spear across the creature's body. I could feel the slime that covered it, and the hard, bony parts of its body beneath me. It squirmed and could have torn me to bloody ribbons, but I shifted the spear and pushed it forward. The razor-sharp blade caught the alien just below its narrow chin, puncturing flesh and piercing up through its face.

The creature broke into a frenzied seizure. I was thrown back but luckily didn't get hurt. The breath was knocked out of my body, and I came up on my knees gasping for air. The alien, however, was still down, writhing on the ground, the spear was in its face and the arrow in its chest. I got to my feet, drew Elaa'zar's hunting knife and circled around the creature until I was closest to its big, curving head. As its spasms slowed, I rushed forward and grabbed the edge of its skull with my free hand. A split second later I rammed the knife blade up under the edge. Blood gushed out, and the alien stiffened. Its eyes were open. They reminded me of volcanic glass, but I had no doubt they could see me. I stabbed the knife as deep as I could make it go, then worked it down the curving arch of its skull.

"It's dead," Elaa'zar said.

His words seemed foreign. I kept hacking and stabbing.

"You did it," he said. "You killed your first alien."

That finally got my attention and I dropped backward, sitting down, but still clutching the bloody knife. I was breathing hard. My chest hurt, but I was elated by the kill. The alien had tracked us down and we had killed it.

"You hurt?" Elaa'zar asked.

"No, not really," I said. "You?"

"It didn't lay a finger on me, thanks to you."

"That was the plan, right?"

"It happened fast," Elaa'zar said. "It could have gone either way. I'd be dead now if you hadn't jumped into it the way you did. I don't recommend that tactic, by the way."

"I wasn't thinking," I admitted.

"You've got the instincts of a hunter," he said.

That was high praise from Elaa'zar. He wasn't the kind of man who belittled those around him or utilized rude insults in an effort to motivate people. But he didn't hand out compliments very often, either.

Once I caught my breath, I pulled the alien's carcass as far from the camp as I could before I had to rest. I dropped into the tall grass beside the alien and stared up into the sky. The stars were bright, and I couldn't help but imagine what it was like up there among them. When I finally regained my strength I cut up the alien's body, just the way Elaa'zar had shown me. I kept the skull after emptying out the organs. Harvesting the larger bones took nearly an hour, but once it was done I collected my bloody treasure and carried it back to the camp.

The night was half spent. Til'da, Zerel'da, and Elaa'zar were all asleep. The hunter still had his bow on his lap with an arrow nocked on the string while he snored in his slumber. I had to respect his resolve.

It was time for me to get some sleep, too, but I was covered with alien blood and gore. I had to search for a bit before finding a spring. For the next hour I scrubbed everything: my clothes, my body, my hair. I was shivering in the cold air as I hauled myself back to camp. There I built a fire and hung my clothes near it, then wrapped myself in the white ram skin and slept hard through what remained of the night.

†††

"You killed it?" Zerel'da asked.

"We did," I told her. With only a few hours' sleep over the last forty-eight hours, I wasn't in a talkative mood.

"I can't believe I slept through that," the girl said. "So, what now?"

"Now you climb this hill and tell us how far we are from Hole-down," I said.

"Sure, OK," she said.

While she scrambled up the hill, I got dressed. My clothes weren't dry, but they were only slightly damp after hanging by the embers of the fire all night. We didn't usually risk burning fires in the daytime. The smoke tended to scare away game, and it attracted the aliens. I didn't think there were more in the area, but we couldn't take that risk. So, we ate some berries and drank the water Til'da fetched from the spring nearby.

Then we tried to move Elaa'zar. I didn't like him being exposed, but the best we could do was to move the floating box. It no longer floated and was extremely heavy. Plus, knowing what was inside made my skin crawl. We pushed it to the side and cut more spruce boughs. Elaa'zar, wrapped in his bearskin, was moved onto the pile of soft branches, but even moving him that short distance caused him so much pain he was breathless and faint.

"We can't carry him to Holedown," I said.

"It's only a few hours from here," Zerel'da said.

"Then you and I can go," I told her. "Til'da can stay here and tend to Elaa'zar."

I gave the mute girl specific, yet simple instructions. She was to dig a firepit and cook the rabbit we had left. She could make a stew that would feed her and Elaa'zar that night, with enough left over for morning. I hoped to be back a few hours after sunrise with help.

There was no need to carry the bone-bag. Instead, I carried Elaa'zar's knife, the spear I had used to kill the alien, and the pouch full of coins. It was enough money to make us a target, so the coins were hidden in different parts of my clothing. Zerel'da carried the alien skull and bones. They hadn't been boiled, which was done to remove the tight skin and bits of flesh that clung to them. It would have to wait. The alien skull was proof of who I was and who I was with.

We made the trip in just over three hours. Holedown was exactly as it was named, a village inside a hole in the ground. We had to climb down a rickety ladder made from old bits of wood and braids of dried grass. It was a village like the others I had seen. Hovels, makeshift booths, and desperate people. The stench was so offensive that I would have lost the contents of my stomach had there been anything in it.

There weren't many people who wanted to deal with a pair of girls, even with the alien skull between us. But a few were willing. I bought a boy the size of a grown man. His name was Ceef'us. He had the typical round face many Heterrids had, and it seemed to me that he didn't understand a lot of what was happening around him. But his mother swore he was good and strong.

"He's been working at the quarry," she said. "Hauling big rocks. He's been to the surface, too, oh yes. He's been up the ladder many times. He loves it up there."

"And he can follow instructions?"

"Yes, he's very smart. I know it don't seem that way, but he is. He just doesn't like to be touched or confined. I could keep him with me, but they'll work him to death in that quarry."

I wasn't convinced he was clever enough to run a trapline or even learn to skin small game, but he could certainly carry the bone-bag. After I had overpaid for the boy, a full sixty marks in silver ten-piece coins, and his mother kissed him goodbye, he didn't seem to understand that he would never see her again. He seemed content to stand still and stare at the ground.

Zerel'da went to fetch the doctor. I was expecting to have to pay someone all our coin to get them to the surface. When Zerel'da returned with an old woman I didn't know what to think.

"This is Sal'ma," the younger girl announced. "She's a healer."

"Was," the old woman said. "People stopped coming 'round once my apprentice was able to do the work without me."

She smiled. The poor woman had no teeth. Her wrinkled lips pressed together, and the skin around her eyes drooped. She was thin with a hump on her back. What had surely been lustrous hair at one time in her life had turned stark white and was very thin.

"Can you set bones?" I asked her. "Man bones?"

"Sure enough can," the woman replied. "I stitch up wounds too. And make a powerful poultice."

"What about something for pain?"

"Lots of ways to manage pain," the woman said. "I don't have the potent herbs anymore. Sold my collection long ago, but I know where we can get everything we need."

"And you're willing to go up top?" I asked. "It's a three-hour walk to the camp."

"Won't lie and say I ain't afraid," she declared, almost as if she were proud of herself for saying it. "But you get me up there, and I can walk just fine."

"You can't climb the ladder?"

"She won't have to," Zerel'da said. "Ceef can pull her up on a sling."

I didn't like the fact that the doctor was old and not fit enough to climb out of Holedown without help. Still, I didn't see that we had a lot of options. Nor was I happy that Zerel'da was making decisions about what Ceef could or couldn't do. It seemed like she was overstepping her boundaries, but I kept my thoughts to myself.

"All right. How much?" I asked the old woman.

"You buy the supplies," she said. "And get me out of this hole in the ground, and I'll come free of charge. I don't need money. I don't plan on coming back."

"You're willing to just leave everything?" I asked suspiciously.

"Lived all my life down here. Used to go up the ladder and stare through the hole at the sky. Never had the courage to climb up, though. And I've been staring death in the face a while now. Then your little helper comes along and gives me the opportunity to see the up top before I close my eyes for good. I'd have jumped at the chance...if I could still jump."

"Can't jump, can't climb," I pointed out. "You sure you can walk?"

"Both legs still work," she said, offering another smashed lip grin. "When do we start?"

We spent the rest of the day gathering what she needed. It cost nearly as much as Ceef'us had by the time we finished. Sal'ma had a shoulder bag that she stuffed with bottles, bandages made of old scraps of fabric pieced together with hemp thread, and lots of powders that I didn't recognize. We slept that night near the ladder after eating roasted tubers and drinking goat's milk. When the sun rose, Ceef'us and I made the climb up the ladder. He didn't struggle even when the rope ladder swayed and creaked under his weight. When we reached the surface, he shaded his eyes and waited.

Zerel'da put Sal'ma in a sling, then carried the rope connected to the sling up the ladder to where we were waiting. To his credit, Ceef'us pulled her up as easily as he might draw water from a well. The old woman had her eyes closed and was holding the rope sling in a death grip, but once we put her feet on the ground, she stood up and looked around.

I remembered the feeling of seeing the surface world for the first time. That had been at twilight, which made the open air seem less expansive. Sal'ma didn't have the luxury of a slow adjustment.

"It's so big," she said in a shaky voice.

"You get used to it," I said, still breathing in the fresh mountain air.

"My eyes won't stop streaming," the old woman complained.

She had tears running and was using both her bony hands to block out as much of the early morning light as she could.

"They will," I said. "We don't have time to coddle you Stay behind Ceef'us. He casts a good shadow."

We set off for the camp. It was a brilliant day, with a cool breeze sliding down from the mountains. I led the way, with Ceef'us and Sal'ma right behind me. Zerel'da brought up the rear. I had given her the chance to stay in Holedown, but she declined, and I couldn't blame her for that. Just a single day back down in the dank, stinking village was too much for me.

It felt good to be in the sunlight again and to stretch my legs. We had to make frequent stops to accommodate Sal'ma, who insisted we call her Sal. She didn't have shoes, and her dress wasn't any better than Zerel'da's, even though it looked like it had once been a fine outfit. Whenever we stopped, I took the time to forage and even show Zerel'da what was edible and what wasn't. We found some really nice morels and enough collard greens to last us for several meals. There were blackberries at one stop and a patch of wild potatoes at another.

It was past midday when we reached the camp. I was relieved that our healer had made it. She was clearly exhausted when we found the old mine. But to her credit, she went right to work examining Elaa'zar.

"The good news is he didn't break his hip," she said with a grin. "It's just a bone bruise, and that'll heal on its own. You the one who splinted his leg?"

I nodded. My father had sprained his ankle once, and while there wasn't a healer in Gipid, the old mothers showed him how to brace it. I had been responsible for keeping the brace tied tightly.

"That was a fine bit of work," she said. "The bone's already starting to heal. Won't ever be as good as before, I suspect. It wasn't set quite right, but he'll be all right, given time and rest."

"How long?" I asked.

"Three weeks before he can walk, and then we'll need to fashion some crutches for him. I think he may have fractured a few ribs, and he definitely has a concussion. But he'll heal in time. I gave him a draught for the pain. It's powerful stuff. He's sleeping it off now."

"Can we move him?"

"I wouldn't," she said. "He needs his rest. And so do I."

We had some food, but needed more. I spent the entire afternoon setting snares and hunting. I came back to the camp with a pair of grouses, which Til'da plucked. As soon as it was dark she got a fire going in the pit. Ceef'us had water carried in the old alien skull. Til'da added the mushrooms and wild potatoes, even some of the greens. She broke the grouses down and added it to her stew. By the time Elaa'zar woke up, he had a very savory dinner waiting for him.

The next two weeks were pleasant. I spent my days hunting. There were small deer in the area, and I managed to harvest two of them. That kept us in meat, despite the fact that Ceef'us had a seemingly unending appetite. He and Til'da seemed like long-lost siblings. They often ate together, both perfectly content with silence.

Zerel'da, on the other hand, never seemed to stop chattering. She and Sal passed long hours every day in unending babble about the most mundane things. I tried to keep her busy foraging and even attempted to show her how to snare game, but she had no interest in learning anything. I took Ceef'us out to find wood for crutches, which I had to whittle into shape. Unfortunately, while Elaa'zar made rapid improvement, Sal was declining every day. She slept longer and had less energy. In the evenings we would talk, sometimes telling stories of life before coming to the surface, and other times sharing what we knew about the Vanj.

"They take people sometimes," Sal said as we gazed up at the stars one night. "No one knows where or why, but they take some people alive."

"They would have taken Zerel'da if we hadn't stopped them," I pointed out. "I found her locked in a cage. Why do you think they take people? More genetic experimentation?"

"The Vanj aren't that evil," the old woman said. "They're animals, highly intelligent animals, but they see us as food. If they wanted to experiment on us, they would do it here."

"On Ferret?"

The old woman nodded. "It's too much of risk to do it elsewhere."

We both sat silent after that and looked up at the stars. There were so many it made me wonder how many beings might be wandering through them.

"All my life I've thought about what it might be like up there," Sal said. "It's hard enough to take in all the space here on the surface. What must it be like up among the stars?"

"It looks crowded," I suggested.

That made the old woman laugh. I felt my face flush. I was thankful for the darkness that hid my embarrassment, and the cool night air that soothed my burning cheeks. When we first arrived back at the camp, I had gotten thick animal skins for both Sal and Ceef'us. The old woman was wrapped in a wolf hide. Her body was painfully thin. She couldn't chew much, but drank the stew broth and sucked the animal bones. It seemed like she was always cold, even with the thick animal fur wrapped around her.

"They didn't teach you about the stars where you came from?"

"Only that they exist," I confessed. "My father didn't think much of anything outside the village. He called it vain imaginings."

"I've heard it called worse," Sal said. "But the truth is there's a lot we've forgotten about the surface world and beyond. I don't have many regrets in life, but since coming up here with you I regret not doing it sooner. I should have done it when I was young enough to really enjoy it."

"We're pretty safe here," I told her. "It isn't always that way."

"Safe or not, it's better than living in a hole underground. We weren't meant for that."

"What were we meant for?" I asked.

That was the question we all longed to know but could never answer with any confidence. We knew the Maston Overlords had stolen our source DNA, but no one even knew where that came from. They broke our genetics apart and rebuilt it, experimenting over and over in an effort to find perfection. When they came up short, they abandoned us on Ferret.

"Out there," the old woman pointed up at the stars, "there are thousands of planets. Each star has them, and while they look close to us, they are separated by distances so vast we can't even fathom it."

"Really?"

"Oh, yes," the old woman confirmed. "And the Vanj are

nothing like the Maston. No one has seen them in generations, but I saw a picture of one in an old book."

"What's a book?" I asked.

"It's made of paper, hundreds of thin sheets of paper, all bound together so you can turn each page."

"Whoa," I said, struggling to even imagine such a thing.

"In that book, the Maston were short, shorter than me even. They were thin, and nearly featureless. They had tiny bodies and big heads with huge black eyes."

I shivered, but not because of the cold.

"They took us from our home world and did their best to make us into something we were never meant to be," she said. "They're monsters, not the animals that hunt us here."

I wondered if she would say the same thing after seeing a Vanj hunt, but Sal never saw one. The next day she was too weak to get up off the bed of grass and spruce boughs we had gathered for her. And late that afternoon, she died. It was calm, almost graceful. She fell asleep and just stopped breathing. I had known it was coming, but it still caught me off guard.

Zerel'da tried to just ignore that it happened. Elaa'zar was stoic as always, and unfazed by grief. I, on the other hand, was emotional. Something about the old woman's death reminded me of my mother. We put her in the deepest part of the mine and stacked rocks around and over her tiny body. The next day we broke camp.

Elaa'zar couldn't do much. He got around on the crutches I had made him, but he couldn't go far without falling into exhaustion. So, I took the bone-bag from Ceef'us, and we fashioned the hunter a litter. Ceef'us carried one end, Zerel'da and Til'da carried the other. We only traveled about five miles from the mine, moving closer to the mountains until we found ourselves a nice camp in a stand of towering pine trees. Ceef'us dug a firepit, and we raked up mounds of pine needles to spread out for beds. There were fallen logs, too, which made good seats and even better heat reflectors. The nights were getting colder, and by fixing our beds between a fallen log and the fire pit, we stayed warm in our animal skins.

"Winter's come on soon," Elaa'zar said. "We'll need more pelts and a better shelter."

"That shouldn't be too hard. You'll be hunting again before you know it," I assured him.

"Not before the snows come," he said. "Small game will get scarce. We need elk, maybe even a moose to feed this crew. And we need a bear, the biggest one we can find."

"I understand," I told him, but in truth I had no idea what he was talking about. I knew winter meant cold weather. Underground the temperature remained constant, but on the surface we experienced the changing seasons.

He put me to work practicing with his bow every day. And while I shot targets until my arms ached, and my fingers bled on the bowstring, Zerel'da was sent in search of willow boughs to make more arrows.

The first snow fell ten days after we made our camp in the trees. It was spectacular, but cold. Everything got wet, which forced us to push in closer to the mountains until we found a rocky overhang to shelter under. Ceef'us moved bushes and fallen trees up to the camp. Elaa'zar oversaw the construction of a camp that would see us through the winter, but yet wouldn't attract unwanted attention. We saw ships land soon after reaching the new camp, but we didn't strike out after the Vanj, even when

Elaa'zar traded his crutches for a walking stick, which he soon made into a spear using a big piece of flat metal that he spent hours grinding down with an ancient file.

Every day I practiced with the bow, and every day I went out to hunt. I saw an elk on the second day and got close enough to take a shot at one on the fifth day. The shot was true, but I still had to follow the blood trail for over a mile to find the animal. It was too big for me to carry back, even after I drained the blood and removed the organs. I had to work late into the night cutting large sections of meat from the bones and storing them in the elk's skin, which I was using like a sack to carry my kill back to camp. By the time I finished I was covered in blood. It made me a tempting target.

The snow that fell and melted in the valleys, stayed in the higher elevations, pushing down predators in search of food. Me and my bag of fresh meat were a target that couldn't be resisted. I was oblivious of the danger above me as I walked under a huge oak tree that had lost all its leaves already. In the daylight I would have spotted the mountain lion in the barren tree, but it was dark, the sky overcast, leaving my trail back to the camp in deep gloom. I was hurrying as well, knowing that being out at night was a risk. I had a hunting bow, a quiver of arrows, and Elaa'zar's hunting knife. But the bow was a poor weapon in the dark, and if something got close enough where I could hurt it with the knife, the odds were much higher that it would hurt me first.

The creak of the tree limb above and behind me saved my life. I heard the sound and turned, backpedaling as I went. The huge animal came at me out of the darkness with a resounding roar that terrified me. In the process of my turn I dropped the bag of meat, and managed to nock an arrow onto the string of the bow. The elk skin hit the ground and flopped open, revealing dozens of cuts of fresh meat. The lion forgot about me and pounced on the meat. Maybe it would have taken some of the kill and escaped, or maybe it would have turned on me to add to its sudden bounty. Only I didn't flee. I set my feet, raised the arrow to my cheek the way I had done thousands of times in practice, and let the bolt fly. I was less than ten full strides away from the big cat, which had turned sideways as it sniffed the meat I had been carrying. I saw its huge gaping mouth open, revealing long, curved teeth. Then the arrow hit. It knocked the lion sideways, the arrowhead burrowing deep between its ribs and into the animal's heart. Instinctively it tried to leap away, only to find its strength suddenly gone. The lion collapsed on the ground and died.

My own heart was still pounding hard in my chest, like a frightened rabbit racing for its burrow when a predator is chasing it. My hands were shaking, and my knees felt as though they might give way. I had to take several minutes to just breathe. The night was quiet, but I listened for any other sounds of danger. Convinced I was alone, my mind wrestled with the question of what to do next. My first instinct was to gather the elk meat and run for home, but could I really leave the lion pelt behind? With the elk meat we didn't need the lion, too, and I certainly couldn't carry both back to the camp, but I could take a few minutes and skin the animal. Mountain lions didn't have thick, luxurious fur, but it would make an excellent pad on which to sleep.

After realizing I couldn't walk away from my accidental kill, I built a small fire. It wasn't big enough to provide much heat, but the light was welcome and the smoke would keep other predators away...or so I thought.

It was late in the autumn and most bears were finishing up

their feasts before going into hibernation for the winter. There were black bears and brown bears in the forests around the mountains. They were all big, all dangerous, but none as ferocious as the grizzled hair browns. The one that attacked me didn't make a sound. I was skinning the mountain lion, trying to preserve the pelt but also working as fast as I could. The light from my little twig fire was minimal, but it was enough to reflect off the big eyes of the most powerful predator in the mountains. I saw them gleaming, and in the darkness it was impossible to say how far away the animal was.

Then I heard the bear sniffle. It was filling its nostrils with the smell of smoke, elk, mountain lion, and me. I stopped skinning the cat and picked up the bow. In a stroke of good sense, I had already nocked a bow on the string. That was the only thing that saved my life. The huge animal charged me. I drew and fired the arrow in one quick motion, then dove to the side. The bear roared in pain, rising on its hind legs as it staggered into the light of my little fire. The arrow was sticking out of its shoulder. It turned its head, the big mouth open in a savage roar, and looked right at me.

There was no time to nock another arrow, and I didn't think an arrow would stop the bear anyway, even if it hit a vital. The bear was massive, easily twice my height when standing on its back legs. I was no match for the animal, but my terror had given way to a rage I didn't understand. I had killed the elk. I hunted the animal down and harvested it. It was my effort to harvest the meat, and now the wilderness predators were looking to steal it from me. I should have run away, but instead I stepped forward. The little fire was between me and the bear. I kicked the small teepee-shaped bundle of sticks that were burning brightly. They flew up right into the bear's enraged face.

I drew the hunting knife as the bear staggered back and ran by it. As I passed the great, shaggy creature, I hacked at it with the blade. It opened a long, shallow cut on the bear's hind leg. It was still roaring and pawing at the embers on its snout. I turned quickly and thrusted the knife hard into the bear's back.

It turned, swiping at me with a massive paw, but I had already pulled the big knife free and jumped to stay behind the grizzled bear. I was so close that I could see the silver hair standing out straight along its back. I stabbed again, this time my knife hitting backbone and bouncing off.

That was the end of my advantage. The bear spun around, and I was forced to jump back to avoid the jaws that snapped at me. I slashed at the bear with my knife, cutting open its nose. That only enraged the beast further and it started forward. I took a chance and lashed out with a front kick. There was no chance I could hurt, much less injure a bear that was twice my size with a punch or kick, but I wasn't aiming for the bear. My boot was made of soft buckskin, and I felt something in my foot snap as it hit the arrow sticking out of the bear's shoulder. My kick drove the arrow in deep. The animal roared, but also dropped its face to the ground. As I limped backward, the bear rolled over and over. The arrow was in deep; nearly three quarters of the length of its shaft was in the animal's flesh. That part that stuck out was broken off by the bear's thrashing around.

If I had my spear handy I could have killed it, but all I had was the knife. By that point I realized that getting any closer to the animal would be suicide. I circled back around to my elk skin. The meat was still there, just waiting to be gathered back up. I snatched the bundle and retrieved the bow and quiver of arrows. I fully expected to go back at dawn, finish skinning the mountain lion, and track down the bear. But I never even made it out of the clearing.

A net dropped over me. It was heavy, and when I tried to run it immediately tangled around my feet. I fell, still unsure what had happened, or what the net was. I was pulling the net, which would stretch but didn't break. Through the links in the netting, I saw a dark shape drop from the trees. It was no more than a shadow, and yet I knew exactly what it was.

I hacked with the hunting knife, but sharp as it was, it did little to the net. Grabbing one link, I sawed at the material with the knife. The strands parted, but I only managed to make a small hole. Meanwhile, the Vanj was facing the bear. The animal, blood flanking its shoulder and the foreleg on that side drooping, reared again. But the bear roared in fury, and I in a panic tried to cut through the net.

The alien sprang forward, caught the bear's good paw in mid swipe, and somehow managed to match the animal's incredible strength. With his other hand, the alien slashed at the bear's throat. Blood and fur flew away. The bear staggered backward and then dropped onto its back. It tried to roar, but only managed to gurgle. The alien pounced onto its back, sinking its long, curved talons into the bear's flesh. It fell again and struggled weakly. The alien grabbed the bear's head and twisted until its neck snapped.

I lay in the bundle of netting, still struggling to escape as the alien turned toward me, and I knew my life was over.

†††

When the alien turned my way, I expected sudden death.

"Come on, then!" I shouted. "You want me, come and get me!"

Only it didn't come and kill me the way I expected. It simply gathered up the net with me still in it and began dragging me back through the forest. You can imagine the torture of being pulled over gnarly tree roots, stones, sticks, and brambles. The alien didn't seem to care when I called out in pain. My clothing was torn, my body covered in cuts and bruises. I was so disoriented, and in such a state of panic, that I didn't recognize where we were going.

The alien reached my camp just before dawn. I was left barely conscious while it activated its camouflage and approached the jumble of huge stones.

I shouted a warning, but it didn't help. When Elaa'zar came limping from the shelter he was hit by the nearly invisible alien who was waiting for him. I saw him crash into the rocks and fall to the ground, where he never moved, Inside the structure, the alien made quick work. I was thankful that I didn't see it, or that the others didn't suffer. The creature was deadly, but efficient.

Soon, all my comrades—Elaa'zar the hunter, Til'da and Ceef'us, and even Zerel'da—were all slain. I was forced to watch as the alien field dressed their bodies, then went about the grisly business of skinning each one. By the time he finished, his ship had flown itself to where we waited. Not that I was simply content to just be alive. At first I was in and out of consciousness. My body was hurting and exhausted, my mind in shock at what had occurred. The hunter had spent decades in the wild, living off the land, making the aliens who hunted us pay for their deeds. But just like that he was dead and all my friends were gone, never to return. And for the first time since being purchased by the hunter, I wished I was back in Gipid, or any of the underground villages. They were nasty places, but they were safer than up top. I would have traded all the freedom and pride

I had discovered with Elaa'zar to be back with my abusive father in that moment.

Of course, I was also cutting the net whenever I thought of it and was confident the alien wasn't watching. By the time his ship arrived I had opened a hole big enough to wiggle through, which I did. The net was still a tangled mess, and by the time I was free the alien had turned its attention back to me. It hissed a warning. I could see my friends, their bodies stripped of their skin, their vital organs, and their dignity. All I had was the knife. Perhaps I could have run away and survived, but frankly, that thought never entered my mind. Brandishing my small weapon, I charged the alien.

I had no expectations of survival. Attacking a Vanj hunter alien with a knife was suicide, and even though I didn't want to die, I wanted revenge even more. But I was in no shape to fight. My mind was foggy, my body weak. I ran right into the alien's grasp. It might have snapped my neck, but instead, it caught my arms and held me up in the air. Its face dripped with the clear, viscous fluid that seeped from its pores as it hissed at me. It bared its teeth, its dark eyes glared into mine, and I knew I was about to die. But instead, it wrung the knife from my grip and carried me to the ship, where it locked me in a metal cage.

I threw myself against the door so hard I was stunned and fell on my back. I didn't see what happened next, but of course I know. The Vanj carried the bodies on board the ship. They view humans as trophy animals and game meat. My friends were put in cold storage and eventually devoured by the cruel aliens, but the Vanj who stole my freedom and killed my friends had an entirely different purpose for me.

CHAPTER 3

SPACE WAS nothing like I expected. It felt like I was in a strange room. Outside that room Ferret fell away, as if it were never really there to begin with. Not that I was aware of its passing. I was still in the cage recovering from my abduction and the shock of seeing my friends killed.

What I didn't know, and couldn't have known at the time, was that my abductor was not in fact a Vanj hunter. The Vanj are a race with specific castes and an unchangeable hierarchy. On the planet Vespa, a hot, humid world, there are kings, breeders, workers, hunters, travelers, and, as I was about to learn, the Fray.

Food and water was given to me in my cage. It was too hot to need a blanket, or even to care that my clothing was in tatters. It took a while for my mind to clear and the realization that I was alive to kick in. At first I felt relief, and then, just like when Tip'un was killed, I felt guilt for being alive when everyone else I knew and cared about were dead.

Sal'ma's words came back to me as I lay in the cage. There was no comfort there, just hard metal and fear. Sal had told me the Vanj sometimes take prisoners. The old woman had no idea why or where, but I soon realized that I was going to find out. At first I thought I would be presented alive to the alien's leaders. Perhaps I would be tortured for information, or dissected for some type of heinous research. Of course, that made no sense since the Vanj had hunted and killed thousands of Heterrids. My companions were hanging on meat hooks in the ship's cold storage. If they needed to experiment or learn something about us, they had more than enough specimens to work with. They certainly didn't need me.

I tried to escape my cage, but it was useless. Without a tool of some kind, I couldn't break free. And even if I had, there was nothing I could have done to escape. The ship had already left the Mige system and passed through a portal that led to a different part of space, one completely controlled by the Vanj. It took less than two days for my abductor's ship to land on a planet that I had never even imagined existed.

Vespa was a dark and stormy place. It was much closer to the system star than Ferret, but with an atmosphere so thick and damp that it grew alien foliage in abundance. The ship I was on landed at a facility that processed the meat from the people who were killed on Ferret. My friends were removed from cold storage and taken into the facility while I was left to swelter in the cage. The ship had two exits, one smaller airlock that I could see, and then a big rear hatch that lowered to form a ramp. Through the rear hatch I could see the facility nearby. It was a big, heavy structure made from huge blocks of stone and covered with dark vines that grew up the sides and over the top. It was the first building I had ever seen, and despite my confinement and bleak future, I couldn't help but marvel at the structure.

The ship had landed on a level area that was free of debris and all fauna. The ground had some sort of stone slabs that were all level with barely even a crack between them. There were other ships there as well, most with tubes and hoses running to them. I could see a team of aliens operating a contraption with several large tanks. It moved between the ships, refueling the engines and replenishing water to the space vessels.

Of course, at the time I didn't know anything. I leaned my face against the damp bars of my cage and stared at the wonders of the alien world. Beyond the cold storage facility and landing area was a jungle with massive trees. The ground was covered with thick foliage. I could see movement in the jungle, but it was along the trunks and thick branches of the trees, not on the ground. The aliens were climbing and jumping from tree to tree. Out of the thick jungle rose a massive object that reminded me of stone stacks that were considered sacred on Ferret. It was dark but seemed formed rather than a natural structure. I had seen mountains before, but this was different. It was built in sections, with those above being slightly smaller than those below. It looked very much like an artificial mountain, and it towered above the jungle canopy.

I must have spent hours watching the place, wondering how big stones could be moved to build a structure, or how long it must have taken to construct the artificial mountain. There were plenty of aliens, hundreds that I could see, all in motion. I saw them come from the building, moving among the spaceships and climbing the trees. I could hear the hissing and shrieking they made. It was awe-inspiring and terrifying at the same time.

But the greatest surprise of that day was meeting Cly've. He was an old man, but clearly a Heterrid like me. He had a bald head and tiny eyes that were set wide on his wrinkled face. They were overhung by little folds of skin that dropped down from his thick brow. His body was thin and stooped. He walked with a short stick for support and wore only a wrap around his waist. He hobbled up the ramp and sat just outside my cage. All I could do was stare at him. After hours spent sweating on the hot, humid world, my mouth felt thick and gummy. I sat slumped against the bars of my cage and watched my captors, expecting to die at any moment. Then came one of my own. He sat and wheezed for a while before he spoke.

"Welcome to Vespa," he said in a gruff voice. "I'm Cly've. Who are you?"

"Azree'el," I managed to say.

That was all we said to one another for a while. Eventually, an alien came past the ship and left a cylinder-shaped container on the ramp. Cly've slid down to retrieve it. I watched him pour water into a little cup that served as a lid on the container. Then he drank it slowly.

"You have to go slow," he said. "You won't want to. You'll want to suck it down fast, but it will make you sick and you'll end up losing most of it. Drink it slow, and let your body absorb it all."

He poured more water into the cup and passed it between the bars of my cage. My hand shook from weakness and dehydration as I took it. He was right, I wanted to suck it down fast, but I forced myself to sip it instead. The water wasn't cold, it was lukewarm. In fact, it was the same temperature as my mouth, and I could hardly taste it. But I did feel it slide down my parched throat in a deliciously exquisite trickle. My body yearned for more. I had to squeeze the cup, and it took all my willpower to sip instead of gulp the water.

"Usk choose well," Cly've said.

"Usk?"

"Your master," he said. "Do you have any idea why you're here?"

I shook my head. The water was helping. I felt better, lighter, but tired. My mouth felt less thick, less gummy, with each sip I took. I began holding the water in my mouth as long as I could before swallowing it. That seemed to have the best effect on how I was dealing with the sweltering heat of Vespa.

"You've been chosen," he said with a smile that revealed several missing teeth. "I was once where you are long, long ago."

"Chosen for what?" I asked, thinking I had probably been selected as the main course of a feast the aliens were preparing. It didn't seem possible that they would let me live, despite the old man sitting next to me.

"To be part of their sacred magic."

"Magic?" I asked. Even among the wonders of the Vanj civilization, having traversed outer space from one planet to another, I was still skeptical.

"Divine magic," Cly've said. "Some of us are more skilled at utilizing it. Others are natural born fighters, chosen to be protectors of the high priests."

"That's why I'm here?"

"Usk saw something in you," Cly've said. "Time will tell if he was right. For now, you must adapt to Vespa. Not all who are brought here can."

Cly've left me in the cage, with only half a container of water left. I spent the rest of the long day languishing in the heat. Hour after hour passed. In many ways it felt like my body was shriveling up like a piece of dried fruit. The hardest part was rationing the water. I didn't know when or if I would get more. Eventually I laid back in my cage and fell into hallucinations of Ferret. I dreamed of the cold nights sitting by a firepit, wrapped in my ram skin pelt, my stomach filled, my muscles relaxed. We used to stare up at the stars and wonder what could be out there in the vast dark expanse.

When one daydream broke I sipped a little water, and then gave myself over to the next fantasy. I had entire conversations with my old companions, even though they were dead and gone. I saw Elaa'zar sitting on a boulder, sharpening his spear. We talked about the Vanj and the best ways to kill them. I imagined that Sal'ma was back with me under a full moon, telling me tales of the daughters of the night. I even saw Tip'un and Rip'un laughing and joking together, supremely confident and happy.

They were pleasant fantasies, and they helped me pass the time. The long day faded into sweltering night. The temperature did come down a little, but not much. There was no cool breeze in the jungle, no relief from my misery. I tried to sleep, but it was too hot and I was too miserable. Eventually, I stopped sweating. My tongue grew thick and stiff in my mouth, despite the sips of water I allowed myself to take. My eyes got so dry I could barely see, and my breathing was painful.

When the sun rose the next day I had only a cupful of water left. I pulled myself upright in the cage and sat in the back corner, watching the sky turn red, then pink, and finally blue. I don't remember finishing that last cup of water, but realizing it was empty was a rude awakening. Panic set in, and I prayed for death. On Ferret people rarely talked of God or religion, and yet I prayed instinctively. Who I was praying to was a mystery, but I begged whatever divine being that existed to let me die. The survivor's guilt I had felt was swept away by a tide of envy. My friends had died and I had lived, only to be tortured slowly in an alien world.

When Cly've returned I was slumped against the wall of my cage, barely conscious. I didn't even notice him limping up the ramp of the ship. My eyes were open, but my vision was blurry and my mind so foggy that I took no notice of him approaching. Nor had I seen the storm clouds that were drifting toward us.

"You're still alive," he said, a little surprised. "I had my doubts about you. It takes no small amount of strength to survive a full day on Vespa with only a little water. Most people gulp down what they've got and die through the long watches of the night. At least you made yours last till dawn."

His words sounded strange to my ears. I heard him, and yet they didn't really reach me. It was like being in the darkness and hearing someone moving around in another room. He unlocked my cage and pulled me out just as the first fat drops of rain began to fall. The temperature of the water was cooled slightly as it fell through the hot, humid air. But to me they felt like a refreshing oasis in the desert. I didn't even know then what a desert was, or an oasis. All I knew as the old man pulled me down the ramp and left me lying in a heap on the paving stones, was that something other than the wretched heat was falling on me. I rolled onto my back and opened my mouth. I let the drops puddle on my eyes and soak into my parched skin. Not enough fell into my mouth to alleviate the thirst I felt, but any amount of moisture was welcome. The rain fell heavily. Cly've stood in it, letting it run down his bald head and into his scraggly beard. I lay in it, exhausted and dehydrated to the point of sickness.

When the storm passed, we were given water, which Cly've mixed with a powder.

"It's salt, mostly," he said, "but some other trace minerals, too. This time, you should drink up. Go slow, but drink it all."

Drinking slowly was hard. Every fiber of my being wanted to suck it all down as fast as possible. Instead, I swallowed little amounts, one after another in a slow but steady rhythm. My vision cleared within moments, and my mind sharpened. I still felt tired, my arms and legs felt as though they had been tied down with heavy weights. The gravity on Vespa was greater than on Ferret, but I wouldn't learn that fact for many days. Most of all, I just felt better. The surge of energy was tiny by any other standard, yet it felt to me like I was shaking off death. I managed to get to my feet and stand on my own.

You might be thinking I should have run at that point. There were no bonds holding me there, so why not try to escape? Surely I could have outrun the old man with a cane. But there was nowhere to go. Should I have run into the jungle that was teaming with Vanj? I was on an alien world, with no way to know if I could survive even one day on my own. And getting off the planet was even more impossible. I could have run back into the ship, closed the hatches, and taken off, only I didn't know how to do any of those things, much less actually fly a spaceship. And even if I could get to space, I didn't know where I was or where to find Ferret. I needed information and time to regain my strength. So, when Cly've hobbled toward the building I had seen my friends' bodies taken into, I followed without complaint.

For over a week I did nothing but work to regain my strength. Every morning Cly've appeared. He took me for long walks. I was given strange fruits and vegetables to eat, nothing cooked, no meat, but it was so hot I didn't want anything else. Inside the big facility were tiny rooms with woven mats on the floor and small basins with running water. That first day I was bowled over by the wonder of turning a knob and seeing fresh, clean water pour out of the little faucet. I drank my fill and poured handfuls over my head and neck. The temperature inside the facility was the same as outside, a constant swelter. But over time my body began to adjust. There were trails through the thick ground cover in the forest. I was sent to walk them at first, then to run. I thought Elaa'zar's daily exercises had been tough, but on Vespa my body became like iron. There was no fat, just muscle and bone. My heart beat with a strength I had never known. My thighs grew larger, my arms and body thicker with muscle. The food I was given was nutritious, much more so than anything I had ever eaten on Ferret. But it was supplemented with powders that I would add to my water and drink. The powders were designed to cause my muscles to grow and my skeleton to strengthen.

I learned about the divine magic, too. At first I didn't believe it, but it didn't take long before I couldn't deny it. Any hopes that I harbored of escape or being free were crushed by the ability of the Vanj wizards. All I could do was obey.

†††

"Today begins the testing," Cly've announced when he brought my breakfast and unlocked the cell that had become my home.

"What?"

"You will be tested for worthiness in the pit of suffering," the old man said. "That's all I'm allowed to say."

"And you did this?" I pressed him, going straight for the bowl of food he had brought me.

"Long, long ago," he said. "I wasn't always an old man, you know."

After my breakfast we went into a room, where I was examined from head to toe by a group of Vanj. It was frightening, as their long claws poked and scraped my skin. My body had hardened into pure muscle and bone, there was nothing soft about me any longer. I was thankful there were no mirrors in the Vanj facility, and perhaps I would have fought the aliens if they had allowed it. But the moment I stepped into the room I felt my stomach flip and I rose into the air.

"Don't panic," Cly've said. "It's the divine magic. You can't escape it."

He was right. I couldn't escape or even control myself. I tried to swim in the air, but it did nothing. The ceiling was high in that room, and nothing was within reach. The group of aliens surrounded me. I hung, suspended before them helpless, while they hissed and growled and made clicking noises. At times they pointed at me or touched parts of my body. I was spun upside down so they could inspect my hair.

When they finished, I was lowered to the ground. It felt strange to be on my feet again, and I was sluggish as Cly've led me out of the room.

"Something's wrong with me," I said.

"You're just adjusting to gravity again, child. You're fine."

"Gravity?"

"You have much to learn," he said. "Gravity is an invisible force, the essence of all magic. Everything exists inside this gravity. You...me...the building...the trees...even the planets and stars. The Vanj wizards have learned to manipulate it."

"How?" I asked.

We were walking from the facility toward a boxy-looking vehicle. My usual daily exercise was being skipped, and I didn't want to complain. I was leery of everything around me and expected at any time to be killed by the Vanj, but even terror loses its potency after a while, replaced by routine. I was fascinated by things that Cly've was showing me, but also struggling to keep up with the demands placed on me. And I didn't mind a disruption of my daily routine, even if the inspection was humiliating. It was still better than running.

We climbed into the back of the vehicle. There were low, metal benches to sit on. Cly've leaned against the wall of the vehicle and stretched out his legs. I sat beside him and did the same thing.

"How do they work the magic?" I asked again.

"You will hear them speak of it in time," he told me. "There are many myths and legends, but the Vanj believe the divine magic was given to them by a divine being. I cannot pronounce the name it had, so I just call it Enlil. The story goes something like this: In the beginning, Enlil desired a place to be created. His most powerful servants, the Fray, spun the universe together in his honor. But Enlil was harsh and cruel to the people living among the stars, and the Fray decided he was not worthy of their creation. Banding together, they rebelled against his rule. It's a story as old as time, is it not?"

"That doesn't answer my question," I pointed out.

"I'm getting to that. Asp was the supreme Fray, the leader of the host or something along those lines."

"Like a chieftain?"

Cly've shrugged his bony shoulders. "Yes, I suppose that's right. It was he who led the fight against Enlil, but before they destroyed each other, Asp taught the Vanj to use the divine magic. It was given to them to help them survive when the Fray were gone."

"Survive how?" I asked.

"Just look around," he said, pointing to the facility. "Just as they lifted you off the ground, they lifted those stones. They can use the magic to power their ships and cross impossible distances."

"What distances?" I asked.

"The space between the stars," he said.

"It's not far," I told him. "I was taken from Ferret and brought to this planet in less than a day."

"Because of the magic, child. You have much to learn. The stars are separated by incredible distances, spaces so vast it would take more than a lifetime to travel between them if not for the magic."

I nodded, but I didn't really understand. I thought of the stars I had watched at night on the surface of Ferret. They were close together. Nothing he was saying really made sense to me at the time. But the ship we were in lifted off the ground with a roar and rose over the trees. I looked out of the open hatch in the back. The jungle canopy stretched as far as I could see.

"Consider this planet," Cly've went on. "How far could you walk in a day?"

"Not far," I said.

"Even in this conveyance," he pointed out as we flew swiftly over the treetops, "it would take days to cross the entire length of the planet."

"So?"

"So, how is it possible to travel from one world to the next in less than a day?" he said. "You can't even see the other planets."

"Luna rules the night sky," I pointed out.

"That is just a moon. Most planets have them. They are barren rocks, child. Vespa orbits a completely different star than Mige. You are no longer in that system."

I didn't understand what he was talking about, but I enjoyed listening to him as we flew over the treetops. It was all wondrously new to me. I had traveled between planets, but that had been in a cage and I hadn't seen anything. Since being on Vespa I had been confined to the ground, going only where my own two feet carried me. The boxy transport was my first time experiencing vehicular travel.

After a couple of hours, we slowed down. I saw other ships flying to and from a massive opening in the forest. When we got closer I could see buildings of all sorts inside the open area, with aliens moving around between them like ants. In the center of the clearing was a circle. From the air I couldn't really make out the fact that it was an amphitheater. I had never seen one before, although I'd heard stories of huge crowds gathering for competitive events. The Heterrids on Ferris had never tried to gather in my lifetime. In fact, most never left the caverns they were born in.

"That's the pit," Cly've said. "You'll have to fight to survive down there."

"Fight?" I asked.

He nodded, and we both looked back at the massive circle on

the ground. I considered myself to be a hunter, not a fighter. The idea made me nervous, but I had been living without hope since being captured on Ferret. So, I felt resigned to my fate. As the ship descended toward the city, I watched the pit where I expected to die.

Once on the ground, we went to a low-roofed building, where I discovered that I was not the only captive from Ferret. There were dozens of people, men and women, each in his or her own little cell. They wore simple shifts that were woven from some type of lightweight material. They watched me as Cly've marched me toward my own cell.

"These are the chosen," he said. "You'll have to win to survive."

"I have to fight them all?" I asked.

"Not all," he said. "But several, at least until you prove yourself."

"Prove what?"

"That you're capable of defending your master," Cly've explained. "We've all done it. Survive long enough and you'll be taken off this world, Azree'el. You might even be lucky enough to learn some magic and see the galaxy. This is you." He pointed to the tiny room.

Inside the cell was a sleeping mat, a wash basin, and a metal pole that was above my head and connected to both sides of my narrow room. I stepped inside and looked around. There wasn't anything inviting about the small space.

"This is where I leave you," he said.

"Where are you going?"

"Back," he said. "I don't watch. I just prepare the new prospects."

"Will I see you again?"

He shook his head. "I doubt it. Forget about an old crust like me, Azree'el. Survival is all that matters now. That and the prophecy."

"What's a prophecy?"

"It's like a prediction about the future," he said. "No one knows where it came from, but an old man told it to me when I was where you are."

"So, tell me," I said.

He closed the door to my cell. It was made of thick wood on the bottom half, with metal bars on the top half. The lock clanked as the door closed. It made an ominous sound. I took hold of the metal. It was warm. Everything on this sweltering planet was hot. Still, I pressed my face between the bars, getting as close to the old man as I could. He was the closest thing I had to a friend, and my emotions were unraveling at the thought that I would never see him again.

"It is said that one day a Heterrid will be freed by the mercy of an enemy," he said, his tiny eyes boring into mine. "That one will return to Ferret to free our people and show them the way of the master."

He stepped back, and I reached out for him. "What does that mean?"

Cly've shook his head sadly. "No one knows," he replied. "Good luck."

Tears flooded my eyes as I watched him leave. Then I sank down onto my sleeping mat and cried.

"You finished yet?" a rough voice from the next cell over asked. "Don't waste your tears. You should drink some water. You'll need it."

"What?" I asked.

"It'll be dark soon. That's when the fights start. Don't waste your strength crying. You'll need it all to survive in the pit."

I wanted to know more, but first I went to the wash basin. It was the same as the one in the facility where the bodies of my friends had been processed into food for the Vanj. The small, bowl-shaped basin had a dark hole in the bottom. From a spigot above, a stream of lukewarm water poured when I turned the knob. I filled my hands with water and splashed it on my face, neck, and shoulders. After washing myself, I returned to the door.

"What's your name?" the rough voice said.

It was weary, but female. I strained against the bars trying to see who the speaker was, but I couldn't see anything but the dark cells that lined the far side of the facility.

"Azree'el," I said. "What's yours?"

"Nee'na," the woman said.

"What is this place?"

"It's a stable," she said. "We're all fighters. You want to survive, then you do whatever it takes, you hear me? You can't hold back, Azree'el, 'cause whoever fights you in the pit won't show you any mercy."

"Okay," I said.

It was hard to take everything in. My voice sounded weak and frightened, because I was. There was no sense in denying it. In fact, I embraced my fear. It reminded me that I wanted to live.

"So," I asked, "how do we get out of here?"

"Only two ways," Nee'na replied. "Either you win, or you die."

"Win?" I asked. "I win and they take me out of here?"

"If you win enough times," she corrected herself. "One time won't do it. But if you win, you'll get a tutor."

"A what?"

"It's a machine. If you want to be selected to be a protector of the Fray you have to learn. That's all we do here. We train to fight and learn. You can't be selected if you can't understand their language."

"Whose language?"

"The Vanj. They call it Common. It's not what they speak all the time. Not the chattering clicks and hisses."

"Oh," I said in surprise. It had never occurred to me that a person could know more than one language.

"You learn Common, and whatever else the device teaches you. Every few days you'll fight. That's what we're here for."

"How long have you been here?"

"I don't know. Can't remember. I got hurt pretty bad early on and things got a little blurry."

"What do you know about the prophecy?"

"I know you'd best forget it," Nee'na said. "There ain't no hope to be found in anything other than yourself in this place. Ain't no friends, ain't no alliances, just you. When they come to take you down to the pit, best get your mind set on killing. Nothing else matters if you're dead."

Once more I sank down onto the sleep mat. I pulled my knees up to my chest. A short time passed and food was brought to my cell, along with a cup. I didn't have much of an appetite, but I drank my fill of water. It was hot inside the stable, just like every other place on Vespa. Heat was a constant, as was sweat. My meal was a small bowl with some fruit and vegetables in it. I emptied the bowl onto my sleep mat to save for later. Along with the food was more of the powder, which I added to my cup of water and drank. The mixture of artificial hormones was combined with electrolytes and trace minerals that my body needed to combat the constant sweating. Cly've had done his best to prepare me for the trial that lay ahead, and I didn't want to disappoint him. And even more than that, I didn't want to die. There was still a glimmer of hope before me. It was far away and out of reach, but even the idea of the tutor device intrigued me. But to get it I had to win the fight I knew was coming. The anticipation of that fight was terrible. In the other cells, the fighters were getting pumped up.

"Oh, yeah! It's go time!" someone shouted.

"Time to bash some skulls," another said with a chuckle.

"I can't wait!" another voice said, though it didn't sound as cocksure as the first. "Can't wait!"

In my cell, I sat in the corner with my knees pulled up against my chest, listening. Compared to the others, I was terrified. It never occurred to me that they were frightened, too, and their arrogant bellows were just another way to deal with how they felt.

The stable fell silent as the Vanj came down the hall between the cells. I got to my feet and looked through the bars. They were headed straight for my cell. Even after all the time I had been captive and seen the alien Vanj, they were still frightening up close. They had long, spindly bodies, almost as if they were all bones covered with tight skin that was various shades of gray. Their skulls curved back over their backs and they had animal faces. One opened my door and the other lifted me slightly off the floor using the magic they possessed. I didn't know it then, but only a select few of them could utilize divine magic. Still, I was once more held helplessly in their invisible grip. The alien caused me to glide out of my cell. I knew better than to try to fight the strange magic. Instead, I relaxed and saved my strength for the trial I knew was coming.

"Good luck," Nee'na called out.

Down the row of cells, the other captives began to hit the doors of their cells with their knees in a slow, steady rhythm. Most pounded the doors softly. They had no chance of breaking them down. The steady pounding echoed through the stable. It was a salute to the fighters who would battle to death in order to entertain the mob. I knew none of that, and didn't even look at the other captives. Elaa'zar always said to remain calm before making a kill. That was a hunting skill, but it was all I really knew. A person can get tense before extreme action is called for. But that only leaves them weary and tense when the time comes to do what is necessary. I didn't want to be so wrung out from worry that I had no energy for the fight. Nor did I want to be tense. Instead, I thought about my friends and paid attention to what was happening.

At the far end of the stable was a ramp that led downward. The alien brought me there. The down sloping tunnel was gloomy and covered with thick vines. It would have been difficult to walk down that slope without tripping or twisting an ankle, but the Vanj seemed to prefer the textured floor to a smooth, clean passageway. The tunnel went down until the light from the stable was lost behind us, and only a dim glow from what was ahead could be seen.

At the end of the tunnel, I could see the floor of the pit, even though I had no idea what it was. Before I could see it, I could hear the roar of the crowd. It all blended together into a noise that sounded like meat sizzling in a hot pan. Beside the entrance to the pit was a rack full of weapons. There were swords, spiked clubs, hammers, axes, and knives. There was only one spear, and it had blades at either end. I had never fought with any of the weapons except for defending myself with my knife. But I had killed, both man and beast. And I was most comfortable with a spear. So, I selected the double-ended weapon, and at a wave from the aliens, walked out into the arena.

The cheering of the crowd increased when they saw me. I'll admit I was timid. The floor of the pit was hard-packed earth that was covered with some sort of white, chalky dust. I learned later that the white dust was put there to make our blood stand out in a more dramatic fashion. You may feel that dueling for one's life is cruel, and in some ways I agree. But it helped prepare me.

I walked out toward the middle of the arena, testing my spear as I went. It was a sturdy weapon, lighter than I expected. In the very center of the wooden handle was an ornate section that was thicker than the rest.

When I reached the center of the pit, I turned around. It felt like danger would be coming for me at any moment. My skin felt hot and itchy down the center of my back. My mind felt numb. I kept turning and turning until at last my opponent appeared. It was a woman about the same size as me. She wore the same shapeless shift that the other prisoners I had seen wore. It revealed her arms, which were packed with tight muscles and protruding veins. Her skin was pale compared to mine. Her long brown hair was tied back to keep it out of her face.

I was still in my rags, the same clothing I had worn on Ferret that had been ruined when the alien dragged me from the forest to my camp in his net. I saw that my opponent had an advantage. I had nothing to tie my hair back with, so I raised the end of my spear and started sawing at my own long tresses. My opponent stopped walking toward me and watched. There was surprise on her face. My act of desperation was actually frightening her to some degree. I can't say how I knew that, maybe I just recognized myself in the other woman. I had been terrified many, many times in my short life. It was one emotion I knew well enough.

It only took a few moments to cut most of my hair. Of course, it was ragged and horrid, but there weren't enough long strands left to get into my eyes during the fight. The other woman started to circle. I really knew nothing of fighting but knew I didn't want her coming at me from behind, so I stayed where I was and turned so that I remained facing her.

Relax, relax, I cautioned myself. *She's too far away.*

It took work. My muscles seemed to tense up all on their own. I shifted my grip on the spear as my opponent slowly angled closer and closer. In my mind I could see Elaa'zar and Tip'un running toward the first Vanj I had ever seen. I remembered the hunter's tactic. He pulled back at the last minute, let the alien try to counter, then rushed in when the Vanj was off balance. I felt a pang of resentment that Tip'un hadn't been instructed on how to attack. But then maybe he had been. Maybe Elaa'zar told him exactly what to do, and the boy simply failed to do it.

My opponent was still ten paces from me when I decided I couldn't wait any longer. The crowd was screaming and jeering. None of their alien noises made any sense to me; it was all a blur. All I could think about was the woman with the sword in the pit with me, and everything else, as wondrous as it all was, seemed to disappear.

I rushed toward her; my spear held ready. I saw the woman set her feet and draw back her sword for a killing stroke. Then I stopped, just out of reach as she swung her weapon in a level stroke that would have knocked my spear aside and opened a deep wound across my chest. The sword swished through the air as I leaned back out of reach and simultaneously drew back my spear.

My opponent was trying to regain her balance when I countered with my spear, thrusting it toward her face. That was a mistake. I should have stabbed toward her thighs, but she saw my attack coming and leaned to the side to avoid it. My feint strategy could have worked, but didn't. Instead, the woman shuffled her feet to move out of my range before I could strike a blow.

The crowd roared. It seemed like it was a million miles away and barely registered in my mind. My opponent made the next move. She dove to the ground, rolling over one shoulder and coming to her knees close enough to land a blow. I brought my spear around to block her attack, but she was fast and I was inexperienced in combat. I stopped her blade, but not before the razor edge scored a minor cut just below my knee. It was very shallow and I hardly felt it. Pushing her sword to the side, I tried to reverse my spear's motion to bring the rear blade up and into her body, but she rolled backward and sprang from her shoulders to her feet in a very athletic move. She landed on her toes, facing me, sword held ready to defend my next attack, but I was rooted in place, just watching her. I couldn't help but marvel at her skill and the gracefulness of her movements. This obviously wasn't her first fight. She stepped back and looked at the edge of her sword. There was just a little blood on it. She raised a finger, swiped some off, and held it up, taunting me.

The crowd loved her antics and loved seeing the blood on my leg, too. It rolled down slowly in hot drips. Fortunately, it didn't hurt to use that leg or to move my feet, which I finally did. My opponent and I circled each other. She was studying me, and I was trying desperately to come up with an idea or strategy for attack. It seemed clear who had the upper hand.

There are pivotal times in a person's life; I know that now.

There are times we discover things about ourselves that we never knew before. We're exposed to something new, or find within ourselves something we didn't know was there. My opponent's next move was that sort of moment for me. She started forward, as if she were going to chop my head off, but then stopped, pivoting on one foot and turning around. She bent her knees as she reversed course, spinning her entire body to bring all her strength and momentum to bear. Her sword was extended to take my legs out from under me, and in a split second I realized that there was more than one way to win a fight.

I jumped, adrenaline and fear fueling my leap. I brought up my knees, raising my feet as high as they would go. Time slowed down to a crawl. As my feet left the ground I could see my opponent's brilliant maneuver. I raised my knees, felt my stomach muscles tighten and sweat rolling down my face. The sword passed harmlessly below me, and I seemed almost suspended in the air. My spear was held across my body in a defensive grip, but I lashed out with both feet the way I had seen Elaa'zar do. I had to turn slightly in the air, felt my body start to fall. The soles of both feet hit my opponent on the side of her head. All my strength was put into that kick. She was knocked backward, her sword went flying out of her hand, and then I hit the ground.

All the air was knocked out of my lungs. Pain was all I could think of for a moment. I had landed flat on my back, my spear across my chest. Rolling to the side, I sucked in air with all my strength, reinflating my lungs. A loud ringing started in my ears, and there were sparks dancing in my vision. I saw my opponent on her hands and knees, crawling toward her sword. My mind was screaming for me to get to my feet and finish her off, but my body just wanted more air. For a full second—an eternity in a fight—I was immobile. I wheezed, drew another breath, then struggled to my knees. It was as if my body had lost all its strength.

My opponent reached her sword and spun around. We were both on our knees, but I could see that one side of her face was swelling. Her eye was only a slit, and her teeth were bared in pain.

The crowd erupted again as she charged me. The woman got on her feet so fast. My body felt sluggish and weak. I was still trying to catch my breath as I struggled to stand. The other woman leaped into the air, a savage war cry bellowing from her, the sword she fought with held high over her head. I staggered forward despite the fear I felt at her attack. My skin tightened into goose flesh, but I moved into her, or actually it was under her. She had jumped so high that I was able to move under her and rammed upward with my spear as she started to descend. It tore into her chest, shattering bone and rending flesh. I pushed her back up and over my head. Then her weight pulled her face down. My spear was caught in her body, and I released it as she fell dead just a large stride from where I stood.

For a moment the world seemed silent and still. Killing wasn't something I felt good about. I didn't know my opponent, but she was like me. Like most Heterrids, she looked very similar to me, with big eyes and a little blade of a nose. The look on her face in death was maybe relief. At least her muscles were relaxed and her eyes closed.

Then the crowd went wild. The sound of their cheering was so loud it surprised me. I looked up and could see the spectators again. There were thousands of them, bobbing up and down, chattering and whooping in delight over the death of a woman who could have been my friend.

I looked around, not sure what to do next, but the need to

make a decision was taken from me. My body rose into the air, not just a few inches off the ground, but high up. I was left spinning above the fighting pit in full view of the crowd, who were, I learned later, cheering for me. When I was lowered, it was toward the ramp that led back to the stables. I was levitated the entire way, which wasn't so bad. I had time to inspect the cut on my leg. It wasn't bad, but I was exhausted from the fight. The anticipation and wrought nerves left me completely debilitated. I was released to my cell and stumbled to the water basin. I drank a cup of water, then dropped onto the mat that served as a bed and fell instantly asleep.

More fights continued in the pit, but I was oblivious to them. And when I woke it was daylight. There were windows high up on the stable walls. They were narrow and wide, allowing in light and fresh air. On the floor beside my mat was a shift like the other prisoners wore and on top of that a small device. It was tiny, just slightly bigger than my palm, and very thin. I picked it up, and the screen on the device lit up. There were letters displayed on the screen, but of course I couldn't read them. I had never even seen writing before.

"Welcome to the Common tutorial program," a voice from the device said.

I turned it over in my hands, astonished at the technology.

"Touch the screen with your finger to begin," the voice on the device said. It was speaking my own language and I understood it perfectly, but I felt almost like a traitor just holding the thing. It was wonderful and I wanted to play with it, but I knew that by doing so I was playing right into my captor's hands. They wanted me to fight and kill. They wanted me to learn their ways, their language, and their customs so that I could serve them. The horror of the fight, and of my bloody victory, flashed in my memory. I had killed another Heterrid. That seemed wrong to me. Shouldn't I have attacked the Vanj? Weren't they the enemy?

I dropped the small device onto my sleeping mat and used the water from the tap to bathe myself. I had to scrub off the sweat, the dirt from the arena, and the blood. There was my own blood of course, and that of my opponent. I wanted none of it, no reminders of what I had done. I scrubbed my skin until it felt raw, using my old garment. Then I put on the new shift. It was clean and felt light on my body, which was sore from the battle. My back ached and my muscles felt stiff. When my meal was brought I ate everything, including the food I had saved from the night before. All that day I drank water and sat in the corner of my cell, trying not to look at the tutoring device.

In the cells across from mine were other prisoners. They were mostly men, and they spent time exercising. They did push-ups and sit-ups, just like Elaa'zar had made me do with Tip'un and Rip'un every morning. They also jumped up to grab the metal bar that was suspended above our cells and connected to the side walls. I saw the other prisoners doing pull-ups, their muscles flexing, their skin shining from the sweat that covered them. It occurred to me that perhaps I should be doing the same exercises. I saw the other prisoners doing stretches. They moved slowly through various poses, twists, turns, and bends. Others pretended to fight. They boxed the air and pretended to knee or kick imaginary opponents. More food was brought, and more of the powder with hormones and stimulants.

I did nothing the entire day but watch the other prisoners and ignore the device the Vanj had left in my cell. It wasn't until nightfall that the woman in the cell next to mine spoke up again.

"You survived your first fight," she said. "Not bad, Azree'el."

"I killed a woman," I said in a soft voice. I moved to the door of my cell and leaned against the bars for the first time that day.

"It's kill or be killed. I'm not sure which is worse, but when it comes right down to it, I don't want to die."

"Me either," I admitted.

"Good. What did you think of the tutoring device?"

"I...I didn't like it. Don't you think it's wrong to just do whatever they want us to do?"

"There ain't no escaping this life, kid," she replied. "Can't go back home. Hell, it wasn't even much of a home to begin with. Scraping by, in constant danger, fighting for the bits of tech we managed to find? Does that sound like a life to you? Even if we could go back, we're no better off. A short life on Ferret isn't what I long for. You'll see what I mean when you learn enough. There's an entire galaxy out there, Azree'el. All kinds of intelligent species. Planets full of things that are much, much better than anything on Ferret. So, yeah, I guess it seems wrong to just go along with the Vanj, but at least they're offering us something more than we could ever have on our own."

I felt shocked by her statement. Part of me hated her for saying it, and part of me wondered if maybe she was right. But I didn't pick up the device again. Instead, I stayed at the door to my cell and watched the prisoners who were taken to the pit for their fights. Men and women, some big, some little, all of them determined and scared. I joined in the tribute to them, banging my knees against my door in the rhythm set by the other captives. We watched the victors return to their cells. The dead were never seen again.

That night sleep was harder to come by. I lay in the darkness staring up at the windows. They were slightly less dark than the ceiling of the stable building. Fear seemed to course through my veins, and my mind wrestled with the idea that participating with the Vanj was a pathway to a better life. Could it be possible? Would we ever be anything other than slaves forced to fight for the entertainment of our captors? There was only one way to find out. And Cly've had said that I might even get to learn about the divine magic. That would be worthwhile, I thought, if I could just live long enough.

The next day I spent half my time exercising and stretching. My body was still strong, but sore, too. I had a bruise on my back, and the muscles there hurt when I used them. I jumped up and grabbed the bar in my cell. Pulling myself up made the muscles in my back ache, but it was a good ache, a reminder that I wasn't helpless. Yes, my body hurt, but that didn't mean I couldn't make it work. I ignored the pain and did pull-ups until all I could do was hang from the bar. That stretched the muscles in my shoulders and back in a way that felt good.

I spent the other half of my day learning from the tutoring device. It surprised me how much I didn't know. The program was broken into little lessons. I learned new words, how to pronounce them, what they looked like spelled out, and took little quizzes that unlocked the next lesson. Little did I know just how hungry my mind was. I soaked up the information and learned the entire series of symbols used in the Common alphabet. It fascinated me to discover that words could be written and messages relayed through the use of different combinations of the symbols. I simply couldn't get enough. That night when the fights began I joined the other captives in paying tribute, but in between I worked through more of the lessons. It wasn't the device that held me enthralled, or the Common language itself, but the sense of empowerment that I felt from learning.

That night I slept better, and the next day devoted myself again to preparing my body and mind. When the guards came, I understood some of what they were saying.

"Prepare yourself," one of the Vanj said. The voice was high-pitched and sounded almost like a small bird chittering away in the springtime, but I heard the Common words. They weren't there for me. Nee'na in the next cell over was levitated out.

"Good luck!" I told her.

"Don't need luck," she replied, but there was note of tension in her voice.

I understood the strain she was under. No matter how prepared a person was, they couldn't deny the fact that they were fighting for their lives. And the only way to survive was by taking another person's life. It was a nerve-wrenching ordeal from start to finish.

Once again I joined in the tribute, banging my knees against the wooden portion of my cell door. For the first time I was able to see Nee'na clearly. She was about my height, but thicker through the shoulders and chest. Her hair was braided and looked lovely, I thought, which made me touch my own hair. It had been hacked off crudely in the spur of the moment. I could feel it sticking out in all directions, but there were no mirrors in our cells or tools that I could use to shape or comb it.

I watched her float away with the alien guards. Then her opponent was taken to the pit. She was much larger than Nee'na or myself. Thick through the arms and legs, with scars that showed where her short shift revealed them. One eye was cloudy white, and her hair was long and wild-looking.

Waiting for Nee'na to return was the first time I put down my tutoring device that day. The fight seemed to stretch on and on. Part of me wished I could see what was happening. Another part of me knew I wouldn't be able to watch it. Two fighters who choose to test themselves and their skills in combat was honorable. Rules of engagement could be agreed upon, as well as victory that didn't leave a person crippled or dead. But that wasn't what we were forced to do on Vespa. We had no choice in the matter. We weren't willing athletes or professional warriors; we were prisoners on an alien planet fighting for our survival. No matter who won the fight, we all lost.

Nee'na didn't return that night. Her opponent did. She barely even looked winded and had a vicious gleam in her eye. I suppose that for some people there is joy in killing. Looking at the large woman, I felt a shudder of fear. But there was no time for mourning. I was the next prisoner called into the pit.

†††

My double-ended spear was still in the weapon rack. I took it and walked out into the arena. There was already a woman there waiting for me, waiting to kill me. She had long arms and legs. I didn't think a person could be that skinny, but she was painfully thin. Her stomach sank in between her hips, and her shoulders seemed to stick out on either side of her neck. She had the round face that many Heterrids possessed. But there was a droop to her features, her eyelids half closed over her big eyes, her narrow mouth curved down.

Her hair was slicked back with water. It hung in wet ribbons down the back of her shift. I walked out of the tunnel with my spear held in one hand. I let the lower blade drag across the ground. It was something Elaa'zar would never have allowed on Ferret. He was always adamant that weapons were tools to be carefully maintained and never used carelessly. I wasn't being careless. I intentionally dragged my spear as my own way of showing the Vanj my disrespect for their spectacle.

There were wet areas on the ground, and in one spot a shallow puddle of dark red blood. Nee'na and I hadn't exactly been friends. There hadn't been enough time to allow us to get to know one another. The circumstances of our confinement didn't allow for that. But she had been kind to me. It had been her last act of kindness. The big woman she fought, the woman with the white eye, had taken her life. The only comfort I had was knowing that Nee'na was finally free.

I have come to discover that most intelligent life forms believe in an afterlife. We were not taught that concept on Ferret. Looking back at the history of the Heterrids, which I didn't know when I walked into the arena that night, was that because we were scientifically designed in laboratories, cloned, genetically modified, tested on, and replicated until there was very little diversity in our DNA, it was believed that we had no soul. Life was all we possessed, and when one died they simply ceased to exist as anything other than the sum of their physical bodies. I didn't imagine Nee'na in some eternal paradise, and I didn't think that if I made a mistake in the fight that I would be whisked away to a different plane of existence. I knew what was at stake, and I was determined not to be the one lying dead when the fight was over.

My opponent, the woman with wet hair, had two daggers. She held one facing up, the other down and back. As I got closer, she began moving slowly sideways. The crowd was chanting something I couldn't understand. Occasionally, I heard a word shouted in the Common language, but most of what the Vanj uttered sounded unintelligible to me.

"You got lucky last time," the woman said. "Won't be so lucky this time."

I didn't speak. The woman with the wet hair must have known my first opponent. Perhaps their cells were side by side the way mine was with Nee'na's. But it didn't matter. I brought the spear up and held it with both hands. It angled from my right shoulder down toward my left calf. My hands fit neatly on either side of the wider, ornamental section in the center of the shaft.

As we got closer, I had to force myself not to tense up. My opponent began to move first one way, then another. And it wasn't just her feet that moved. Her body swayed back and forth, up and down. Her arms were in constant motion, the daggers flashing from the huge bank of lights that illuminated the pit. It was a hypnotizing dance, her long arms twirling, her bony hips swaying. But I managed to shake myself from the spectacle and stepped forward, jabbing at her with my spear.

She jumped back to avoid my weapon, then spun to the side and leaped in my direction. I was surprised at how fast she could move. Her legs didn't appear to be strong, but they were. If I hadn't jumped back, she would have come down within striking distance. Instead, she only put herself in the range of my spear. And I had learned my lesson from the first fight. I didn't strike at her head or shoulders, but rather at her lower legs. The tip of my spear cut into her leg just below her right knee. It clipped the top of her shinbone and severed part of a tendon that connected to her knee. She staggered back, limping for a moment. The crowd screamed at the sight of blood.

There was a look on her face of sudden panic. She turned and tried to run away, but the damage to her leg was worse than I thought. After half a dozen struggling steps she fell. In the attempt to catch herself, she ended up cutting her side open with her own dagger. Moaning in pain, she attempted to crawl away, but there was no place to go. As I stalked her down she finally gave up and lay still.

"Make it quick, sister," she said in tremulous voice.

I did. My spear thrust was strong and true. It severed her spine high in the back of her neck, cutting deep. Her body spasmed hard one time, then lay still. The crowd actually booed and hissed. Not over my kill, but that the fight had gone so wrong. But that was the danger of fighting. One mistake could cost a person everything.

I ignored the crowd and walked back to the tunnel. The guards levitated me back to my cell. I ate, I drank, and I slept, but I was not at peace. Finding a way out of the stables and off Vespa became my highest priority.

I'd love to say that the next day I was set free, but of course that didn't happen. The days continued in an unwavering rhythm of food, rest, exercise, and learning. Six days after getting my tutor device, I could read Common. It was a simple, intuitive language. Every letter of their alphabet had meaning, and every word was a combination of those meanings to create a kind of picture that defined the word. For example, the first letter in Common meant first, leader, or head of. The second letter meant house, or building. Those two letters together formed the word for father. By learning the alphabet and the meanings of the letters, a person could make out writing in the simple language. And I was hearing it spoken too, first by the device that was teaching me the language, and then occasionally by the Vanj who brought us food and brought us to the fighting pit. I even heard words I could understand from the crowd that occasionally screamed out in Common. *Fight* and *kill* were often heard in the arena.

When the guards came to get me for my third fight, they spoke to me in Common, and I spoke back.

"Prepare yourself," one guard said.

"I am ready," I replied.

It was true. I was taking full advantage of my time by that point. Survival wasn't enough; I needed to prove myself and my abilities. I alternated my days between hard exercise, stretching, and shadow fighting. I didn't have a spear to work with, but I thought about how to use the double-ended weapon in combat, and practiced moves to teach my body how to carry out the attacks.

"You have progressed rapidly," the alien said.

I was already floating, held firmly in the grip of the divine magic. The alien approached me, looking into my face with dark eyes.

"Tell Usk I am ready," I said.

It was a gamble. I didn't know any of the aliens, but Cly've had used the name Usk and referred to it as though it were the alien that captured me. I had no frame of reference. I didn't know if the fighters who showed the most skill in the fighting pit, or with their language skills, got selected for something else, but I knew I didn't want to stay in the stables fighting for my life and few days' rest. There was no way to escape and nowhere to escape from, so I took the only chance I had and dropped the one name I knew.

"Usk selected you?" the alien asked.

They were in no hurry to move me down the tunnel to the fighting pit.

I nodded. "I am ready."

"We shall see," the alien said.

Their faces were so foreign and so terrible that I had no way of knowing what the Vanj staring at me meant. But a moment later we were descending the tunnel to the fighting arena. When they released me from their invisible grip I selected my spear and stepped out of the tunnel. It took a moment for my eyes to adjust to the sudden glare of bright lights. The crowd was chanting loudly in their own language, which I didn't understand, but it was clear they were excited. And I could see why. Across the dirt floor of the arena was the big woman with one white eye, the same woman who had killed Nee'na. She was big, almost like a man, With broad shoulders and thick arms. Her hips were wide, and unlike the last opponent I had fought, the woman with the white eye had plenty of muscle. She was thick from her chest down into her thighs. And she stood with a club on one shoulder. The fat, striking end of the cudgel was pierced with spikes that stood out in all directions.

I was struck with fear. I didn't want to die. The big woman had killed Nee'na and she was going to try to kill me, too. All my planning and strategy seemed worthless in the face of what seemed like an unbeatable opponent. I had to take a deep breath and steady my nerves as I walked slowly toward her. She stood still watching me, grinning maniacally. I didn't know if she was the most fearsome and deadly of all the fighters in the stable, but at that moment it seemed that she was.

Anything can happen in a fight, I told myself. *Don't panic, keep her at bay, and let the weapon do the work.*

It was the same advice that Elaa'zar had given me when we were hunting big game. Whether it was with a throwing stick, a bow, or the heavy spears we used against the Vanj, the idea was to harness the tool's killing power and deploy it wisely. When I was less than twenty paces from the woman I swung the double-ended spear around and rolled my shoulders to loosen the muscles I had there. Unlike my opponent who was thick with muscle, I was more wiry. But that didn't mean I didn't have strength. In fact, I was stronger than I had ever been in my entire life. It flashed in my mind what my father would think if he could have seen me at that moment. He would be afraid. He was a coward who didn't mind slapping me around when I was just a helpless child. But I wasn't helpless any longer.

"Time to die," the woman said, her voice deep and gravelly, as if she were recovering from a head cold.

"Not if I have anything to say about it," I replied, trying to sound confident.

"You don't," the bigger woman said.

The crowd fell into a hush as I started to circle the other woman. She held her club lightly with one hand and didn't move. It occurred to me that with so much muscle she would probably tire quickly. I feinted as if I were going to charge her and she still didn't move. Her hand shifted slightly on the club she held, and that was all. Her other hand hung at her side. Her feet were shoulder width apart and she didn't even shift her weight onto the balls of her feet. It seemed as though she were entirely unfazed by having to fight me.

The crowd began shouting and I suppose cheering again; it was hard to tell which. The noise grew louder, but that was all I was certain of.

"They love a spectacle," the woman with the white eye said. "I like to put on a good show, so try not to die too fast."

I didn't reply. Instead, I started toward her, walking calmly. The big woman never moved until I was within striking distance. My spear was about as long as I was tall. By holding it in the center I could just about double my reach. When I was close enough, I shifted my weight to the balls of my feet, bent my knees slightly so that I was ready to spring away when the big woman attacked. Then I thrust my spear forward. To my complete surprise, she caught it with her free hand. I hadn't thrust as hard as I could, and certainly hadn't put my weight behind the move, but it was still shocking to see her grab the spear blade and stop its motion. There was blood welling on her fingers.

I started to shove the weapon forward. It seemed like the right thing to do at the time. But Elaa'zar had taught me that if an animal bites you, pulling away would only make things worse. Even though we instinctively want to pull away from the bite, it was better to push in. With the big woman in the arena, my instinct was to shove the spear forward, and in so doing I would shift all my weight forward. But if I got any closer I would be in the range of her heavy, spiked club. So, despite my instincts to show her how strong I was and prove that grabbing my spear had been a mistake, I pulled back instead. At the same time I pulled down on my spear. The sharp blade laid open four of her fingers in the process.

The big woman looked at her bloody hand, then held it up to the crowd. The Vanj went crazy. Maybe it was the sight of human blood, but I think it was seeing the big woman totally unfazed by my attack and the wound on her hand. Still, it seemed like the perfect time to attack, which is what I did.

My spear was already low, and I swiped it at the big woman's knees. She immediately countered, swinging the heavy club in an almost effortless fashion. It stopped my spear and nearly knocked the weapon from my hands. She followed up with a step in my direction, but I immediately jumped back, thinking she could swing the club faster than I expected. It was a keen observation, and one that probably saved my life. The big woman seemed slow, plodding, methodical. Her weapon seemed heavy and unwieldy, but in her hands it wasn't. I circled around and tried to attack on her left side, away from the club. She calmly stepped out of the path of my thrust, only she wasn't quite fast enough. My spear cut a shallow groove into her leg. I spun the weapon away as she tried to grab it again.

There was a frown on her face at that point. Not from the pain so much as the frustration at seeing my strategy of staying outside her reach. I continued to circle, forcing her to move her big feet. The crowd was chanting something in a pounding rhythm that matched the beating of my heart. Fear was playing at the edges of my consciousness, but I did my best to stay focused on my opponent. Several times I darted in, thrusting or slashing, but never close enough to cause any real damage. My goal was to keep her off balance and force her to work for the kill. I hoped to wear her down in time, but she was no fool.

I saw her knees bend and her weight shift to the balls of her feet. Her toes seemed to dig into the ground as she prepared to engage with me. It took all my mental energy to stay loose and relaxed at that moment. When she charged it was like one of the giant grizzled brown bears on Ferret. The club was held ready to strike, and I waited for it to move. There was no doubt about the outcome of the fight if it landed. Even a glancing blow would shatter bones; the spikes would rend my flesh. But I was ready. I kept my spear held low, and when the big woman started her swing with the big club I dove to the ground, rolled over one shoulder and came up on my knees just out of reach of the woman...but she was in range of my spear. I thrust it hard into her leg. The tip plunged deep into the muscles of her thick thigh. The moment I felt the spear hit bone, I shifted my weight and slashed the blade out the back of her leg.

It was a wicked strike. The big woman could tell it had hurt her. But instead of stumbling away from me, she fell toward me. Once again my spear saved me. I still held it with a wide grip. The white-eyed woman fell against it and pressed me back. Heaving with all my strength I managed to shift her weight as we fell, pushing her over my head. I rolled to the side just in time for her good leg to hammer into the side of my head. For a moment the world turned upside down and everything was blurry. When I got control of my senses again I saw her wide foot coming at me again and managed to get my spear up. The metal blade severed all her toes except the biggest one. It didn't completely stop the kick either, but did shift it so that it hit my shoulder and threw me onto my back.

The edges of my vision were dark, but there was also a voice of panic in my brain shouting for me to get up and get away from the big woman. I started to sit up just as the wounded woman brought the club swinging at me. All I could do was throw myself to the side. Several spikes raked my back, leaving shallow cuts, but didn't do any debilitating damage. I rolled away from the club and got to my knees. The big, one-eyed woman was breathing hard. She was propped on her left elbow and attempted to swing her club at me again. I had my spear and thrust it toward her face. She threw up her shoulder and the spear pierced deep again. It wedged in her shoulder joint, and I had to wrench it hard to free the blade. Blood flew, and the woman screamed. It was a hideous, agonizing scream. I got to my feet and saw the bloody mess she had become. It made my skin crawl and I felt nauseous.

"I'm not though with you yet!" she snarled.

Fear and anger and the drive to survive the fight came together, propelling me into action. I surged forward and drove the spear into her chest. She was trying to hit me with club at the same time, only the killing stroke robbed her of her strength. The spiked club fell from her fingers as she was driven back to the ground. Only a little portion of the blade was sticking out of her chest, the rest was buried deep, having shattered her sternum and punctured a lung. Blood flew from her mouth as she bellowed in pain, and her right hand grabbed the spear blade to pull it free. But all she managed to do was cut her hand.

Standing over her, I felt grateful to be alive. She looked at me with so much hatred it chilled my blood. All my anger and fear drained away in an instant, leaving me with only a sense of loss. The woman was a Heterrid, taken against her will from Ferret and forced to fight for her life on Vespa. Perhaps, under different circumstances, we could have been friends. She died with her eyes open, and I pulled my spear free.

The crowd went wild. Once again I was levitated into the air. I could feel the warm blood on my back from the cuts the spiked club had left there. Exhaustion set in on the heels of the adrenaline that flooded through me during the fight. I was grateful to be weightless, and knew that if the Vanj wizards set me down again I would collapse on the spot. But I didn't fall, and they left me spinning slowly for the crowds to see for several minutes. And then I was returned to my cell. I made it to my mat before I collapsed.

I can't say how long I lay there before I was able to think

clearly. As usual, I had saved some fruit on my sleeping mat. It was a bundle of small, green oval-shaped fruit. They were juicy and burst in my mouth the moment I bit down on them. I let the juice flow down my parched throat as I sucked on the meat of the little fruit. It was sweet and slightly sour. It seemed wonderful as it flooded my dry mouth. After I had eaten them all, I slept.

And the next day the cycle began again. The only change was that my tutor device, after having completed all the language lessons, began to teach me about planets, stars, and space. It was utterly mind-blowing. Sal'ma's thoughts about the stars, and Nee'-na's argument for the vastness of space were nothing compared to the little device that could show pictures and videos. The lessons were taught in Common, and I was quickly growing accustomed to the new language. I didn't know at the time that few of my fellow prisoners in the stable had worked through the language lessons. For many, it didn't come so easily. I was fortunate to be young enough and eager enough to learn the material, yet old enough and strong enough to stay alive. Elaa'zar had taught me well. He had seen the potential in me and honed my strengths. My father had said that I had no talent and had practically given me away to a complete stranger, yet that stranger had prepared me to survive in a dangerous world. The ideas and strategies he planted in me on Ferret were bearing fruit on Vespa in circumstances he never could have imagined.

The three-day recovery period passed by in a flash. And I had trouble sticking with my exercise routines because I found the information about the cosmos so fascinating. It made me wonder where my people had first come from. It wasn't Ferret—we all knew that—but there were other worlds in the galaxy and other intelligent life forms. The Maston Overlords had stolen us from our true home, tampering with our genetics until we no longer resembled the people we had once been, and finally discarded us on Ferret.

In my mind, the information I was learning was the way out of slavery. If I could get free, then maybe I could travel to other planets. There were places with huge cities where people lived peaceful lives. All I had to do was find one of those and get to it. It was a dream without much foundation in reality, but as I studied the cosmos on my little device, it took root in my heart. Somehow, some way, I had to make it a reality.

I had been a prisoner in the stable for two weeks when I was taken to my fourth fight. My spear had been cleaned of the blood and gore the big woman with one white eye had left on it. I took up the weapon and walked boldly into the arena, never realizing I was in for the fight of my life.

†††

The girl across the arena from me looked almost exactly like me. The only real difference was our hair. I had cut off most of mine, while hers still flowed in long, gentle waves around her head. She was armed with a short, thin sword. As I approached, she raised it and kissed the blade. That was when I saw her tongue was split down the middle and her teeth were filed to sharp points.

I never twirled my spear. The weapon felt good in my hands, but I didn't spend enough time with it to do anything fancy. Instead, I nodded at her and wondered what she was. It seemed clear that she wasn't like anyone I had ever met. And she proved that a moment later when she ran toward me with such abandon and confidence that I couldn't help but take a step backward.

When she was only a half dozen paces from striking distance she feinted one way, then the other, before leaping toward me.

For some reason I felt rooted to the spot. Perhaps I was paralyzed by fear. I won't deny how I felt in that moment. The spear seemed heavy and clumsy in my hands. I felt like a child fighting an adult, even though as the girl got closer to me it seemed to be just the opposite. I was young, but my opponent was clearly younger. Still, she jumped like an agile cat, flying several feet off the ground and bringing her sword down toward my head. All I could do was raise my spear in both hands and hope the handle was strong enough to stop her weapon.

The collision split my spear in two and sent me staggering back. And before I even knew what was happening, my opponent dove to the ground and threw a low, sweeping kick that knocked my feet out from under me. I landed hard, but the impact seemed to wake me up from the spell I was in. Throwing my feet up, I rolled backward over my shoulder and got to my feet at the same time as my opponent. There was just enough time to adjust my grip on the broken spear, which had been transformed into two long-handled swords. The younger girl was like a tornado of danger. She came at me, then changed direction by spinning off her back foot. She brought her sword around quickly using all the momentum of her spin. But I was ready for that and caught her blade on one of mine. I then stabbed at her with my other sword, but as soon as our blades clashed she leaped away.

I didn't know it at the time, but she was using magic against me, and to boost herself. All I knew was that she was dangerous. The crowd was on its feet, screaming so loudly in anticipation of our battle that it hurt my ears. But there was no time to worry about the aliens in the stands. I took off after my young opponent.

We clashed again. She slashed low with her sword in a graceful swipe that I leaped over, then she ducked under my counterstrike. I had just enough forethought to hold my spare sword in a protective position, which saved me from a devastating cut I never saw coming.

Once more when her strike didn't land, she backed away, a frown of concern on her face. I stalked forward, cognizant of the fact that I could make a mistake by pressing her, but I wanted to keep her off balance. She was too fast and too agile to let her have control of the fight. With an easy spin of the sword in my left hand, I switched it to a down-facing, defensive grip. Then I raised the other sword in my right hand so that it was ready to strike.

When I got close enough, my opponent thrust her sword at me, which I easily batted aside, then stepped forward as if to slash down at her. She raised her weapon to block my attack, but instead of slashing with the sword, I kicked her in the chest with a front kick I had been practicing in my quarters. She was strong, but not quite as big as I was. The impact knocked her off her feet and sent her crashing to the ground. With a surge of hope of finishing the fight, and maybe propelled by the roaring crowd, I closed in on her. My sword came down in a hard strike, but she rolled out of the way. My sword hit the ground instead of her, and her own weapon shot up toward me in a hard, well-aimed thrust. I flexed my hips forward, but the blade still caught and left a jagged cut in the small of my back.

I moved quickly away, pretending the wound was worse than it was. My opponent rolled to her feet, her forked tongue and pointed teeth protruding from thin lips. I let her close on me while I feinted a limp and did my best to look frightened. It wasn't hard, and the younger girl moved in quickly. I swung out with my right-handed, upright weapon in a clumsy slash she easily avoided.

As we fought I studied her moves and tendencies. I had already guessed what her reaction to my clumsy slash would be, and she didn't disappoint. But I spun around, avoiding her counterstrike and slashing with my left-handed, downward-facing sword in a backhanded move that she didn't see coming. But she was still fast and able to turn the killing blow into a minor scrape across her shoulder.

We were both bleeding, both breathing heavily, and without saying a word, we began to circle one another. I didn't need to limp, and discarded the feigned injury. I wanted to take the fight to the younger woman, but I couldn't risk an even exchange. My opponent had only one sword, but she used it with cunning and speed I could hardly match. But I was learning, and knew I could move faster, with more force, and greater rapidity. All I needed was an opening, and eventually I found it.

She occasionally glanced past me at the crowd of roaring Vanj. Even though I couldn't understand their language, it seemed obvious that she was their favorite in our match. And the younger girl seemed to thrive on the thrill of the audience. When she looked past me I jumped to the side, and as soon as my feet touched the ground I charged at her. She turned, coming face to face with me, and raising her sword defensively. Twisting my body to the side, I swung both of my swords, slashing and turning, with one blade high, the other held low. The younger girl deflected the high blade and attempted to jump over the low one, but she didn't quite make it. My sword cut across the top of her foot, severing the tendons there, and causing her to fall onto her side.

That should have been the end of the fight, but she jabbed at me with her sword from the ground. The point of her weapon gouged into my thigh and stabbed my hip. It didn't break the bone, but it hurt bad enough that I shouted in pain and went tumbling backward. Even though her foot was injured, she managed to rise to her feet and leap on me. Her momentum was powerful enough to knock the sword from my right hand when she slashed at me. Her body crashed on top of mine, knocking the breath from my lungs and making sparks dance in my vision, but I raised my left arm and sliced with the remaining sword under her right arm. Blood gushed over me, and the girl screamed as she rolled away from the pain. Her sword dropped behind her with her right arm dangling uselessly from her shoulder. Blood soaked her shift and she was helpless to stop it. I might have finished her off immediately, but I was struggling to catch my breath and moved away from her to get the chance to do it.

Somehow, when I got to my knees, she was already up on her feet with her sword in her left hand. Her attack came fast, even though her feet never moved and her legs were still. She shot at me like an arrow from a bow, slashing her sword at my throat. All I could do to avoid it was throw myself backward. Her slash missed my throat by a hair's breadth. I felt the wind from its pass by my chin. She crashed into me, but stayed on top of my body as we fell. Somehow she was floating. I thought one of the wizards was helping her, and there was no doubt that magic was at play. But I still had one sword and slashed it at her to keep her at bay. She rose several feet in the air, rotated her sword so that it was pointing down, then dove at me. I jerked to the side, but the sword sliced open my shoulder and severed the thin strap of my shift on that side. Screaming, I punched her hard in the side with my right fist. She recoiled from the pain of my punch and I grabbed her wounded shoulder. With a jerk, I pulled her to the side and rolled over on top of her. She still had a sword, but I pinned her arm down with my sword, the blade cutting deep into her left wrist. At the same time, she rose and tried to bite my neck with her pointed teeth. In my effort to stop her I threw my head toward hers and smashed my forehead into her nose. I heard her teeth clack as they came together. She was knocked backward, and I rose on top of her. With only my right hand free, I hit her. Pain reverberated through my hand and up my arm, but I had opened a little gash in her cheek with the punch. In return, she opened her mouth and hissed at me.

I dropped, thrusting my forearm under her chin. Her teeth clashed again, snapping onto her forked tongue. More blood fountained up. Her nose was gushing, and with her tongue severed her mouth was filling with blood. I had all my weight on top of her. She tried to buck me off, but I held on and continued pressing my forearm into her throat. For a moment it was a struggle of pure desperation. And then she tried to breathe, but her airways were clogged with blood. It flowed into her lungs as she inhaled. Her entire body shook with a wicked, desperate frenzy that was more than just the pain I had caused her. She choked to death on her own blood and died beneath me. Her body writhed for a moment, then went still. I didn't let go, fearing a trick. My own shoulder and hip were aching. Suddenly my entire body spontaneously rose from the young fighter.

Higher and higher I flew, all the while struggling to catch my breath and come to terms with the fact that somehow I had survived.

†††

When I arrived back at my cell, there was a clean shift neatly folded on my sleeping mat, along with some kind of cream in a tube. I had never seen a simple squeeze tube before, and once I drank my fill of lukewarm water and regained some of my strength, I studied it intently. The writing on the tube was in the Common language. I was fascinated by it. Simply having something that I could read using the skills I had learned was very empowering. And discovering that it was medicine was exciting, too. I squeezed out the cream and massaged it over my wounds. The pain began to diminish slightly.

That night I slept hard, and when I woke up there was a Vanj waiting for me. The door to my cell was open wide, and the alien sat patiently just inside. It was hard not to panic. Even living among the aliens for weeks hadn't changed the way their hideous appearance made me feel. I sat up, glancing around the tiny cell for a weapon I knew wasn't there.

"You have done well," the alien said.

Its voice was a husky, scratching sound, but the words in Common were spoken slowly and deliberately for me to understand. I nodded slightly, but didn't speak.

"You have proven to be resourceful," it continued. "Let us see if you have the strength to wield the gift as well."

I had no idea what the gift was, and I was still exhausted from my battle the night before, but I got to my feet. The alien was squatting, its long legs folded backward, its arms folded neatly against the sides of its painfully thin body. Up close to the creature, I wondered how its thin neck supported the weight of its head. The Vanj skull was long and curved, all its vital organs inside. I had seen and even handled a decapitated alien skull. Elaa'zar had removed the organs right in front of me, peeling off the tight flesh that covered it, and used the skull like a kettle to boil the alien's bones in.

"Come!" it commanded.

It turned and left my cell open. I followed, walking under my own power. The wound in my shoulder ached as the strap of my new shift rubbed against it. Pain lanced through my body with each step. I had cuts on my back, thigh, and shoulder, along with a variety of bruises. My arms and legs felt heavy, but the alien was walking quickly down the passageway and I struggled to keep pace, ignoring the agony my body was in.

For the first time since arriving in the alien city, I was taken from the stables out into the sunlight. I had to squint and shade my eyes with one hand. My escort didn't seem to notice or care. It just kept moving, the long legs striding so fast I nearly had to jog to keep pace.

We left the stable and crossed into a round building with a domed roof. I might have been mesmerized at the sight of it if not for my constant pain and nagging fear. Nothing about the Vanj was good. I had no expectation of anything positive happening in the new structure the alien led me into. Nor did I bother with entertaining ideas of escape. There was nowhere to run to in this strange world, no way to get back to the planet I thought of as home. So, I followed and waited to see what new horror awaited me.

Inside the dome was one huge room. The floor was stone, and light came in from high windows just below where the ceiling began to arch upward. On the walls beneath the windows were curtains, and in the center of the huge room was a set of thick floor pads. The alien went straight to them and turned around to face me.

"Sit!" it ordered.

I was only too happy to sit down and stop moving. Every fiber of my being was crying for me to stop and rest. The pads were thick and soft. Part of me wanted to lie down and close my eyes. They were the most comfortable things I had felt in weeks. After being captured and dragged by the alien in a net, then locked in a cage and sleeping for weeks on the hard ground, the mats felt luxurious.

The alien pulled out a feather of some sort from somewhere on its body. The Vanj didn't wear clothing, and I had no idea where the feather had come from, but it was suddenly there in the creature's long, talon-like fingers. It was a brilliant blue color with a black quill.

"Look at this feather," the alien said. "Concentrate on it until you can feel it in your mind. Don't just think about it. You must sense it in a way that you never have before, and send it flying out of my hand."

Part of me wanted to laugh at the ludicrous suggestion, but I had to admit that I had been levitated myself by the magic of the Vanj. They had lifted me in the air to carry me to the fighting pit, and after my victories I had been levitated high enough that even the aliens at the top of the amphitheater got a good look at me. If they could work their magic on me, perhaps, I thought, I could do something with the feather.

I stared at it hard, trying to sense it the way the alien had instructed. It didn't take long for what I thought was my fatigue to kick in. The room began to rock and sway around me. I was sure I was falling asleep. It felt as though my consciousness was letting go of my physical body, and the only times I had ever felt that sensation was when I closed my eyes to sleep. It was like the moment just before you drift off, a sort of lightness to your entire body as you finally relax into sleep.

I shook my head, trying to ward off the drowsiness I thought I was feeling. There was a sense of futility to the effort, and more than a little embarrassment, too. The light, wavy sensation returned. Something seemed to be moving all around me. I shook my head again, afraid I was about to pass out.

"Stop fighting the magic, little one," the alien said. "Move the feather. You can do it."

It was oddly encouraging. I imagined the feather moving, and it was if I could feel the wavering energy around it letting go. It was so tenuous, so delicate, and yet, as I severed the strands of motion that seemed to make the feather waver in the alien's claw, it moved. It wasn't much, just a slight lift for a moment. It could have been from the breath of the alien for all I knew, but I not only saw the movement, I felt it, too.

"Yes, yes, that is it. Release the feather from its bonds. Surround and lift it into the air with the strength of your mind."

I was all in at that point. Perhaps under other circumstances I would have laughed it off, or been embarrassed, but we were alone in the big room. My fatigue fell away, and my pain was forgotten. All that seemed to exist in the universe was the feather and the strange sense of motion that was rolling in waves around us. I wasn't sure, but I thought I could feel it holding us down. I willed the feather to be free, to float upward, and once again it shivered in the alien's hand.

"It isn't enough to break the bonds that hold us down," the big Vanj alien said in its husky voice. "You must enshrine the object in your own will."

The instructions didn't really make sense and my progress was slow, but the alien didn't give up or even get impatient with me. Minutes turned into hours. I sat very still, sweating in the heat, struggling to wrap my mind around the little feather. Eventually, my senses picked up the delicate strands coming from the quill. I can't say how it happened, just that my awareness deepened. And I imagined a gap around the feather. Only then did it float up into the air.

"You have the talent," the alien said. There was no delight in its voice, or sense of triumph in the declaration, just the recognition of what I had achieved. "What is your name?"

"Azree'el," I said.

"I am Usk, but you will call me Master."

I was too tired to get defensive, and too thrilled at having touched the divine magic to be upset by the alien's demand. He brought me to another building, and I was given a room with a shower. It was my first time to be able to stand under running water. I was given food and more of the medicinal cream. Instead of the plain shift that the fighters wore, I was given a skirt and a vest that laced together. In the room was a mirror that allowed me to see my own reflection without being distorted. I was given a pair of scissors to work on my hair, and freedom to roam through the building where I was being housed. It was completely empty except for me; the other guestrooms were vacant.

Instead of a sleeping mat I was given a proper bed with a soft mattress and blankets. It was still too hot to need them, but having come from Ferret where such things were practically nonexistent, I understood the luxury of them. My fortunes had changed. I was no longer just a slave expected to fight for the mob's entertainment. My ability to learn and the willingness to throw myself into the task had set me apart. Of course, my innate fighting skills were recognized, too.

The next day I was put through a rigorous schedule of training. In the morning I was sent running for over an hour. Then I spent another hour training with an old man named Urii'us. He was missing three fingers from his left hand, and his body was so stiff he had trouble moving around. But he was an expert with the double-ended spear I had fought with in the arena. Under his tutelage I learned the proper techniques for using the weapon against a variety of enemies. We also studied fighting with short swords. It was exhausting, but illuminating. I had no desire to return to the fighting pit, but if I had, there was no doubt I would have been much more efficient in dispatching my opponents.

After training in the morning, I spent the rest of the day learning to sense and control the divine magic. Of course, I had a thousand questions that were never answered. The Vanj didn't teach me magic as much as force me to grapple with the strange, invisible forces day after day. I learned to feel it flowing at all times, and to keep track of the things around me. For instance, when I trained with Urii'us he sometimes sent multiple opponents against me. I learned to sense them and their movements in the flow of the invisible magic.

I wasn't allowed to utilize magic during my weapons training, but I used it to help me keep track of what was happening. Even during the evenings when I was alone in my room, I could sense whenever someone else entered the building. And no one had to teach me that I could use the power to defend myself. If I could move an object, I could stop an object, or a person for that matter, from getting close to me. In the evenings I practiced forming a protective shield around me as I did my daily stretches that helped work out the soreness from my long runs and sparring practice with the double-ended spear.

Four months passed in a blur. There were times when I was so incredibly lonely that I cried myself to sleep. Yet, I was learning so much, and there was no doubt that I was being groomed for something. Occasionally other people showed up in the building that was my official home. They were almost always elderly, most so old my mind could barely comprehend it. Had they been left on Ferret they would certainly have died much younger, but the elderly visitors were like Cly've. They, too, had been abducted from our world and taken to Vespa as prisoners. Unlike me, they weren't taught the divine magic, but they often knew a lot about it. Some weren't interested in spending time with a young woman in training. Others were only too happy to have some company. They told me of their lives on Vespa, usually as trainers like Cly've. It made sense that getting the lay of the land and adapting to life on Vespa was easier done by another Heterrid than the alien Vanj. Most of the visitors had vivid scars from their time in the fighting pits, of which there were several across the larger enclaves of the Vanj on Vespa.

Some were workers inside the temples of the alien world. The Vanj didn't worship a god, but rather they worked to evolve into one. When the first visitor explained this to me, I thought he was mad.

"They think they can become a god?" I asked, trying not to giggle.

We were sitting outside on a little elevated platform near the power converters. It wasn't designed for that purpose, but most of the visitors who came to the building I thought of as my home but was really just a hotel of sorts for the humans in the city, knew of the space. It was isolated, but sometimes the evening breeze blew in so that it was comfortably cool. In fact, it was one of the coolest places I had found since being brought to Vespa. We sat on the edge of the platform, our feet dangling, the breeze ruffling my short hair as we talked.

"That is their belief, and from what I've seen they aren't far off the mark," Jaa'san explained. "You know of the magic."

I nodded. Of course I knew of it, the Vanj were teaching me to use it. I still didn't know why, and to be honest I didn't care. I had discovered the invisible power and wanted more of it. But that didn't mean I needed to tell everyone that I was learning to use it. That nugget of information I kept to myself.

"They can do things that defy the imagination," Jaa'san continued. "Some say they can even extend their lives forever. To become immortal and live among the stars, that sounds like a god to me."

It was certainly something to think about. I wanted to go back up into space, to travel through the stars. My first experience had been less than desirable. I'd been locked in a cage and abandoned to grieve the loss of my friends. I still grieved for them at times, but the pain was fading, and the more I learned of the divine magic, the less I thought about the life I had lost on Ferret.

After four months of training, I was ready for the testing. Usk met me in the domed building and told me what was to come.

"Tomorrow you will face the first of your trials," he said. Being immersed in the Common language had made me fluent. I didn't have to translate the words in my mind as I heard them anymore. Even in my dreams people spoke Common.

"I am ready," I said, partly because I felt I was, and partly because I knew that was the expected response.

"You will be tested both physically and in the magic skills you are being taught. Do not disappoint me."

"No, Master," I said, bowing in deference.

But I had no idea what I was agreeing to. If I had, my response would have been completely different. They say ignorance is bliss. That night I slept fitfully, mostly from excitement. Had I known what lay ahead I wouldn't have slept a wink.

CHAPTER 4

THE NEXT MORNING I rose early, only to be told to wait. Impatience was hard to deal with. It wasn't just the testing I was anxious to have behind me, but I was dying to know what would happen once I passed the first trial. But the day wore on and on with no word on what the tests would be, or even when they would be given.

It was hot that day. I felt stressed as the sweat beaded on my forehead and ran down my face. Midday came and went, then the afternoon turned to evening, but still there was no word. Finally, after waiting the entire day, Usk arrived at the domed building where I normally did my weapons training and lessons with the divine magic.

"It is time," he announced.

Before I could even ask *time for what,* I was lifted into the air. My first instinct was to fight back, to pit my meager skills with the magic against his own. It would have been a useless exercise, and I knew I was supposed to face a trial, so I did my best to relax.

When a person is completely out of control they can waste energy and focus on futile struggling, or they can conserve their energy and try to learn what dangers they face. It didn't take me long to find out what my danger was.

Usk levitated me high into the air and over to the arena. I could see the aliens already packed into the stands. They cheered raucously as I was lowered to the sandy floor. My spear was there waiting for me. One end was lodged into the floor of the pit, the shaft and secondary blade stood pointing at the sky. As soon as my feet touched the ground the hold on me released and I could move freely. I took the spear, pulled it free of the sand, and immediately began expanding my awareness of the divine magic's ebb and flow. What happened in the stands didn't interest me at all. But from the opposite end of the arena from where the prisoners were kept, a metal door opened on well-oiled hinges. The door didn't make a sound, and neither did the three animals that came racing through it. They were short creatures, covered with spotted fur. They had powerful legs and long claws on their wide paws. Their heads angled down toward their mouths, which were filled with sharp fangs. Each one had a tail that was as long as their bodies and ended with a spike. I felt their presence before I heard them, or saw them coming.

The crowd, on the other hand, saw the animals and quieted down. The sudden drop in volume was ominous. I turned to face the creatures. All three were moving so fast that normally I wouldn't have a chance. But a lot had changed since I'd been sold to the hunter Elaa'zar. I bent my knees, held my spear ready, and waited for them to leap toward me. They did, extending their claws to rip me shreds before devouring my flesh....only I didn't let them. I flung two of the animals high by grabbing them with my control of the divine magic and boosting their jump so that they flew well over my head. The third was a little behind the others. It jumped too, but I pressed it down, piling the weight of the divine magic onto the creature. It fell to the ground at my feet, squirming to get free. I speared it easily, the blade of my weapon severing the creature's spine and penetrating its vital organs. It shivered and died, its blood staining the sand.

I had just enough time to turn as the other two animals raced back toward me. They were intelligent hunters and separated to come at me from two different angles. I let one come, the other I held back. It was hard to divide my attention, but I managed. It felt a bit like holding a heavy weight away from my body with one hand, while I tried to do some delicate work with the other. The third animal raced in, fangs showing in its open mouth. I dove to the side, rolled over my shoulder, and swung my spear in a level slash that opened the animal's side from shoulder to the back haunches. It screamed in pain, limped away, and collapsed.

Finally, with just one animal left, I turned to face it. The creature was in a frenzy, probably from me holding it back, but maybe also from the smell of blood. I knew that many animals had a powerful sense of smell. Elaa'zar had claimed that bears could smell the blood of another animal, or a person for that matter, from half a dozen miles away.

There was plenty of blood in the arena. The sand soaked up most of it, but around the two dead animals there were puddles of it, dark and sticky. I let the frenzied animal come at me, only it was my turn to jump. I leaped into the air, boosting myself with a push of divine magic. I came down right on top of the animal, driving down with my spear held ready. It punched into the creature's back, pushing it down through its stomach and driving the blade into the sand beneath it. The animal roared, its front paws scrambling to get free, its mouth full of pointed teeth snapping in my direction, but I stepped out of reach. The creature's back legs didn't move, nor could it get free from my spear. Its beautiful pelt was getting marred by its blood. I reached out, took hold of the spear, and pulled it free with a sudden jerk. In one fluid motion I spun the weapon and chopped the blade down on the back of the animal's neck. Its head rolled away.

I didn't relish the kill. On Ferret I would have been ecstatic to have killed three large animals at once. The pelts and meats would have been worth a small fortune. But on Vespa things were different. I had a feeling that the animals were just a warmup to the real danger.

Before my training had begun, I'd fought a younger woman who used magic on me. She wasn't very strong. Her control of the divine magic was elementary at best, and I had killed her. It made me wonder who I might be fighting and if they would be as fortunate against me.

I didn't have to wait long. The bodies of the animals were removed. I felt two different Vanj working magic and levitating them out of the arena, but the sand was still stained with their blood. From the stables came a tall, older woman. She walked confidently across the sand and carried a long, straight sword in one hand and small shield in the other. I could see scars on her legs and shoulders from past fights. They were a reminder not to take her for granted, but I was excited to put all my hours of training to the test.

The woman didn't disappoint. She was fast and strong. There was no circling one another or hesitation on her part. She came right at me. I tucked the spear under one arm and let her come. Of course, I could have used the magic to levitate her off the ground or pin her down on the sand, but I didn't think that was what I was supposed to do. And that intuition was confirmed a moment later when a blanket of divine power settled over the arena's fighting area.

Usk hadn't been very involved in my training and only came around occasionally to make it clear that when I was fighting someone with the same ability to control magic, we would nullify one another. I felt that same feeling as the older woman approached. It didn't come from her, though, but from another being somewhere in the crowd.

The woman with the sword dashed forward when she was only ten paces away. I let her close the distance until she was nearly in range with her long blade. Then I thrust my own weapon straight at her. She raised her small shield just as I anticipated, but I drove my weapon forward so hard she couldn't merely bat it aside. Her feet were still moving forward, her sword arm upraised as she prepared to counter my thrust with a wicked chop, but my blow knocked her backward. She stumbled, off balance. I moved forward, easily avoiding the slash of her sword, which wasn't well timed and didn't have any real power behind it. She was trying to ward me off, but I wouldn't be denied.

With a flip of my spear, the lower blade slashed across her thigh. Blood flowed and the woman grimaced in pain as she continued stumbling back, limping from the pain. I spun the spear around and slashed at her left side. She blocked with the shield, but the power of my blow shook her. When she countered I deflected her blade and threw a front kick that landed against her belly. She nearly doubled over and I smashed the shaft of my spear into her face. Blood flew up in an arc as she flopped backward.

When she hit the ground her head came up, eyes wide with fear. I could have rushed in and landed the killing blow, but instead I stood back and let her get up again.

Blood covered the woman's face. Her nose was bent at an obscene angle, obviously broken. Her eyes were wide with fear. Even her teeth were stained red.

I let her gather her strength. She made no feints, just stepped forward and slashed hard with her sword. I dove to the ground, rolled over my spear, then thrust it up. Maybe it was the pain, or maybe she was simply resigned to her fate. I thought she could have jumped to the side, but maybe the pain in her leg was too great. That wound bulged, thick muscle protruding from the gash. My spear came up and sliced deep into her side. She staggered away, grunting with pain. I barely heard the roar of the crowd. I was watching my opponent face death. She did it with dignity, a grimace on her face and her sword in her hand. With a pivot on her good leg she slashed at me again, but I stepped back. I couldn't use my magic against her, but it still informed me of things I couldn't know without it, such as the exact reach of her sword. The tip of the blade swished through the air just below my chin without actually touching me. Then I shoved my spear forward. There was nothing fancy or skilled about the attack. A spear is a brutish weapon at times. The flat spear blade had a sharp point that sliced into her chest, slid between her ribs, and punctured her heart. The woman didn't scream in pain the way you might expect. Instead, she sighed, almost as if she was relieved, then died before her body hit the sand.

More blood stained the arena floor. The crowd was screaming. I could see the aliens hopping and waving their long, taloned hands. Some were even crawling over the others in their excitement. It was a scene I'll never forget. It still sickens me to think about it. Those weak, pathetic animals had an insatiable taste for Heterrid blood. And I couldn't help but wonder what they would do if I were coming after them.

There wasn't much time to consider my dark fantasy. Almost immediately the woman was whisked away and the doors opened to reveal my next opponent. I remember thinking he was the biggest man I had ever seen.

Each of his legs were as thick as my waist, and his chest was so broad it seemed impossible to me. His shift was torn at the middle and tied around his hips. I could see the stomach muscles and the fibers of the thick pectorals across his chest. His hair was black and long. He had a red band around his forehead to keep the hair out of his eyes. On each wrist he wore a stained leather cuff. He was some sort of freak of nature, at least I thought he was. It never occurred to me what the Vanj hormones might do to a person.

He walked out into the arena slowly. As he did, he leaned his head from side to side to loosen the thick muscles above his collar bones. For a weapon he carried a thick bladed sword with a handle long enough to allow him to wield it with both hands. The crowd was chanting in their own language. I don't think it was my opponent's name, but he raised his sword and pumped it up and down in time with their chants.

"Unbelievable," I said out loud, not that anyone was around to hear me, or even could have heard me over the roar of the alien crowd. Still, I simply couldn't believe what I was seeing.

The man stopped his arrogant strut twenty paces from me and drove his sword blade first into the sand. He began rotating his shoulders and flexing his muscles while he stared at me. But it was his arrogant laugh that drove me into a fury. I snatched up my spear and flung it at him. The double-ended weapon wasn't meant to be thrown like a traditional spear, yet it flew like a bullet. I might not have looked it, but the past four months of daily training had left me stronger than even I realized. The spear flew fast. It would have killed most people, but the big man managed to dodge out of the way. The keen edge on the leading blade did score a minor cut on the big man's left shoulder as he dove to the floor of the arena.

The spear continued on another twenty paces beyond the man before falling into the sand and sticking fast. I followed it, sprinting toward the man, who rolled onto his knees. The arrogance was gone from his face, his eyes wide with shock, but he managed to get moving to cut me off from my weapon. We reached his wide sword at the same time. He reached for the weapon, but I jumped up and came down with my foot extending into a downward kick onto the side of his knee. His leg bent in toward his other with a pop that I could hear over the roar of the crowd.

He collapsed at my feet, screaming in pain. With one hand he grabbed his injured knee and with the other waved the sword in a clumsy fashion to ward me off. I walked away from him, turning my back as if I didn't fear him at all. The man was defeated. His ruined knee made it impossible for him to stand. His heavy sword was nearly useless to him. When I reached my spear and pulled it free, he was levering himself onto his good knee with his sword. I turned to face him and saw sweat rolling down his face. Sand stuck to his body, which didn't seem so menacing now that he was injured.

"Give me a clean death," he said. "One these monsters will talk about tomorrow."

"Why do you care about them?" I asked.

"That's all I have," he said.

It was sad to me, pathetic really. He was strong, but everyone has a weakness. He relied too heavily on his sword in battle, and on the impression his big, muscular body had on his opponents.

"You live to kill our own people," I said with a shake of my head. We had to shout to be heard over the crowd. They weren't happy with the way the fight had gone, but I didn't care. I wasn't there to entertain them.

"I fight to live," he insisted, clearly in a lot of pain.

The knee I had kicked was already swelling. He managed to get up onto his good leg, but couldn't put any weight on the other. He swayed, still keeping his sword up, but I knew one swing would offset his weight and send him toppling back down.

"This isn't living," I told him.

He raised his sword over his head in both hands as if he could still fight. I stepped forward and thrust my spear with its longer reach straight into his heart. The big sword fell behind him, and he crumpled to the ground. The look on his face was sad, but I didn't feel sorry for him. Perhaps the man had made the most of being a slave. He clearly did whatever it took to become a behemoth, which probably meant killing who knows how many other Heterrids. I understood the futility of their situation, but I didn't condone giving into it. They couldn't escape, but they didn't have to embrace their lot in life, either.

I left him lying in the sand, and it was clear the mood of the mob had turned against me. They were booing and baring their teeth at me. I didn't smile, but deep down inside it felt good to defy my captors. The big man's body was levitated away, and I used the sand to remove his blood from my spear. There was no way of knowing how many people I would have to fight and kill, but I assumed that when the testing was over I would be taken to another place, maybe even off world. Part of my training had been an education on the wider galaxy. I learned about other planets, other intelligent races, and the heresy of the Scion. They believed the divine magic was a gift from an all-knowing deity and forced their beliefs onto entire worlds. Part of my instruction was in recognizing and eliminating the Scion at all costs. And so, I couldn't help but hope that once I survived the night in the arena that I might be taken off Vespa. That would be a gift in and of itself.

Finally, my new opponent arrived. She looked like me. Most of the people from my world looked alike. It was a condition of the selective breeding and genetic manipulation from the Maston Overlords. There wasn't much diversity in our DNA when we were abandoned on Ferret. Those survivors mated and produced children, but it wasn't unusual for people to have very similar features. I thought my new opponent and I could be sisters. The only real difference between us was our clothing, and the fact that she still had long hair. She even carried a double-ended spear just like mine.

Don't get cocky, I reminded myself. My first few fights had been against opponents who weren't at the same skill level, but I got the impression the woman approaching me across the sand of the arena was different. When she twirled her spear my intuition was confirmed. The weapon spun in her hands and around her body in a highly practiced fashion. The crowd roared its approval, while I watched her and hoped to find a weakness. None seemed to exist.

Just outside thrusting range we began to circle one another.

My use of magic was still being dampened. It was frustrating. The younger woman I had fought and defeated before my training with magic had begun used it against me in our fight. I remembered feeling encumbered and seeing her leap higher than it should have been possible to jump. But my own abilities were being countered by someone, somewhere. It left me completely unable to utilize the magic against my opponents.

Some fighters just charge straight into battle. Others like to probe for weaknesses and take their time. My opponent belonged to the latter group. She feinted several times at attacks trying to get me to jump off balance or do something stupid. But I was well trained with my spear. I knew what it was capable of, and what to do against just about any attack. Not that the weapon was foolproof. Any weapon was deadly, and as dangerous as the person wielding it. I let my opponent take her time. As we circled I held my spear close in a defensive position, waiting for her to make a move or to open herself up to an attack. She feinted thrusts and slashes a few times, and even pretended to leave herself open, but it was a trap. I didn't so much recognize the tactic as much as I sensed the danger of the woman. We seemed to be equals physically, and if anything, she seemed to be even more trained with the spear than I was. And that gave me an idea.

I stepped toward her. It was a threatening move, but I still held my spear perpendicular to my body in a wide, two handed grip.. Thinking my move was an attack, the other woman spun around and brought her spear up and back down in a powerful chop that might have cleaved my skull in two had I kept moving forward. Instead, I stayed just out of the reach of her blade. I couldn't manipulate things with my magic, but I could sense her movements and those of her weapon in the flow of the invisible force. I knew just how close to get to prompt her into action without putting myself in danger. Instead, I raised and extended my spear as if I expected to block her strike with center of my shaft. And just as I hoped, her blade cut through the wooden handle cleanly, but missed my skull and the rest of my body on its downward trajectory.

After the single strike I stepped back. My opponent was smiling, as if happy with the result of the encounter...at least until I rotated the two separate ends of my broken spear. I had gone from a single weapon to two long-handled short swords. I brought one up in my right hand, and rotated the other down in my left. My opponent's eyes narrowed as she realized I had intended her to sever my spear all along. Perhaps she had trained with the spear, just as I had, but I also trained with two swords.

I dug my toes into the sand and kicked it up at my opponent's eyes. She blinked rapidly and stepped back. I charged in. She brought her spear across her body to defend herself. I brought the sword in my right hand down in a high chop. She blocked the chop and I turned, slashing with the other sword. It slid under her weapon and across her stomach. The cut wasn't deep, but it shocked her just the same. We separated again long enough for the woman to touch her stomach with her left hand. She lifted the fingers, glanced at the blood on them, then looked at me. There was fear in that glance. And then she charged at me.

People respond to fear in different ways. Not everyone runs from it; some run toward it. Some people are so intent on not being afraid that they look for danger and move toward it. The woman came at me with her spear twirling over her head. I slid forward, then danced back as her spear swished through the air where I would have been. She continued forward, rotating her weapon around so that the rear blade slashed toward me. I blocked with the sword in my left hand and threw my shoulder toward her. She turned and we rotated past each other. Reversing her weapon's momentum, she slashed the spear toward me again. I blocked with my right hand sword and when she swiped the low end toward me again, I threw a kick that landed just below the blade of the spear, stopping it cold, while at the same time slashing my own sword up the shaft. The metal of my sword was the same leaf-shaped design as hers, and honed to a razor's edge. It slashed across her hand, severing three of her fingers before she jerked away.

Backpedaling to get away from me, I stepped over her severed digits to pursue. My opponent tried to hack at me with the spear, but I blocked it with my own weapon. The shock of the two blades clashing nearly made her drop it. The pain was just starting to register from her wounded hand, and holding the spear was difficult with just her index finger and thumb on her wounded hand. Blood was flowing freely. I swung my sword in a slash at her shoulder. She blocked, but it was like landing a physical blow to her body. The shockwave through the shaft of the spear was clearly painful. She wanted to get away from me, to regroup and figure out a new way to attack, but I didn't give her that freedom.

The crowd was roaring, but it was all just white noise to me. I swung my swords with each step, battering her weapon again and again. To her credit, the woman resisted me as long as she could, but she was growing weaker with each pump of her heart. Blood gushed from her severed fingers and eventually she could no longer hold her spear with that hand. Her once powerful weapon became a liability with only one hand to hold it. To my surprise, she threw down the weapon, turned her back on me, and ran. I had no idea where she hoped to run to.

At the same time the magic counteracting my own power vanished. It hadn't come from the woman I was fighting, but whoever was acting to stop me ceased once my opponent fled. I let her run for a few seconds. In truth, I felt sorry for her. She knew she was going to die and was trying to escape that terrible fate. I certainly took no pleasure in killing my fellow Heterrids, but that was what my captors demanded of me.

In time I would learn to use the divine magic like a weapon in its own right, but at that time all I could really do was levitate objects and defend myself. Reaching out with my new senses, I took hold of the fleeing woman and lifted her into the air. She stiffened, perhaps thinking she was being rescued. It made sense, since the Heterrid fighters were levitated to and from each battle in the fighting pit. But I turned her to face me as I reeled her in. The realization that the fight wasn't over caused her to panic. I put her out of her misery quickly with a hard blow to the neck. The short blade of my sword cut deep, severing her spine. She died instantly, and I lowered her gently to the ground.

I fully expected another opponent, but instead I was levitated out of the arena. The crowd couldn't decide if they loved or hated me. I saw several fights break out in the stands as the aliens argued about my performance. But I hadn't done it for them. And despite the victory over my opponents, I didn't feel good. There was no elation, no thrill to my achievement. It was over, and all I could think about was what might be coming next.

"You did well," Usk said, his raspy tone guarded. "But that was only the first trial. There will be others."

"Can I ask a question?" I said.

"You have earned the right," he replied. "Ask what you will."

"What is it you are preparing me to do?"

It was the question that had been on my mind since being brought to Vespa. The aliens devoured Heterrid flesh. It was a delicacy for them, and nearly every person caught or killed on Ferret was given over to that use, so it made no sense for the Vanj to train me in their magic, or with weapons. The mob in the arena certainly hadn't been pleased to see me dispatch their favorite fighters with relative ease. I had stopped three beasts and three of my peers without sustaining an injury, and the crowds didn't like it.

"Those of us with the gift have many purposes," Usk said calmly. "And every student has a master. I am yours, and I in turn serve mine. When called upon to fight the Scion heresy, you will serve as my proxy. Your job will be to protect me and kill the members of the Scion sect. Once we leave this planet, Azree'el, we will be in danger. No other place in the universe is safe for us."

Safety was an illusion. That was a principle everyone on Ferret grew up hearing, and in my own life it had proven true. My father wasn't safe, my village wasn't safe, joining the hunter Elaa'zar hadn't been safe, and nothing about Vespa was safe for me. I had fought in duels to the death on several occasions, but I didn't feel it was the right time to point that out to my master.

"That is why we have trained you," Usk continued. "In a battle with the Order of Scion, our magic will be countered by their own. Your kind has proven to be skilled warriors with the proper training. I am pleased with your progress, but until you have faced the great trial on Fierocite you will not be ready to face our enemy."

I had been returned to the domed building in the same way I had been taken. We stood just inside the entrance. The interior was completely dark, as was most of the city. The Vanj didn't need light to see the way I did. My own building was one of the few with lights on inside. But I didn't return to the room that had been my home during training. Instead, Usk took me to a section of the city where large ships were lined up in neat rows. I had seen and heard the vessels taking off and landing from there. And while much of my education had involved space, I knew next to nothing about space travel.

Usk led the way into one of the ships. Red lights lit the corridors of the vessel. Metal walls, decks, and ceilings were left unpainted, the raw metal looking cold and harsh. Along with the wiring and pipes were thick vines that snaked across almost every surface. I was taken to a small room not much different from the one in the building where I had stayed during my training.

"This is your quarters on the ship," Usk said. "Look after it."

"Yes," I said without really thinking. After months of training, I was accustomed to taking orders.

On the back wall of my room, which was large enough for a narrow bed, a desk with an attached stool, and a comfortable-looking lounge chair, was a round window. It protruded from the ship far enough that I could lean into it and see an unobstructed view of that entire side of the vessel. Dim lights had come on in the room when I entered, and there were none of the vines or flora in my small quarters. Attached to one side was a small lavatory with a shower stall.

Usk left me there in the semi-darkness to explore my new living quarters. A switch on the wall allowed me to increase the light. I turned it up brighter, then back down. I was so enthralled with the ship that I barely noticed the powerful bubble of magic that was formed around it. Moving to the window, I watched us lift off. There was no sense of movement, no roar of engines. I knew enough about divine magic to realize that it was being used to propel the ship. I also knew that most of the vessels I had seen landing and taking off from the city where I was trained had used loud engines. Likewise, most of the ships I had seen land or leave from Ferret had made noise, but the ship Usk and I were on was silent.

I looked out the window and watched the dark city grow small. There were lights on at the arena; no doubt more fighters were battling to the death as I left Vespa. The sight of it made me feel ill, but I was also very excited to be leaving the sweltering planet. It felt like my life was finally taking a turn in my favor.

†††

"Why are the Scion heretics our enemy?" I asked.

We had been in space long enough for me to clean myself up and sleep. When I woke up it was much cooler than it ever got on Vespa. I had learned that space was a cold place, so cold, in fact, that without protection no life could survive. There was also no air to breathe. It made me a little concerned, but the moment I stepped out of my room I found the rest of ship hot and humid. A short search of my room revealed environmental controls that were displayed in the Common language. The cold in my quarters felt good, but I dialed up the temperature a little anyway, then I went in search of Usk.

I found the Vanj wizard in a much larger room that was covered with vines and flowing plants. The metal floor and walls were completely covered, and only the dim red lights—emergency lighting, I would come to learn—illuminated the area. There were wide windows in the large room that showed the vessel moving swiftly through space. After watching for a while in silence, I asked the question that had been on my mind since learning about the Order of Scion's existence.

"Magic is divine," Usk said. He was curled up, his arms and legs pulled tight against his body as he perched in what looked like a nest of some kind. It was hot in the room. My skin prickled with it after only a few moments inside, but Usk seemed cold. "It is the strength of the gods, but the Scion heresy denies the existence of all but their Creator deity and his vaunted offspring."

"So, who cares what they believe?" I said.

"They do," Usk replied. "If theirs was simply a difference of opinion they would not be our enemies, but instead they press their beliefs on the entire galaxy. Anyone who wields magic outside their sect is seen as their enemy, and they slay or imprison all who disagree with them."

I was beginning to see why the Order of Scions were feared. Not that Usk ever seemed afraid, but the very fact that I was being trained to protect the Vanj revealed that their fear existed. They were still stronger and faster than I was. Their talons were natural weapons, and Usk was much more powerful in his use of the divine magic than I thought I could ever be, so the idea of having a guard seemed odd. Of course, the Vanj were aliens. I couldn't begin to understand their logic.

"To defeat them you must be prepared," Usk said, moving for the first time since I had entered his chambers on the ship. He held out a long, black-bladed dagger. "Do you know what this is?"

"A knife," I said.

"It is a bladed weapon, yes, but it is not iron, or steel, or bone. This is Cidian, an exceedingly rare material that is both difficult to find and to mine. Touch it with your sense of magic and you will see that it is truly unique."

I did as I was instructed. In space there was less substance to distract me from the sense of magic all around me. It existed in space, but the divine magic seemed to both cling to and emanate from things. And while it hadn't stood out to me on Vespa, I was starting to see that various substances felt different in my magical senses. I could feel the vines beneath my feet and the steel decking of the ship. Both felt unique to my sixth sense, not just living and inert, but the metal was more dense, with a greater pull on the flow of magic around us than the vines had.

Likewise, the black dagger felt completely different from anything else on the ship. I could feel the hull of the vessel, the pipes that moved the air, and the electrical currents pulsing through the wiring. Usk didn't use the ship's engines, but the vessel had other systems working, specifically those that controlled the lighting and the temperature on board. I could even feel the big, complicated engines on the ship, each one with thousands of parts. When I really pressed in I could feel the individual nature of each part, but nothing was like the Cidian dagger.

"This material can be used to create the most potent weapons in the galaxy," Usk continued. "It holds an edge that never dulls. It can cut through metal and bone without breaking. It is the weapon of choice for our enemy, and therefore we must utilize it as well."

"This is mine?" I asked, pointing at the dagger.

"No, black Cidian must be mined for oneself. You will have to find it for yourself in the world we are approaching. That is your second trial. Find the Cidian, move it, forge it into a weapon. You will have seven days. If you do not return to this ship with a Cidian weapon in that time, I will leave without you."

I didn't speak. Fear was playing at the edges of my mind, but so was hope. I was being taken to another world to find the strange metal, but would failure really be so bad? Usk would leave and I would be forgotten. I had to consider the fact that maybe, just maybe, that would be a better alternative to living as the Vanj's slave.

Of course, I knew nothing about this new world. And when I saw it through the ship's wide windows, I realized that staying there alone wasn't an option. In fact, I wondered if I could survive for seven days on the alien planet. From space it looked like a block of ice, all white and blue. I could see the storm clouds swirling in the atmosphere. The place looked completely inhospitable.

"This is Fierocite," Usk said. "The air is thin and cold. Prepare yourself, Azree'el. Finding the Cidian will not be easy. Mining and forging it will be even harder."

It wasn't exactly a pep talk, and I left Usk's chamber on the verge of despair. Over my months on Vespa my body had adapted to the heat. Going to a freezing world would be difficult.

There were storage compartments built into my quarters. Panels on the walls opened up to reveal shelves full of supplies, mostly towels and blankets, but there were clothes, too. I found thick pants, a long tunic, and a heavy coat. There were soft boots that were a bit too big but with straps to secure them around my legs. In another compartment I found a large pack with thick straps that fit over my shoulders and around my stomach. I stuffed food and blankets into the pack. What I couldn't find were mining tools of any kind, or weapons. When I asked Usk how I was supposed to get the Cidian, his reply opened my eyes to the true nature of the divine magic I was learning to use.

"You have many resources at your disposal," he said, "but not so great as the divine magic. If you are worthy to be my student you will need nothing else."

That didn't exactly make sense to me, but it was a challenge I was ready to accept. I still wore the warm clothes and carried the pack, but set out from the Vanj ship prepared to use my magic to find, retrieve, and forge the Cidian.

What I wasn't prepared for was the icy blast of cold I felt the moment I passed through the magic bubble around the ship. I left through a hatch and stepped onto the snow. The sky overhead was dark with thick clouds. Snow was swirling, both from the clouds and from the wind, which blew the icy crystals in thick drifts. My boots crunched in the snow. I had only experienced snow once on Ferret. Then it had seemed beautiful. On Fierocite it seemed harsh and unpleasant. Still, it didn't seem so bad outside the ship. But the moment I passed through the magical barrier I was hit with the full, unrelenting force of the cold, stormy atmosphere. It doubled me over like a physical blow to my midsection, and the thin, cold air made my lungs burn.

Turning around, I looked back at Usk's ship. There were no encouraging gestures. The alien hadn't left his nest on board the warm vessel, and the hatch I had passed through was already closed. There would be no help from the Vanj. My ideas about being left on this planet were dashed, too. There was only one hope. I had to find the Cidian and get back to the ship as fast as I could manage it. Only I had no idea where the rare metal could be found.

For several minutes I stood blinking in the extreme cold, unsure where to go or where to start looking. There were mountains around me, barren, jagged peaks that were covered with ice and snow. Nothing looked inviting or safe. I realized the second trial was even more deadly than the first had been.

I picked a direction and started moving. That was all I could think to do. The oversized boots I found on the ship were rugged, but not waterproof. It didn't take long before the cold invaded my feeble efforts to keep it away. Not even five minutes into my second trial and I was wishing I was back on Vespa. I never thought I would miss the unrelenting heat until I was buffed by the freezing winds on Fierocite. My lungs burned, the lining of my nostrils grew stiff, and my feet felt like blocks of ice. But my determination pushed me forward. For a solid hour I climbed higher and higher into the mountains. It was more taxing on my body than the hard runs and daily weapons training on Vespa combined. Yet my will was stronger than my muscles and bones, so I pushed on.

After an hour I came to a little cave. It wasn't much, just a crack in the side of a mountain that I could shimmy into. The area opened up slightly once I got inside. It was littered with old tree limbs and small bones, obviously an animal den of some kind. There were no trees in the mountains, and I could only guess that maybe Usk had taken me to Fierocite in the dead of winter. But thinking of the frozen planet from space, I considered that maybe it was always winter here.

I gathered some of the old branches and kindled a fire. To my delight, the cave warmed up enough that I could actually think. Usk had taken me to the frozen world to mine Cidian. That meant the rare material wouldn't be found just lying around. Mining meant digging. Unfortunately, I had no tools for digging.

What I did have was the divine magic, which I immediately put to use. Maybe I would get lucky and there would be some

Cidian inside the cave. Of course, there wasn't any. I was surrounded by solid rock. It felt dense in the divine magic, but there was no sign of the Cidian. That meant more searching. Outside the storm was raging, and it seemed futile to go wandering through it blindly, but I had never stretched my senses in the divine magic farther than my immediate surroundings. Yet I knew I could sense things beyond my immediate confines. On Vespa I could be in my small room and sense others in different parts of the building. I could expand my awareness in the vast domed structure until I could identify everything inside, even the smallest devices, mats, and cleaning tools.

The odds were high that I would need to search a vast area in the mountains to find the Cidian with my magic. I wasn't sure if I was strong enough to do it, but there was only one way to find out.

Sitting with my back to the stone wall and my cold feet stretched toward the little fire I had made, I closed my eyes to focus my attention on the magic. It was flowing all around me. I had the same, almost disembodied feeling as when I first learned to use the divine power. It was an intoxicating sensation. Outside the cave I could feel the snow falling. The flakes were so tiny and had almost no presence in the divine magic, just the slightest downward pull. I could feel the flakes being blown by the wind. There were a few different kinds of hardy scrub bushes on the mountains that I hadn't noticed before. Like the snow they felt delicate, but larger, and more fibrous. I could feel the short little branches coming together and just below the surface, their roots spreading back out. I could feel the rocky soil around the roots—but no Cidian.

The effort was exhausting. And after my first attempt to find the rare mineral, all I could say for certain was that there was none nearby. The back of my little cave continued into the mountain. I explored that with my magic too, but found nothing that would help me. It was doubtful I could have crawled through the narrow opening very far, either.

I ate a little of my food and let my body relax. Soon, it would be necessary to push on. What I had discovered was another cave, a little larger than the one I was in. My goal was to reach it before night fell. There would be no way to push on in the darkness. I was still in the lowest parts of the mountains, but ground was uneven and slick. I couldn't risk a fall, or a broken leg. Not if I wanted to survive, and certainly not if I hoped to pass the second trial.

When the fire died, I moved on. The storm had only grown worse. I could see only a few paces in any direction, but my magical senses gave me the lay of the land. That left me to struggle up the hillside, avoiding danger. The snow was frozen and stung any exposed skin that it struck as it was blown around by the wind. I cut one of the blankets into long strips. Some I wrapped around my hands, others I wrapped around my head. It wasn't ideal, but it helped.

The climb to the second cave took hours. It was almost night by the time I reached it. The entrance was nearly covered by a drift of snow, and I had to shimmy through it. My clothing was frozen on the outside and damp on the inside. Fortunately, there was more debris for building a fire. I was busy gathering it up when the animal who lived in the cave returned.

I had hunted plenty of creatures and killed often in my short life. But I had no weapons, just the pack of blankets and food. The animal who entered was short but wide. It had white fur, a long, vicious-looking snout, and claws that were as long as my fingers on each paw. It growled at me, then charged. There was no time to consider the situation. The cave was large enough that I could take eight or nine steps from side to side and twice that many from the narrow opening to the tiny crack in the back wall. I backed up, but that only seemed to encourage the animal. When it jumped, I batted it back with my magic. That was the one resource I had, and it finally occurred to me that I wasn't helpless. The trial wasn't just a treasure hunt. I was learning to rely on the divine magic and use it in a variety of ways.

I levitated the animal. It hissed and shrieked at me. My heart was pounding inside my chest as I looked at the creature. It was about my size, not as long as I was tall, but its body was roughly the same size as my torso. Using my magic, I slammed it hard onto the floor of the cave. Bones shattered, but it didn't die instantly. I continued piling on the magic, crushing it down until the animal couldn't breathe. Killing it took a minute, but once it was dead, I used my magic to pull out the claws. After I got a fire going inside the cave, I levitated the body of the animal out. I would have liked to skin the creature, but there was no time to tan its pelt. Instead, I used its own claw to cut it open and harvest the tender meat along its spine. With that done, I levitated the creature away from my cave. The last thing I needed was more predators in the area.

That night, I roasted the meat and ate my fill. It was greasy but didn't taste bad. I had certainly eaten much worse fare in my home world. The animal's fat was what I needed. It warmed me from the inside, and I managed to get a few hours of sleep after disrobing and wrapping my body in the blankets from my pack. They were damp, too—everything was—but I hung my clothing on sticks and put them as close to the little fire as I could get them.

The next morning they were mostly dry, for which I was grateful, even if they did stink of campfire smoke.

The storm had blown itself out, but one look outside the cave and it was obvious another was coming. I made the most of the relative calm that morning, climbing higher and higher on the mountain. The second storm was nearly on top of me when I sensed the first tiny bits of Cidian. The only problem was, it was deep underground. I could sense a cavern in the mountain, like a bubble deep inside the thick stone. I stopped climbing, huddling in the cold to let my sense of the divine magic flow into the ground. It was odd trying to feel deep into the ground. The sense of motion I normally felt in the waves of magic power were dampened to the point that I wasn't sure if what I was sensing was really accurate. But I didn't stop, not when the winds began to pelt me and the snow fell thick around me.

Finding the Cidian wasn't enough. It had been just a glimmer at first; the way it interacted with the divine magic was unique. There was a strength to it, but it also felt light, which made it difficult to discern the full extent of the strange substance. I had to stop my climb—which was getting steeper and steeper all the time—to really concentrate and make sure of what I was sensing. But finding the Cidian was just the first step to retrieving it. The substance was buried deep inside the mountain. The cavern around it was plain enough in my sense of the magic flowing through the solid rock, but how could I get there? From the cavern were many cracks and crevices.

For a solid hour, while my body shuttered from the cold, wet, stormy conditions, I searched the nooks and crannies of the underground cavern, pushing my control and awareness of the divine magic harder and farther than ever before. It was exhausting.

Several times I was forced to backtrack when a crevice or passageway narrowed so much that it would be impossible to move through.

I wasn't large, but my body was dense with the muscle I had built up on Vespa. Squeezing through tight spaces wouldn't be easy. Eventually, I did find a passageway to a cavern, but it began on the far side of the mountain. The only positive element about it was the fact that the cave I sought was slightly below my current position, and with the wind coming from the north, I could move to my right and let the mountain shield me from the worst of the storm.

The trek around the mountain took half a day, so it was fully dark long before I reached it. With the wind whipping hard around the mountain, and no fuel that I could use to keep a fire going, there was no chance of building a torch. The clouds were thick, so no light broke through from the heavens above, leaving the mountainside in total darkness. Fortunately, I was learning to rely more and more on my sense of the magic around me. I could discern the ground and the snow that covered it, even the areas where the rocks were loose or jumbled, and of course the dips where a person might slip and injure themselves.

The cave was like a beacon. As long as I was moving toward it, I could trust that I was making progress. It was a slow, cold slog, but eventually I reached the cave. It was small, just another crack in the thick stone of the mountain. Unlike the others there was no debris inside, just snow that was blown in from the continuous storms. My entire body was shivering, which I knew was not a good sign. I needed to warm up before trying to rest, otherwise I would just continue to descend into hypothermia. So, I pressed deeper into the cave.

For several hundred feet I was pressed in on both sides by jagged, unforgiving stone. I walked sideways, shimmying, ducking, and crawling over obstacles. My tired, frozen body was stiff and didn't want to respond to the arduous demands I was putting it through. Fortunately, the farther into the cave I went, the warmer it got. Not that it ever really felt warm, but it wasn't as cold. When I finally reached a slightly bigger opening, I shrugged off my backpack, pulled off my wet clothing, and wrapped myself in every blanket I had.

That night I had no trouble falling asleep. I was completely exhausted, too tired to even eat anything, before closing my eyes and surrendering to unconsciousness.

There was no way to know how long I had slept. It could have been an hour, or ten. Deep in the mountain there was no light, no real way to judge time. All I knew was that my body was aching and half-numb from the stone floor I was sleeping on. It wasn't smooth or level, but undulating and in places sharp. I had bruises from my bodyweight pressing down onto the unmovable stone. Getting up, I found my clothes were still wet, but not frozen. Since there was no way to speed up the drying process, I left them there and moved on with only a blanket over my body. I cut a hole in the center for my head and tied the damp blanket around my waist with the same strip I had used as a scarf.

Deeper and deeper I went into the cave. Having been raised in the caverns on Ferret, I wasn't afraid of the dark. My eyes were useless, but my magical senses were finely tuned. In fact, it probably helped that I couldn't see. I was gaining control and a growing sensitivity to the magic around me every minute that I was completely dependent upon it. Despite the hardship and suffering I had to endure, I found myself grateful for the trial. My confidence was growing stronger. Even if I failed the challenge and had to find a way to survive on the frozen planet, I felt capable of being able to do it.

The passageway leading to the deep cavern wasn't level. At times it descended sharply, and at other sections I was forced to climb. It was rarely so wide that I couldn't touch both sides of the tunnel at the same time, and there were a few areas where I was forced onto my hands and knees to get through. My sense of the divine magic saved me from getting lost. There were numerous offshoots and side passages. But there was no need to kindle a light or mark my way. I could sense the big cavern and the Cidian it held. My passage to it was certain, even if I couldn't see anything.

Eventually there was light. It was dim and red. The temperature rose dramatically when I reached the big cavern. I came out of the passage onto a raised portion of the cavern. Below me were cracks in the stone. Heat and the dim, red light came from them. Among the cracks the Cidian was littered among the various types of rock. Some of it was coarse and brittle, other sections much harder. The Cidian was in narrow veins, like bolts of lightning that trace in crooked lines across the night sky. For a while I didn't move. Reveling in the warmth of the cavern and studying my surroundings, I made a plan.

My first thought was to climb down to the Cidian, but then I realized I still had no way to get it out of the floor of the cavern. It wasn't laying loose like diamonds on a jeweler's velvet cloth. The rare metal was still in the ground, and I had no tools to break it loose. I certainly wasn't going to get anywhere trying to dig through rock with my bare hands.

Instead, I decided to rely on my magic. The Cidian reacted to the magic differently than the stone around it. They were bonded together with magical ties, and even though it would take me hours of work, I could sever each individual one. But with the materials separated, I still had the problem of pulling the Cidian free. Because it was crooked and twisted through the other rock, it wouldn't come out. The only option left was to break the Cidian into tiny pieces. I had used the divine magic to levitate objects and pin them down to the ground, even crushing the life out of the animal who attacked me in its den. But pulverizing metal was not something I was certain I could do.

I sat down on the ledge and ate a small meal. Drinking water and getting some fuel inside my body helped. Then I cleared my mind and focused on the Cidian, drawing all the magic I could muster to weigh down on the rare metal. At first nothing happened. I could feel magic flowing around me, doing what I willed it to do, but the Cidian was too strong. I closed my eyes and steadied my breathing. There was no need to rush the process. How much time passed, I can't say. I was so focused on the task that everything else seemed to fall away. Sweat ran down my forehead, trickling over my eyelids and making the skin at my temples itch, but I ignored it. I paid no attention to the hard floor of the ledge, or how the rock seemed to push through my backside and into my bones. Eventually I grew tired, but pushed through the fatigue. And finally, after what seemed like hours, the Cidian shattered. It didn't fracture or crack up, but crumbled into millions of tiny bits. I drew the powdered mineral up out of the floor of the cave and was thrilled by the amount of it. Using divine magic, I pulled the pure Cidian into a ball, packing it tightly together.

My next task was to forge the rare metal into a weapon. I had been giving that task some thought as I made my way up the mountain. I knew what I wanted to make, and it's not really surprising, a double-ended spear. I wanted the metal blades on each end to be as long as my forearm, with a slight swell in the middle before curving gently down to a point. Double edged of course, with a median ridge. The unique idea was to make the spear from two separate pieces that could lock together. The lower part of one handle, the pommel, would insert inside the other and lock together with a twist. Then, I could use the weapon as either a double-ended spear or as two long-handled swords, as the need required. It would also help me to carry the weapon on my person.

But I had never forged metal before. All I really knew about it was that the smiths on Ferret used forges to get enough heat through the material before pounding it into shape with heavy hammers. I had to consider what that really meant. The heat was clear enough, and I could get that from the vents in the cavern floor. Down those shafts nearly a hundred feet was a pool of molten rock. All I had to do was lower my ore down the shaft using the divine magic and I could get it as hot as I wanted. But I had no hammers, no anvils with which to work the metal once it was hot enough. But what did those hammers accomplish but to apply pressure to the material? I could bring great forces to the material using divine magic, compressing it from all sides with enough force to forge the powdered Cidian back into a whole.

I was ignorant of the mineral and of what actually took place during the forging process. But forming the powdered Cidian into the two blades and connecting them with a long, thin tang was simple. The divine magic moved the powder according to my will. All I had to do was imagine it, and the material would convert into the proper shape. Lowering it into one of the floor vents was easily done. I had sensed the Cidian from the far side of the mountain, so levitating it a couple of hundred feet from where I was located on the cavern ledge was not a problem. Judging the heat was a different matter. Using all my concentration, I focused entirely on the Cidian until I could feel it moving at the atomic level. The hotter it got, the fast the electrons orbited the nucleus. Letting them spin faster and faster was easy enough, and when they were rushing at a fever pace I applied magical force against the weapon. To my astonishment I felt it flow together, the individual bits melting and joining the others in a semi-liquid form.

Without really knowing what I was doing, I drew the spear back up out of the vent, levitating it high into the cavern, and set it spinning to rapidly cool the rare material. It was instinctual. When I thought about it, I remembered the smiths on Ferret plunging their metal creations, from knives to cooking utensils, into buckets of water to cool them down. I had no buckets of water or access to the copious amounts of snow outside the mountain. My only option was to spin the weapon. It was perfectly balanced and easy to spin. I felt the heat coming off it and the material hardening. For a long time, I left it spinning above me. I wanted a potent weapon, not one that would shatter on impact, so I took my time with the process.

When I was convinced the weapon was finished, I levitated down and took hold of it. The metal wasn't very heavy at all, but it was strong. It took a lot of force to sever the long, thin tang that connected the two spearheads, but once that was done I felt a sense of relief. My second trial had been accomplished, and all that remained was to find my way back down the mountain to where Usk waited.

I went slowly back through the tunnel. Fatigue clung to me, but I feared that I had been inside the mountain too long. I found my clothes, still more damp than I wanted, but put them on anyway. Damp clothes were better than no clothes. The spearheads were wrapped in a blanket and stowed in my pack before I made my way back toward the entrance to the cave.

The temperature seemed to drop with each step. It didn't take long for the cold to seep into my bones again. By the time I reached the entrance to the cave I was shivering again. But to my surprise, the sun was out. It was the first time I had seen the sky without a thick bank of clouds. The sky on Ferret and Vespa had been shades of blue. On Fierocite it was a dazzling white. Stepping out of the cave and looking around, I could see more of the mountains than ever before. They were stark but beautiful. The ice glinted in the sunlight, making the tall peaks look like crystal.

For hours I descended, making my way back around the mountain as I went. By afternoon another storm was brewing in the distance, but I could see down the mountain and even make out the snow-covered spaceship that had brought me to this frozen world. There were snowdrifts built up around the vessel, but I knew if I pushed my pace I could reach it by nightfall.

Going downhill was much less strenuous on my body, but perhaps even more dangerous. I had to slow my pace several times. It wouldn't do to break my leg, or worse, my back or neck, within sight of the ship. I passed the caves where I had taken shelter the first day and even discovered the body of the animal I had killed. It was frozen solid and didn't appear to have been tampered with. I levitated the carcass and used the divine magic, which I was more practiced with, to separate the hide from the flesh. Normally when skinning an animal there is plenty of flesh left on a hide. Bits of tendon, cartilage, and fat clung to the pelt, which had to be dried so that it could be scraped clean, but with using the divine magic I got a completely clean skin. I also harvested the two long bones that ran down the animal's back. They were just big enough to make handles for my swords. The last step was to remove the brain so that I could properly tan the hide.

I rolled the harvested materials inside the animal skin and returned to the ship. The fact that it was still there was the only proof that I had accomplished the task in the allotted time. Usk met me inside just as the new storm rolled in. It was dark by that time, and while the wind howled outside I unveiled my Cidian blades to Master Usk.

"Well done," he said, an even, calm tone in his husky voice. "You have passed the second trial. Only one remains."

"What is it?" I asked, shivering both from cold and from excitement.

"The third trial is to slay a Scion heretic. Do that, and you will become my apprentice. There is much still to learn about divine magic, Azree'el. You have only just begun to understand the true nature of the power we possess."

CHAPTER 5

I WAS grateful for the ship's running water. A hot shower felt good, along with a hot meal and plenty of sleep. When I woke up we were in the Arendi system. The planets were inhospitable, but the system was home to a trade center. I'll admit I was shocked by the existence of a huge space station full of aliens buying and selling goods from different worlds. It was a shock to me that Usk would be welcomed in such a place. To me he was monstrous; a hideous creature who instilled fear in those who saw him. I also knew him to be smart and powerful in the control of divine magic. But there was much about the universe I still needed to learn.

"What is this place?" I asked the Vanj when I reported in the next morning.

"Arendi," he replied. "Here we will resupply and prepare for your final trial."

"Are the Scion heretics here?" I asked, suddenly feeling very uncertain about the test.

"No," Usk replied simply.

I felt a little better. Fighting was something I was familiar with, and even good at, but it was hard not to fear that the Scion warriors were more dangerous than anyone I had ever fought. And while I felt better physically after my second trial on Fierocite, I wasn't ready to be thrown into my final trial right away.

Usk gave me instructions and a bag of coins. He docked the ship and had the batteries that worked the vessel's life support systems recharged. I went aboard the space station and paid for the services. It was a simple exchange. We didn't need liquid fuel, but we did get the ship's air and water tanks topped off. Once I paid the dock workers, I had a full hour to explore the station. Everywhere I looked there were kiosks with vendors selling goods of all kinds. I barely made one loop around the lowest deck before I needed to get back on Usk's ship. It was a wonderland of diversity, and there was so much to see and try. Food of all kinds, clothing, weapons, armor, games, and all sorts of devices for entertainment. But the most common goods were those for ships: parts vendors with common vessel upgrades, boosters, shield generators, atomic converters, power generators, even food prep machines. Maybe the most incredible thing of all were the robots. Most looked like bulky machines, but they moved and performed a variety of functions. I could have spent hours watching them. The bots did everything from ship repairs to simple cleaning.

It was the most incredible place I had ever seen. There were vendors from different planets. Some looked similar to me, but most were completely different. Some wore breathing masks, and others suits that covered their entire bodies. Everything was displayed in the Common language. I could read and understand all the different beings from different planets.

There were more vendors on the upper levels of the space

station, along with a casino and entertainment deck. There were even rooms to rent, although most of the beings stayed on board their own ships.

I made only one purchase for myself, a small crafter's kit. It contained a straight-edged saw, files, small chisels, and a tube of industrial strength adhesive. It was just what I needed to complete my double-ended spear handle.

Back on the ship I couldn't help but reflect on how much my life had changed. I had gone from a frightened girl with no real future to becoming a space traveler and seeing things I had never imagined.

For the next several hours I worked to complete my new sword handles. The two long bones were hollowed out. Using the industrial adhesive I had bought, I mounted the blades onto the long handles by inserting the tang into the bone. The lower ends were carved to fit one inside the other and lock together. It was a simple design, but efficient. After tanning the animal skin, I cut several long strips from the belly of the creature, which had no fur on it. These I wrapped around the bone handles to provide extra grip.

With my weapon finished, I used the rest of the animal pelt to make myself a long cloak. The fur from the animal was used to line the upper portion. The ship itself wasn't a cold place, but the trade station on Arendi had been much cooler. In my quarters was a wall mounted, full-length mirror. During my months of training my hair had grown to my shoulders. I liked the way the fur-lined cloak hung around me and hid the swords.

For well over an hour, I practiced with them. Locking the two handles together created the same type of double-ended spear I had used in the arena on Vespa. The Cidian was surprisingly lightweight, as were the bone handles. It made the weapon easy to use and fast. The balance was perfect, and I found myself more excited about the weapon than I had thought. There was a satisfaction in having forged it myself, and a sense of pride in knowing what it had taken to obtain and create the Cidian blades. And the animal bones represented something about me, an homage to my past life on Ferret. Even though I served the Vanj I was still a unique person.

Two days later we entered the Basque system. Usk summoned me to his chamber with the wide windows as we approached a planet.

"Pyrenee," he said, waving a talon at the blue and green planet we were approaching. "The people there are simple farmers with no extra-solar ambitions."

It made me think of Ferret, and I felt a sense of sadness for the inhabitants of the planet.

"It is under the protection of the Scion heretics," Usk continued. "They know we're here."

"They do?" I asked, suddenly feeling nervous.

"Yes," Usk said. "And we will destroy them."

I didn't want my fear to show, but I was afraid. Maybe the heretics had been built up in my mind to monumental proportions. Still, it was hard not to fear our mortal enemies. I had fought to death many times in the arena, and in every instance, my instincts had seen me through. But going to fight the Scion felt different, more dangerous, more difficult somehow.

The ship descended toward the planet swiftly. In the upper atmosphere, Usk's magic bubble around the ship was buffeted by friction and surrounded by clouds of smoke. When we burst through the smoke, the planet was so close it filled the windows.

Everything was green, with blue rivers and lakes. We passed over herds of animals that had to number in the hundreds of thousands. It was an awe-inspiring world, so rich with resources I thought I understood why the inhabitants had no ambitions beyond their planet. No one on Pyrenee would go hungry. The vast herds feasted on wide, green plains that were rich with grass. Surely anything planted on this world would flourish. I could see why it would need protection.

Usk landed the ship on a wide plain. Across the way was what looked like a building, and I could sense the protective bubble of magic around it.

"Prepare yourself," Usk ordered. "This will not only be a test of your physical prowess but of your mental strength as well. Remember, the heretics will seek to draw you into their foolish beliefs. They may be very convincing, but to fall under their sway is to lose yourself completely."

"I'm ready," I lied. I didn't feel ready, but I was anxious.

"There is one master, one apprentice. Be on your guard at all times. I cannot protect you."

That seemed a bit unfair. Usk wanted me to protect him, but he wouldn't lift a finger to save my life. The Vanj thought of themselves as superior to every other race. They pursued godhood with a singular devotion. I was to be a watchdog, nothing more, just a bodyguard to my master. There was never any mention of my ascension, or that I even could achieve the same mastery over life and death that would make me divine. Nor was there any talk of freedom. I had seen what awaited those who survived long enough. They were returned to Vespa to tutor or train others. That would not be my life. I would serve Usk as long as there was more that I could learn, but eventually I would be free. I would find a way to traverse the stars and do as I thought best. But first, I needed to pass the third trial.

"I understand," I replied. No one had shown me any help since being abducted from Ferret. Why should things be any different now?

I made my way to the hatch that led off the ship. It was a double-door system. Only one ever opened at a time, and only if the other was closed and sealed. It was an indication of how fragile space vessels truly were. They could never risk being exposed to the hard vacuum and intense cold of space. It was also a testament to the incredible power of divine magic. It could not only lift the huge vessel into outer space, but it propelled us across the vast distances between systems in what seemed like no time at all.

Leaving the ship, I stepped out onto Pyrenee. The grass was soft and lush, the ground soft beneath my boot. It was a warm world, with a cool breeze blowing and fresh, oxygen-rich air. On Ferret I hadn't known anything about air other than I needed to breathe. My instruction on Vespa had taught me that planets have atmospheres that are made up of all sorts of invisible gases. Some were beneficial, others weren't. It was clear from my first breath on Pyrenee that it was the type of planet with a rich, life-sustaining atmosphere.

I was still standing outside the ship when my enemy appeared. There were two of them, just as my master said there would be. One was an alien with a wide head and three eyes on short, fleshy stalks. Its legs were thick with muscle and bent at the knees. The thick body was balanced on the powerful rear legs that seemed designed for jumping and had a short, thick tail that stuck out behind it. The alien's arms were folded in close to its body but didn't seem nearly as powerful as its legs.

Beside the three-eyed alien was a strong-looking male. It had four arms and four legs. It looked like it was half man, half beast, the upper body was shaped like my own, with two extra arms. The lower half was wide with two sets of legs. I started toward them, keeping my own magical shields up. The planet was almost intoxicating. I felt wonderful just walking across the flat, grassy plain. The sky was bright blue with the occasional white cloud drifting across the expanse. The sun was warm, but not hot, and the breeze caressed my face and made my cloak billow behind me. I lowered the fur-lined hood and let the sunlight wash across my hair and skin.

"This world is not your home," the three-eyed alien said in a high-pitched voice. He spoke Common, and his voice carried easily across to me.

"Perhaps it should be," I said without really thinking.

"The Fray are not welcome here," the four-armed alien said. "I am Xandor, four-year member, eighth of my kind. This world is under the protection of the Order of Scion. You may join us, or leave in peace. Anything else will result in your death."

"Or yours," I replied calmly. To be honest, the sweetness of the planet was whisking away every other thought and feeling. I was no longer nervous or apprehensive about fighting the Scion heretics. "We are not weak-willed imbeciles. You will not convert us to your false religion."

"The mandates of the Creator are not for the weak," the three-eyed alien said.

"Master Bomba, let me deal with this traitor," Xandor said, his teeth clenched.

"We do not look for violence," Bomba said, still addressing me. "Why have you come here?"

"To destroy you," I said.

"That is a fool's errand," the three-eyed alien replied. "But if a fight is what you desire, we will accommodate."

Xandor drew two blades, his four arms reaching across his body in a dramatic cross-draw. The swords were long, narrow blades. He held one to each side of his body in a two-handed grip. I moved the cloak back off my shoulders so that it hung like a cape and left my own swords free. I drew them out, then linked them together into a double-ended spear, which I spun around my body. It was a dramatic display, a show of skill with my weapons, but it also helped to loosen up the muscles in my back, shoulders, and arms.

"This is your last chance, Fray!" Xandor declared. It was a pompous proclamation from an arrogant heretic.

"Does he always talk so much?" I asked with a smirk.

That set him off. The four-legged alien galloped toward me. I set my feet and held my spear ready. It was obvious right from the start that Xandor was just testing me. He was rushing toward me, but angling just enough to be out of reach of both his swords and my spear. I didn't move. The first assault wasn't with a fist or a blade, but with magic. I felt the attack on me as an invisible force tried to punch through my defenses. If Usk was doing anything other than protecting himself, I couldn't sense it. Fortunately, I was strong enough to recognize and fend off the alien's magical attack.

At the same time, Xandor rushed past me. He swung the sword that was on his right side. It swished through the air but wasn't close enough to hurt me, and I didn't even bother to block it. My own magical senses gave me a strong understanding of spatial awareness. There was no doubt that Xandor's attack was nothing but a distraction so that his master could disrupt my magic. But Usk had warned me of that.

"You have no reason to attack us," Bomba said. "We are not your enemy."

"You are heretics," I replied.

Xandor had slowed to a trot but still hadn't turned around. I could sense his movement and didn't need to turn and watch him.

"We are believers in the Creator. The Power and the Knowledge we share comes from him. Has your master told you of the one true Father and his exalted son?"

"He's told me enough," I said, which wasn't really true. I was fascinated by the Scion heretics and what they believed, although it seemed farfetched. In truth, I didn't mind hearing more from them before the fight began in earnest.

"The Creator wants harmony among us," Bomba said. "He desires that we seek justice and love mercy as we walk with him in this life. That is why we offer you this chance to come with us. Come and learn more about the one who sustains the entire universe."

"Thanks, but I'll pass," I said. "Why should I trade one master for another? If your Creator is so great, why is there such chaos and pain in this life?"

"The universe was corrupted by evil," Bomba replied. "Be careful who you serve, young one. Not all is as it seems."

"Good... evil...are these not just words we make up to describe the things that happen to us? Why should I be enslaved to your god?"

"He is the only god; all others are imposters."

"Spoken like a true believer...or maybe a coward who fears the edge of my blade."

"We have no fear!" Xandor said, charging me once again.

"Join us," Bomba called out.

He sounded sincere, but I knew he was just trying to distract me. Xandor was charging straight at me this time, but I still didn't turn around, even as my hands tightened on my spear. The time for talk had passed and the fight was about to begin. My entire mind shifted to that reality and my body tensed like a spring under pressure.

Xandor's swords were made of black Cidian. They absorbed the light, which made them hard to see. They were like sword-shaped voids, but I wasn't looking at them. I felt his approach, the same way I felt my way through the caverns in the mountain on Fierocite. My magic showed me my enemy, and I felt him extend his long sword straight at me.

At the last possible moment I jumped to the side, rolling over one shoulder as Xandor's blade cut the air where I had been standing. Coming quickly to my knees, I thrust my spear at the alien. He was fast in one direction but didn't have the agility to bounce to the side and avoid my counterstrike. The tip of the spear caught Xandor in the hip, right where the powerful leg muscles bunched. The weapon cut easily through his flesh, leaving a deep gash in his rear haunch that caused him to stumble, then limp as he slowed and turned around.

"I'll make you pay for that!" he hissed.

"Come and collect," I replied.

"Bring her in alive, if possible," Bomba called out, but Xandor had a rage in his eyes that told me he wouldn't obey his master. I wondered if I could obey a similar order from Usk, but my master was nowhere to be found. This was my third trial, and I faced the Order of Scion alone.

Xandor was moving slower, partly because of his wound, but more out of respect for my abilities. He came toward me, pretending to charge and probably expecting me to dive out of the way again. I got the sense that he was not new to fighting, but it appeared that he relied on his strength and appearance to cow most adversaries. But I wasn't frightened by the alien or either of his swords. I stood my ground. When he advanced, I swayed out of reach of his first slash, then caught his second on the edge of my spear's metal head. The Cidian blades smashing together sounded more like two rocks than metal. No sparks flew, but neither weapon gave ground, either. Xandor was strong, much stronger than me, so I didn't push back as he forced his sword forward. Instead, I slid to the side and flipped up the bottom of my spear. Xandor had two weapons, but he obviously didn't respect the double blades on my spear. I gashed the front of his left foreleg just above the knee. He shouted in pain as he jumped backward. Perhaps it was from moving backward, or maybe the fact that he had two wounded legs, but Xandor stumbled awkwardly and I pressed in on him.

He swung his swords to keep me back, and I wisely stayed out of his reach, but my spear was longer than his weapon. I shoved the front blade toward the alien's body. He tried to parry and failed, and my blade slid over one forearm and gouged him in the side. Xandor had bright green blood. It flowed from his wounds and his face twisted into a grimace of pain.

I pretended to attack his head. It was a simple ploy, but one Xandor didn't see coming. As I raised my spear in the direction of his head, he knocked it backward with considerable force. I used the momentum to once again swing up the bottom of my spear. It chopped into his body between his front forelegs. It was a deep, debilitating wound. I tried to pull the spear free but it was lodged too deep. Xandor fell back and tried to pull me with him, but I twisted my end of the spear and pulled it away from the other.

"Back!" he screamed, lashing the air with his swords.

"Prepare to meet your Creator," I said.

I was about to rush in and finish Xandor when a rock the size of my head jumped from the grassy soil and shot at me like a bullet. Fortunately, I still had my shields in place. I couldn't use magic against my opponents, who were nullifying the mysterious power, but I managed to stop the rock. More debris flew at me. Some of it was from the grassy plain, and some from the alien ship. But the projectiles couldn't touch me. What they did manage to do was divert my attention long enough for Xandor to pull my sword free of his body. He dropped the weapon and crawled back toward his ship.

The four-armed alien still had both his swords, but he was holding them with just one hand each, and using the other two limbs to help move him away. I didn't know if he could be saved, but I knew my trial was to kill the heretics. Mercy was not a virtue to the Vanj. I followed Xandor, picking up my fallen, bloodstained sword.

"You have proven yourself," Bomba called to me. "You master can take Pyrenee...for now. But mark my words, we will return."

"Maybe you should stay," I said.

It was my turn to charge my opponent. I ran straight to Xandor, batted away his clumsy slash that was meant to stop me, and rammed my second sword straight into his throat. There was a look of pain and fear in his eyes as he dropped both swords and reached for mine. I yanked it free. He tried to hold back the tide of blood, but it was impossible. Xandor toppled to the ground, never to rise again.

"Why? What did Xandor ever do to you?" Bomba called.

He was moving toward the opening that led into his ship, and I was following at a jog. The vessel started to rise, but it moved slow enough that I jumped and caught the edge of the hatch that Bomba had gone through. I was lifted into the air and didn't dare look down as I dangled from the side of the ship. There was a sense of heaviness to my body that I couldn't counter, but it wasn't enough to keep me from pulling myself up and into the ship. All those pull-ups in the stable and during my months of training had paid off.

The Scion ship was nothing like ours. The floors, walls, and ceiling weren't metal. Nor did they seem to be constructed. The ship looked more like a natural formation, although the walls were straight and the passages just the right size for me to easily walk through. It only took a minute to find my way into a large, empty room. One wall was missing. Through it, I could see the bright green, verdant planet growing smaller as the ship rose into the air.

The three-eyed alien called Bomba was there, too. He stood waiting for me, his tiny arms still folded against his body, but on his feet were artificial claws made of Cidian.

"It is not too late to surrender," Bomba said calmly. "The Order of Scion will help you to see the way forward."

"After I killed your apprentice?"

"That was done in ignorance," Bomba said, but there was a strange sound to his voice. It took me a moment to realize that the loss of Xandor grieved the three-eyed alien. "It can be...forgiven."

"I do not seek forgiveness," I told him.

"We may not seek it, but we all need it," he said sadly. "I will fight you if that is your desire, but it is not mine."

"You can just surrender," I said, mocking the Scion heretic. "My master will show you the error of your ways."

"Your masters know only selfish ambition," Bomba declared. "They do not serve a higher calling than themselves. Surely, you can see a better way."

"We are free to choose what we do and how we do it," I said, but there was little conviction in my voice. The truth was, I had very little freedom. "No ancient mandate directs the decisions of our lives."

"The way of the Creator is good," Bomba said. "Helping others is a joy like you have never experienced."

That wasn't the case. I had known the joy of helping my friends. I had learned to trap and hunt. I saw what my work could do to sustain the people around me. Even taking our finds back to the underground villages on Ferret brought the locals such excitement and delight that I felt joy. Nothing like that had happened since going to Vespa. I couldn't help others, only hurt them. I didn't provide anything, I only worked to prove myself. But once I completed the trials, things would be different. I would be accepted and become an ally instead of a servant. It took some effort, but I dismissed Bomba's arguments for the Order of Scion.

I locked my swords together and started toward the alien. He didn't retreat as I expected. Nor was there a powerful magical attack. He simply waited until I got close, then leaned back on his wide tail and lashed out with his legs. They were longer than they appeared, and I was forced backward. I stabbed at him with my spear, but he deftly parried with one foot. The claws strapped to his feet were thick and seemed clumsy. They certainly would have been on *my* feet. Yet, Bomba worked them with a finesse that was skilled and graceful. He blocked my spear, batting it to the side and using his tail to slide toward me. Then, with a pivot on his down foot, he lashed out at me with the other.

I was forced to dive to the floor. It wasn't slippery, but it was polished smooth. I fell on my side and slid out of reach. He might have been able to pounce on me before I got back up, yet he didn't.

"This is madness," he said. "If you kill me, the ship will plummet back down to the surface. You'll be killed."

"Not likely," I replied.

"What about the crew? There are a dozen people on board who can't save themselves. Would you let them all die?"

"They are heretics that force others into their false religion."

"That isn't true. No one is forced to believe in the Creator. And even if it were true, that's still no reason to slaughter the innocent."

I was back on my feet, twirling my spear slowly as I thought about how to attack next. "Your kind must be extinguished from the universe."

"Surely you don't really believe that."

"What I believe is that you are in my way," I told him. "There is only one path to my destiny."

"I'm offering you a different path."

"You are poisoning my mind with your lies."

Reading the look of an alien you just met is hard, but I'm pretty sure there was sadness in Bomba's three eyes. His arms were longer than I thought, but very thin. He reached down and unfastened the Cidian claws that were strapped to his feet. Then he stepped back away from them and spread his hands in an inviting gesture.

"I offer you freedom from the violence that fills your life," he said. "Nothing more. Come with me and I will show you the Order of Scion, but I will always give you the choice to decide what you want. Nothing will ever be forced. You can leave any time you want."

My short life to that point had been one of privation, struggle, and fear. There had been temptations, of course: the urge to steal what wasn't mine, the desire to rebel against my father, and the desperate need to find something that would help me survive a little longer. But never in my life had I been tempted by something that sounded wonderful. Was the Order of Scion actually willing to give me what I really wanted? Magical power was good, and defeating my enemies was intoxicating, but what I really longed for was freedom. I wanted to explore the galaxy and return to my people to show them all the things I had discovered. And even though it seemed farfetched, I could imagine getting what I wanted if I stuck with Usk long enough to gain the power I needed. But maybe I was just fooling myself. Maybe, like the old ones who had taught me on Vespa, the best I could hope for was to survive long enough to grow old.

Bomba was offering me what I wanted right now. He was offering to take me away and give me freedom. I wanted it so badly that my entire body trembled at the very thought of it. But then I remembered Usk's warning:. namely, that the enemy would test me physically and mentally. I had no reason to believe Bomba. I had just murdered his apprentice. He wouldn't give me freedom. It was all a lie, just a trick to make me lower my defenses.

"You lie," I snarled, my hope suddenly transforming into rage.

"I wouldn't..."

Those were his last words. I charged straight at him, and to my surprise he didn't resist, not even when I shoved my spear into his chest. There was a look of bittersweet regret in his eyes and a sadness that didn't seem to be for himself. Then he died, and the ship fell.

The sudden dissolution of the magical bubble was surprising. I was lifted off my feet as the ship plummeted back toward the ground. I was still holding my spear, which was still wedged in Bomba's thick body. Outside the wind screamed, and it tried to suck me out of the missing wall. I pulled myself down and used Bomba's body like an anchor. Closing my eyes, I pushed out a protective bubble around myself, expanding it. The effort was new and not easy, but I had summoned a great deal of magic to forge my swords. And dire need is a great motivator.

I can't say why I didn't just throw myself out of the ship and levitate to safety. Maybe I didn't want the crew to die. I hadn't seen them, but as my bubble of magic spread through the ship I felt them. The ship, if it could be called that, was more like a land-based structure, and had many rooms. And there was no requirement in my instructions that I save the ship. But something in me wanted to feel like I was more than just a destructive force.

Killing the Scion heretics was one thing, but if I was going to be free one day, I needed to control my power and put it toward beneficial use. Somehow I managed to get my magic all around the ship to break the ties of magic that was pulling us down toward the planet. We slowed and finally hovered a few hundred feet above the surface. The strain on my mind was almost painful. It was like holding up a heavy weight above my head, but my strength was waning. I could feel the ship wanting to fall. I let it descend and managed to settle it on the ground before I collapsed.

I don't think I fainted, but I came close. The big, bright room dimmed, and sparks danced in my vision; for a moment I had no conscious thought. It was like waking up. And when I came back to myself I wasn't alone. Eight short aliens were in the room. They could have killed me before I regained my senses, but they just stood watching in awe...maybe with a little sadness, too.

Getting to my feet, I hesitated as a wave of dizziness passed over me. I was suddenly starving, and my throat was dry. The spear came out of Bomba when I yanked it. The diminutive crew were weeping, but none of them tried to stop me. They were heretics, I suppose, but they weren't a threat to anyone. If Usk chastised me for letting them live, I would just have to live with it. In that moment I felt almost ashamed of what I had done.

After wiping the alien's blood on his clothing, I walked to the missing wall and jumped out of the strange ship. When my feet hit the ground and the cool breeze ruffled my hair, I was filled with a sense of gratitude for being alive. I think it was the planet. It was impossible not to feel good on Pyrenee. Up to that point in my life, I had always imagined going back to Ferret, but if I had a choice, I would have made my home on Pyrenee. It was such a beautiful and vibrant world.

The walk back to Usk's ship took nearly an hour. We had come down several miles from where we had taken off. Along the way, I saw a flock of woolly sheep. That's when it hit me that there were no predator animals on Pyrenee. The locals surely harvested the animals as they needed, but they also tended to them and helped them to grow. It was a world that existed in harmony, and I wasn't part of it. In fact, I was an abomination. That fact was driven home when I saw Xandor's body left to rot in the field near Usk's ship. Death was my only companion. To be near me was to be in danger. It was all I knew, all I had ever been good at.

The realization filled me with a melancholy that I tried to hide from my master. Usk didn't exactly congratulate me or cheer my accomplishment. He acknowledged that I had passed the trial, and nothing more.

"You are a Fray warrior," he said in a cold voice. He was already raising the ship into the air. How he did it so effortlessly was amazing to me after straining just to keep the Scion ship from crashing.

"What will we do now?" I asked.

"Now we go to see my master," Usk said. "I have been searching for a new apprentice far too long."

I wanted to ask what happened to the last apprentice, but I was too afraid. Besides, it was obvious. There was only one way out...death. So far I had managed to avoid it, but that wouldn't be the case forever. All it took was a single mistake. If I wanted to live I needed to give myself completely to divine magic and learn all I could. Even if took a decade, or the rest of my life, I had to be willing to submit to my masters and devote myself to the skillful use of magic if I was ever going to be truly free.

I watched us leave Pyrenee in the Basque system with more than a touch of sadness. I had fought, I had killed, I had passed my test, and yet it felt like part of me was being left behind on the beautiful planet. The trip to nowhere took long enough for me to see to my weapons and clean myself up. When I was next in Usk's chamber, all I could see through the big windows was a giant void. Darkness seemed to gobble up everything. So far, despite the conditions of space, I wasn't afraid, but seeing the black hole gave me an icy sense of dread. Normally, I saw thousands of stars, but near the black hole, there was nothing except another ship.

Usk brought our vessel right up to the other ship. They were about the same size, neither one large nor impressive. And both had been made for space voyages, unlike the Scion ship, which seemed more like a home than a vessel for traversing the galaxy. For the first time since coming on board the ship with Usk, the alien left his domicile. The graceful way he moved over the thick bed of creeping vines made me feel clumsy and out of place.

There was no need for a docking tube to transfer from one ship to another. Usk formed a magical bubble around us and levitated us through space. It was the first time I had seen anyone do such a feat. Levitating other things was something I had worked on right from the start of my training. And on Pyrenee I had formed a magic bubble around the Scion ship and levitated it somewhat to keep it from crashing. But it had never occurred to me that I might levitate myself. Had I known that, I wouldn't have spent so much time and energy climbing the mountains on Fierocite. For that matter, I could have kept the freezing cold at bay, too.

For a few moments, I was obsessed with my ignorance. How I could have accomplished so much but missed such an elementary ability was embarrassing. Once we were on the other ship, Usk released his magic and we walked through the dim passageways. His master wasn't there to greet us. We made our way through his ship, which seemed no different from ours. Metal decks, faded signage, nothing but the most basic systems online, but no creeping vines or steaming atmosphere. It wasn't exactly cold on the ship, but it was much cooler than on Usk's vessel.

I have been shocked by the appearance of many aliens. The Vanj are frighteningly hideous. The three-eyed Scion heretic Bomba was a striking figure, but Usk's master was shocking in a completely different way. He was beautiful and as much like a Heterrid as any being I had seen, except for the third eye in the middle of his forehead. He had golden skin and golden hair. There were very few lights on in his ship, but they weren't needed, because the alien actually glowed. I was shocked at the sight of him, and when he spoke his voice had a melodious quality that left me feeling a little breathless.

"Usk, my friend, you have returned at last," the master said. "And you have a new protégé, I see."

"Master," Usk said reverently, bowing before the golden man.

I quickly emulated my Vanj superior. and noticed that even the master's feet glowed. They were bare; he wore a simple robe that hung nearly to the floor. It was white, with a thick golden sash tied around his waist. The garment was open from midway up his stomach, and the V-shaped section revealed golden skin and the sharp contours of muscle. There was no hair, no markings on his chest. Unlike the men on Ferret, he had no facial hair either, just a narrow but strong chin, delicate features with perfect symmetry, and three eyes that formed the points of a triangle, all framed with golden-colored hair.

We stood, and I felt myself trembling a little. The alien was staring at me. I didn't know what he was capable of. In truth, even though I knew the Vanj believed that mastery of divine magic could make them gods, I didn't really believe it. Powerful, yes, maybe even immortal, but gods? No, I hadn't believed it until I saw Usk's master.

"We present ourselves to you, master," Usk said, his husky voice low with reverence. "This is Azree'el, my apprentice. She has just completed her third trial and is ready to serve you."

"Impressive," the golden man said. "Azree'el, that is a spectacular name. There is power in a name. It's more than just what we are called, you know. Our name is who we are to the universe; it is the representation of our being. Guard your name, Azree'el. Better to be feared than dismissed, or to have some failing mar our name. My name is G'all Gotha. You will remember it, I believe."

"Yes, master," I said, bowing again.

He walked around me. Usk backed away. It was the only time I had seen the Vanj wizard act afraid. I was intoxicated by G'all Gotha's presence. He ignited all my senses. Even the way he smelled seemed wonderful to me. Usk, on the other hand, seemed cowed by the golden man's presence.

G'all Gotha studied me, and I felt incredibly self-conscious. He wore that fine white robe, while I was clad in mismatched clothing that was too big for me. Only my cloak was really mine, and my swords. He reached out and ran a hand across the soft fur that lined the hood of my cloak.

"Impressive," he said. "Where did you find this fur?"

"On Fierocite, my lord," I said, not quite knowing why I called him that. He was Usk's master, which made him my superior, but the word "lord" seemed more fitting.

"There is no market there," he replied.

"I harvested the animal," I explained. "And used its pelt for my cloak and my swords."

"They are unique," he said.

When he reached into my cloak to draw my swords out of the scabbards on my belt, I felt shivers run down my spine. He stepped back, locked the swords together and spun the double-ended spear.

"Impressive design," he said. "The balance is perfect. You are a craftsman, Azree'el. I can see why Usk selected you to serve him."

He uncoupled the swords and handed them back to me. I slid them home as the golden man turned to Usk.

"She defeated a Scion warrior?"

"Warrior and master," Usk said. "I did not interfere."

"Very good. We can hope to exterminate that heresy from the universe soon. Our plans are proceeding quite well. You can help," G'all said in a casual tone.

I had no idea what they were talking about specifically, and from the way the golden man spoke I didn't think it was all that important. "But you'll need a different ship. Go to the Osir system and steal one of their bombing vessels. Are you familiar with them?"

"Yes," Usk said.

"Then you know taking their ship won't be easy, but it must be a functioning vessel. The hour of our victory is drawing near. Obtain the new ship and be ready to take on mercenaries. The final battle is approaching with haste, we must not fail to be prepared. Go now, and contact me when you have it."

"Yes, my master," Usk said with another bow.

I bowed again too, then followed Usk out of the ship. I'll be honest and say I was captivated by G'all Gotha. Never had I seen such a man. He was beautiful, wise, and encouraging. Had he asked me to stay and be his slave I would have said yes. I don't remember much of what happened leaving his ship, or of the voyage we took to the next system. The image of G'all Gotha filled my mind. He wasn't a Heterrid or even the species we had been taken from, although he looked like a Heterrid man. Two arms, two legs, his hands and feet, even his face looked normal, except for the third eye. I had heard old women in the cavern villages speak of using their third eye, but it was just folklore. Some women claimed to have powers such as seeing into the future, but it wasn't real. Maybe the stories had some basis in fact, though. The golden man with the third eye was real, and if he had claimed to be a god I would have believed him. If he had demanded we fall down and worship him, I would have.

In time my memory of him faded somewhat, but he certainly left an impression on me. My thoughts of escape were wiped away. The only desire I had left was to return and see G'all Gotha again. I can't say why. It wasn't just a young woman's crush on a handsome man, although I found him to be beautiful in a way I never knew possible. Nor was it simply a desire to serve him, although I wanted to do that, too. I wanted to make him happy, and I would do anything to achieve that goal. What I didn't want was to be sent away on another mission. No, I wanted to be near him all the time. Leaving his ship felt wrong somehow. I would obey his command, but it didn't seem right to have found such a being and to leave him so quickly.

While Usk flew our ship to the Osir system I remained in my own quarters. Normally, I tried to keep busy. After weeks of captivity on Vespa, I had learned to exercise in small spaces and to be content with very little to do. But after meeting G'all Gotha I sat alone thinking of him. I wanted to memorize how he looked, but it was a poor representation. I could see his form, even the way his skin glowed, but the sense of his presence wasn't right. On his ship G'all had been utterly captivating, and try though I might, I couldn't recapture that feeling.

Eventually, Usk called me to him. We had a task to do, and pining over the golden man with three eyes wasn't it. I left my quarters reluctantly and joined Usk in his sweltering chamber.

"This is Osir," he said.

We were far from the system, but I could see lights in the distance. There were thousands of them, some moving, others stationary. In the expanse of space, the lights formed a line on the planetary elliptical plain. Osir was a small, white star. From our position, I could see a couple of gas giants beyond the star and some smaller planets that had rings of light around them. It took my mind a moment to realize what I was seeing.

"Each light is a ship?"

"A ship, or a space station," Usk said. "The Os are an expansionist race with high technology."

"They build ships?"

"Yes," Usk said. "All kinds of ships. They are militaristic. Taking one of their bombing vessels will not be easy."

None of that except it not being easy computed in my brain. I had seen my own people huddled in underground caverns. I had seen the Vanj in their sprawling cities, and even their airfields where dozens of aircraft came and went on a daily basis. But they weren't a race of high technology. All their vessels were stolen from others, even the ship we occupied. And I had no idea what a militaristic race would be like. But I was soon to find out.

CHAPTER 6

THE MISSION WAS SIMPLE ENOUGH, but to carry it out was a much more complicated ordeal. Usk formulated a plan that I wasn't entirely sure would work, but he was the master and I was the apprentice, so I did what I was told.

In my spare time, before my third trial, I had explored the ship. There wasn't much to it, a dozen or so smaller cabins that reminded me of my cell in the stable on Vespa. A larger, obviously shared bathroom facility made me feel fortunate that I was the only Heterrid on the ship. It was interesting to me that our vessel seemed made for my kind, but I could find nothing on the history of the ship. All the signage was in the Common language, and most of it was faded from age. In the part of the ship that Usk called *engineering* were large batteries. By large, I mean they were the size of my personal quarters on the ship. They were just big blocks near several other mechanisms and tanks that held air and water. I recognized the life support system console, and the heating system was run almost constantly.

Against one wall was a series of switches that powered the various systems on and off. Beside them was one big red lever. Usk had ordered me to throw it. I pulled the red lever and everything stopped running. The lights went out, and the heating unit that normally ran all the time to pump warm air through the ship stopped. The air scrubbers stopped humming, and the water supply shut down. The ship was dead in space. Normally, I might have been frightened, but I didn't need to see to find my way back to Usk's command center. My sense of the divine magic was as useful to me as my own eyes. When I returned to where Usk waited and watched, I could see that we were moving forward through space.

"Why do we need to turn off the power?" I asked.

"Because we want to appear to be a dead ship," Usk said. "The Os will send salvage crews, which in turn will supply us with a vessel that we can fly into their shipyards with."

"And then we just take whatever we want?"

"After a fashion," Usk said. "They will undoubtedly try to stop us, and we will be forced to slaughter them."

That sent a shiver of doubt through my mind. It was disturbing to think that we would just kill random beings. I had no trouble killing those who attacked or opposed me, be they Heterrids or another race. But we would be stealing from the Os, so of course they would try to stop us. I had no qualms about stealing, either. It wasn't uncommon for the strong to take whatever they wanted from the weak on Ferret. I didn't like it, but I didn't find it morally repugnant, as some races do. But even from a distance, I could see that the Os were a highly populated race. There could be hundreds, maybe thousands of them, in opposition to us. I was afraid that Usk was being too bold, perhaps even careless, as well as I feared how many of the aliens we might have to slay to carry out our mission.

The only thing I was certain of was that I wanted to succeed and return to G'all Gotha. Part of me wanted to please him, but another part of me just wanted to be near him again. It wasn't passion or romance, it was a strange obsession with what he represented. Not just power, but a power unlike anything I had ever experienced, or even imagined to exist. Some Heterrids believed in gods, some even carved idols from soft rock, or molded them from clay, but they were just dull figures. There was no life in the idols, no sense of power, and none that I saw ever filled me with wonder. G'all Gotha, on the other hand, was a spectacular being. The Vanj feel they are superior to other races. I didn't know whether to agree or disagree. On Pyrenee I encountered two aliens that seemed neither superior nor inferior to myself. They were different, but that was all I thought of them. G'all Gotha, on the other hand, was spectacularly different. I had felt his power and his presence radiating from him like the glow from his perfect skin. I was entranced by his voice and filled with a desire to be in his presence. I can't say why, or what I hoped for. But I still wanted it, and if I had to kill ten thousand Osians to do it, I would kill them.

I was a patient person. It was a virtue borne first of slow, skillful stalking of prey through the forests on Ferret, and then from the hours of sheer boredom that being a captive inevitably resulted in. We had set a trap, and all that remained was to wait for the Osians to stumble into it. But that took nearly ten hours, and by the time they arrived, the ship we occupied was cold enough to turn water to ice. Usk remained in his place with a bubble of warm air around his alien body. I had done the same for a while, but eventually, the air got stale. Better to be cold than to suffocate. And physical exercise did much to warm my body.

When the Osians arrived it was a relief of sorts. They came in spacesuits that made them seem bigger than they were. Usk struck quickly, ripping through their spacesuits with his talons and smashing them to the deck with divine magic before they could call out for help. We raced across the tube they had attached to our ship from theirs. I followed Usk, my swords held ready, but they weren't needed. While our ship had no gravity, theirs had artificial gravity and full life support systems. We raced in, with Usk using his magic to slaughter the Osians. They were bi-peds but only as tall as my shoulder and with slender bodies. Their faces were dark green, their eyes vertical slits on their oval faces. Their eyes had no lids. Usk had no trouble crushing skulls with his magical power. I felt the force squeezing the aliens and saw their bodies on the floor of the salvage ship. It felt odd to me, somewhat frightening and perhaps wrong, but was just a tiny blip in the midst of my surprise and wonder.

The ship itself was so different from anything I was used to. The floors were polished to a high shine. Everything was bright white with reflective chrome fixtures. Usk seemed to know right where he was going and I followed him, my defensive magic ready. It saved my life when a door to my right opened and an Osian opened fire on me with the first gun I had ever seen. We knew of such weapons and told stories about them on Ferret, but the Vanj didn't carry them, and we no longer had the knowledge of how to make them. The Osian gun was a dark, pointed thing about the length of my arm from shoulder to fingertips. It narrowed considerably until the end was just a round length of pipe, from which small metal slugs pumped out in quick succession. It was loud in the confines of the ship. The bullets it spewed would have torn through me, but my magic crushed them to the floor before they could reach me.

For a moment I didn't move. Nor did the Osian man. He just kept shooting, as if he could will the weapon to overcome my magical power. It couldn't, and after the novelty of what he was doing wore off I grasped the weapon with my magic and yanked it from his hands. It was heavy and hot. The controls felt small to my hands. I wasn't sure how to work the weapon, so, I flung it at him with the strength of my magic. The alien saw it coming and started to dodge away but wasn't fast enough. The gun hit him in the side of the head with enough force to knock him senseless. Perhaps I should have followed Usk's example and slaughtered the alien. He was certainly willing to end my life, but he fell to the gleaming deck unconscious, and the door to the room closed. So, I left him there and hurried to catch up to Usk.

The salvage ship was much larger than our own. Most of it was filled with mechanical devices. There were extendable arms used to clamp onto derelict vessels, and a variety of unmanned autonomous explorer drones. In addition, I saw machines used to clean the air inside a ship, and another that would patch a hole in the hull of a space vessel. It occurred to me that the Osians must have recognized the ship we were in. Maybe not that specific spacecraft, but the make and model for sure. Otherwise, they would have been more cautious, but they appeared to know what they were going to find on board, which was why they sent in a team instead of a drone to search the vessel. That had been their first mistake.

Usk quickly took control of their ship. There was no reasoning with him. Some of the Osians wailed in terror and probably begged for their lives in their own squawking language. Usk ignored them all, preferring to silence them permanently. There was no mercy or kindness in the Vanj. They had no empathy for anyone else, not even others of their own kind. I'm not even sure if they possess a full range of emotions. Usk killed indiscriminately, then sent the ship flying back toward the activity from which it had come. He didn't bother towing our ship along. He had discarded that vessel without a second thought.

I joined him on the command deck. It was the highest point of the ship, which although large, didn't have a large crew. There was a single pilot station and a few small consoles on the command deck, which was surrounded on all sides by windows. One console projected a hologram of the space around the ship. Usk didn't bother with the controls to maneuver the vessel, using his magic instead, but I went to the hologram to admire it.

Whenever we got within fifty miles of another vessel it, too, appeared in the hologram. Using my magic, I confirmed everything I saw on the ship. It was made from a steel alloy. I wasn't practiced enough in recognizing different substances with divine magic alone to know exactly what it was constructed of, but the hull felt familiar to me, as did the retractable arms and mechanical devices in the large cargo area of the salvage ship.

The communications console squawked with the sounds of incoming communications. I didn't understand it, and Usk didn't pay it any attention. The point was to get close to the type of ship he wanted. Everything else was secondary. I felt him conjure a defensive bubble around the ship. Normally, his magical bubble was just a barrier to hold in our ship and the air around it. It severed any hold a planet's gravity or other magic might have on the vessel, allowing him to move it at will in any direction and maintain a sense of gravity as well. But he formed a very powerful bubble around the salvage ship, and it didn't take me long to understand why.

We were flying toward a very neat formation of alien ships. They were pointed at one end, some bigger than others, all bristling with what looked to me like pipes, but which I was beginning to understand were guns and cannons. The salvage ship had no problems getting close to the formation, but once the other ships started popping up on the holographic display the Osians knew something was wrong. They opened fire. Laser light flared in the darkness of space. By that point we were close enough to see their world. It was silvery with thick bands of ships and satellites circling around it, but the entire thing looked to me like it was no bigger than a marble. The laser flashes were like lightning, illuminating the darkness around us for a moment, then disappearing. In the flash of light, I could see our ship. It was oval in shape and looked like a crab. The interior was fancy, but the exterior was completely utilitarian. There were pipes and vents and mechanical fixtures in ugly clusters on the outer hull. I saw stains from where dark fluids had leaked out, and where the pollution from the exhaust vents had discolored the metal around them. The actual ship seemed much more used and dirty than the hologram that depicted it.

The lasers didn't reach us. They were bent by Usk's magical shields and sent streaking off in different directions. I saw one laser bend away from us and strike another vessel. It flashed and part of the ship simply vanished, leaving a gaping hole that vented all sorts of gases and debris. It was impressive, to say the least. Our magic was stronger than their laser weapons, yet they were deadly. When the lasers didn't work, missiles were fired. They came streaking toward us at great speed, but not nearly as fast as the laser fire.

"Stop those missiles," Usk ordered.

I was certain his own magical shielding could do the job, but an order was an order. And, to be honest, I was excited to join in the action. Reaching out with my magical senses was easy enough. Reaching far enough to feel the missiles racing toward our ship was a strain. They were nearly fifty miles from where I stood on the command deck of the salvage ship. It took a moment for me to push my senses out that far. I was used to keeping a tight rein on my perceptions. There were times when I opened myself up to the ebb and flow of magic that I felt a person could get lost in it. Stretching my power around the Scion ship on Pyrenee had been difficult, but reaching out to the missiles was just as taxing. Fortunately, I could see the missiles. They were far away, but visible, and I gave them my entire focus. Once I got a hold on one of them, I simply pushed it toward another. The two missiles clashing together caused them to explode and set off a chain of explosions as the shockwave of the first blast triggered the others, causing a mass detonation.

"Very good," Usk said.

"Which ship are we going after?" I asked.

"One of those on the lower rank," Usk said.

The Osian ships were all built along the same design. They had a V-shaped hull, but with different armaments, engines, and oversize. The armada was formed up in ranks. The ships on the bottom weren't the biggest—that was reserved for those in the middle, out of which swarms of small fighter craft began to fly. They poured out, so tiny to my eyes they were like gnats.

"It is time to make our move," Usk said.

"Yes, master," I replied, not sure what he had in mind, but he was already leaving the command deck and I followed.

"Once we are on the ship, your task will be to protect me while I fly us out of the system," he said. "I will shield the ship; you will shield me. If you fail, we both die."

The words echoed on the ship as we passed the bodies of the dead Osians Usk had already slaughtered. Their presence drove the warning home to me. Usk led us to an airlock. I had to join him in the small space, which was clearly designed for smaller beings. It was tall enough that I didn't have to stoop, but Usk did, and his massive skull barely fit inside. I was crammed into the corner of the airlock, but still closer to the Vanj than I had ever been before. I was close enough to smell the acrid stench of his body, and some of the clear fluid that covered him got onto my cloak.

He formed a bubble of magic around us, but let the hard vacuum suck us out of the airlock. Once we were outside the ship he expanded the bubble, and we drifted apart from one another. The alien was in complete control, moving us up and away from the salvage ship. Another barrage of missiles had been fired. As we flew through space I watched the missiles close in on the vessel. They hit in a series, blasting long sections out of the hull. There were at least forty missiles, but the salvage ship was so big that it only shuttered under the heavy missile bombardment and kept moving toward the armada.

We were traveling even faster than the missiles had flown, only it seemed like we weren't moving at all. Inside the bubble Usk held air, heat, and gravity so that it appeared to me that the galaxy was moving around us while we stood still. We dropped toward the rear-most bomber vessel in the fleet. Within just a couple of minutes after leaving the doomed salvage vessel we were skimming the surface of the military bomber. It was even larger than the other ship we had stolen, and as I extended my sense of magic inside the ship I could feel hundreds of Osians hurrying about their business.

Usk took us around to the bottom of the vessel. I saw the long Bombay doors. They were shut and sealed against the harsh vacuum of space, but near them was an emergency hatch. We flew to it, and Usk used his magic to open the airlock. Once more we crammed ourselves together, and when the airlock cycled open the slaughter began.

†††

The crew of the bomber wasn't expecting us, but they were dutifully at their stations, awaiting whatever orders came down. On the lowest level of the ship were two sets of heavy equipment movers and what looked to me like thousands of eggs in tall racks. The bomb bay filled the entire lower section of the V-shaped ship, with racks of various bombing munitions stretching away into the arms on each side of the V.

More to our focus was the bomb bay crew, a group of eight Osians in bright orange coveralls. They were technicians and certified munitions handlers. Only two were qualified to run the bombing apparatus itself, and none were armed. They looked up in surprise as we entered the ship, and I immediately raised a magic shield around us. But that wasn't enough. Usk could move fast when he wanted to, his long legs quickly outpacing me. I had to run to keep up. The crew quickly armed themselves with whatever was handy, tools mostly. The first of them, a tall alien with long arms and a heavy wrench in one hand, charged toward us. I drew my swords. The rest of the crew backed off when they saw my black Cidian blades, but not the Osian with the wrench. He was focused on Usk, and I have to admit I admired his bravery. Charging a Vanj isn't easy. They're big and strangely hideous, like a weird skeleton with a huge head and the jaws of some kind of animal. Yet the man was undeterred, and I had to leap in front of him. He swung the wrench as if he expected to swat me away like a bothersome mosquito. Instead, I blocked the wrench with the flat edge of one sword and opened his stomach with a slash of the other. His entrails spilled out and he staggered back. To his credit he tried again, stepping on his own intestines in the process. There was no strength in his long arms. Without even trying I severed one and left him on his knees while his life's blood, which was a dark blue color, poured out onto the gleaming white deck in front of him.

"Kill them!" Usk ordered. "Leave none of them alive."

It was a tall order. I couldn't leave Usk, and none of the other crewmen were attacking me. That meant I needed to use my magic. I had never really formed a solid defensive shield and attacked someone with magic at the same time before. It was like doing something different with each hand, but somehow I managed to send a wave of powerful magic against the crew, who had hurried to the aid of their wounded companion. It was a futile gesture on their part. There was nothing they could do to save the wrench-wielding fighter, but having them close together made my strike easier to accomplish. The wave of magic slammed into them like an invisible hammer. They were knocked back and most were wounded. There were broken bones and some were knocked unconscious, but that wasn't good enough.

"I said dead," Usk snarled, whirling around to face me. "Either do that or you're no use to me."

"Yes...master," I said.

We had just reached the top of a metal landing that gave a good view of the bomb bay, and also led to another passage inside the ship. I turned. The crew were sprawled beneath me. I poured my magic down on them. The helpless crew tried to scream but couldn't draw the breath. I kept adding more and more pressure until I saw them die.

Maybe that seems wicked to you. And maybe before I had been abducted by the Vanj I might have agreed. With the hunter Elaa'zar no kill went unused. We harvested all we could from every life we took. Even the small game were skinned, their flesh consumed, their bones fashioned into tools that we either used or sold in the small, underground villages that depended on us for their very survival. Killing the Osians just to get their ship seemed at first to be evil. We attacked them, after all. They were just defending their ship. But they were warriors. They weren't merchants or travelers. They were military professionals who, if given the order by their superiors, would have dropped devastating bombs onto their enemies. Those bombs wouldn't have differentiated between the innocent and the guilty. They would have been used to kill enemy fighters and anyone close to them. Maybe on a scale in some banal criminal court what I did could be seen as immoral, but it didn't take me long to move past it. I didn't have time to worry about the dead, not when the living Osians were still trying to kill us.

Through the hatch and into the main part of the ship were more crewmen. Some were armed with laser pistols. My defenses held strong against their small weapons fire, and I quickly learned exactly where to apply pressure to the Osians that would inflict the most damage. Their necks were strong, but their skulls were thin, almost delicate. Some even wore protective helmets. I could reach out with my magic and crush their heads the way a person might crack an egg on the side of a pan. It didn't take massive strength, and certainly not imagination. Compared to crushing their bodies, or cutting off their air supply, smashing their skulls was child's play.

We made our way through the tight passages and up two more flights of stairs before we reached the command deck. All along the way I slaughtered the crew. Those who showed their faces, and those who hid from us. It was a trial by fire for me and my control of magic. More than once I shattered a wall panel or crushed a conduit pipe with a clumsy strike. It was taxing to keep moving, keep my shields up around myself and Usk, and to fight the Osians. I had to expand my awareness. It was like trying to see in the failing light.

My magical senses reached into every room, corridor, and compartment of the ship. Some of the crew escaped using the emergency pods that were designed for that purpose when red lights began to flash in the corridors of the ship. At the same time a wailing voice was piped throughout the ship. Usk didn't seem to mind. He had already surrounded the vessel with his own magical bubble and was accelerating quickly away from the armada. Some of the ships, especially the small fighter craft, followed. When we reached the command deck I saw a much larger holographic plot of the V-shaped bomber and the ships pursuing us. The tiny ships were fast, but it was obvious from the hologram that we were already pulling away. The technology in their engines was no match for the divine magic that Usk was using to propel the V-shaped bombing ship, and I could already feel the power building that would take us out of their star system.

"Search the ship," Usk ordered. "There can be no survivors to threaten us or sabotage this vessel."

"As you wish," I said, not really sure why I said it. Maybe I was getting used to thinking of Usk as my master. I had been a slave for some time, a captive held against my will and forced to fight for my life. But since leaving Vespa my perception of my own life had changed. Meeting with G'all Gotha had changed it even more. My own ambitions seemed like child's play. What did being free really mean, anyway? What I wanted more than anything else was to return to the glowing, god-like man and bask in his presence.

Over half of the ship's escape pods had been used, and none of the Osians were left alive. When I returned to the command deck I found that Usk had already been at work. He was settled on the highest point, and a tangle of spreading vines was already beginning to snake around him. Where they came from or how they grew so fast was a mystery to me. There was no divine magic involved, and I assumed it was a Vanj tradition that held very little interest to me.

"There are no survivors," I told him.

It would have taken hours to search the entire ship without magic. But no one could hide from my magical senses. I could feel the entire vessel, every hatch, component, compartment, and all the personal items neatly stowed away in the various staterooms. I had found the largest and claimed it for myself. The Osians were not much different physiologically: they slept in beds, used showers to bathe, and ate similar food to what I was used to. I had even stopped in the engineering department to adjust the temperature and humidity on the command deck to Usk's preferences.

The ship had several large freezers in the galley section. I put some of the dead into it and tried not to stare at the bodies of the officers that my master had already ripped to pieces and fed on. Their remains were bunched in the corner, and I could smell what I guessed was their blood. It had a coppery twang, just like Heterrid blood.

"Very well," he said. "Only one chore still remains."

"To return to Master Gotha and report our success?" I asked, already daydreaming about seeing the golden-skinned alien again.

"No, we must acquire a communication crystal," Usk said. "From the mines on Gaul, in the Caledonian system. They are guarded by the Scion heretics, but without it we cannot communicate with my master."

"Then we shall retrieve one," I said confidently.

"It will not be easy," Usk said. He actually sounded nervous for the first time since I had become his apprentice. "They will nullify our magic. Retrieving the crystals will be dangerous."

"Is it necessary?"

"G'all Gotha has commanded it," he snapped. "We will obey."

I didn't argue further. There was no point to it. Usk didn't see me as an equal, and I knew nothing about the crystals he was saying we needed. And above all, if G'all Gotha had commanded us to get it, I would. In my mind it was that simple. But with nothing left to do until we arrived at Gaul, a planet I knew nothing about it, I would settle into my new surroundings.

Leaving the command deck, I took a short flight of stairs and came to what had surely been the captain's quarters. I knew nothing about militaries or who was in charge of big warships like the bomber, but I had a strong knowledge about the ship we were on. Just like the ship we had left, and not so different from the salvage ship we had been aboard for a short while, there seemed to be a hierarchy that was easily measured by the amount of space one had. There were bigger rooms than the one I chose for my own quarters, but they were filled with many bunks that were built into the walls. My new surroundings were lavish in comparison. There were three rooms, one built for bathing, one for sleeping, and the outer room was for entertaining guests. It had several pieces of furniture for sitting, all of them stuffed with padding to make them comfortable. There was a large desk, but it had very little on it. Behind one wall panel was an entertainment console with a large display screen, and behind another was machinery that produced refreshments. I smelled an amber colored liquid in a crystal container, but it burned my nose and made my eyes water.

In the sleeping chamber were two storage compartments. One was lined with military uniforms, which didn't interest me. The other held an array of personal items. Clothing, blankets, and trinkets that obviously had meant something to the previous occupant, but nothing to me. What was interesting were the sets of clothing. I found a matching set of dark pants and shirt. The fit wasn't perfect, but the material was highly stretchy. It covered my body and still allowed me to move freely. Plus, I liked the way it looked on me. There was a mirror in the compartment that allowed me to see myself. I wondered what Elaa'zar or my father would think if they could see me in the alien clothing.

Eventually, I got bored with pilfering through the goods left behind by the crew. I slept for a while, then found something to eat. The galley was stocked with foods for a crew of over a hundred, and there was plenty to sustain me. When I got back to the command deck it was hot and steamy. The spreading vines had made considerable progress. They formed a nest of sorts around

Usk, who was sitting with his limbs pulled in close underneath his massive, curved skull.

"Are we there yet?" I asked.

"We are in the system," Usk said. "I have not detected the Scion threat as of yet."

"Perhaps they are no longer here."

"Don't be deceived," he hissed. "The Gaul mines are one of only a handful of places in the galaxy that the crystals can be found."

"What's so special about them?"

"They allow for messaging between systems at speeds that are much faster than any technological or even magical apparatus can achieve."

At the time I had no knowledge of communication systems. I was still learning so much. But I had learned that the speed of light was the fastest measure in the galaxy, according to the digital tutoring device I had been allowed access to on Vespa. And that even at the speed of light the distances between star systems required years, sometimes hundreds of years, to traverse. It was a marvel of the divine magic that Usk could use it to speed between them. My experience with communication between groups separated from one another was being given a scroll with a message from the elders of one underground village to be delivered to another. As a hunter on the surface of Ferret, Elaa'zar had sometimes taken the messages, which he delivered when we arrived at the village it was addressed to. Sometimes that took days, and other times it took weeks.

"With a communication crystal we can get orders directly from Master Gotha," Usk said. "No matter where we are in the galaxy."

That was impressive to me, and also very intriguing. Of course, anything to do with the glowing alien got my attention.

"How?" I asked.

"How the crystals function is unknown," Usk said. "Many believe they are connected via a different dimension that is outside of time and space."

I knew nothing of dimensions, and all that really mattered in my mind at that time was the fact that G'all Gotha could contact us. I was smitten, but not romantically. The allure of G'all Gotha wasn't physical, it was emotional. Being near the glowing alien had made me feel things I couldn't explain. All I knew was that it was a wonderful experience that left me feeling good in a way I never had before.

The command deck of the V-shaped bomber was different from our previous vessels. It had no windows. The command deck was in the middle of the ship, but the walls were all high-resolution display screens that were linked to cameras on the hull of the ship. On the command deck we could see a dim, red star in the distance. Closer by was a planet, although it looked more like a moon to me. It was gray and dull, the only features were vast deserts and impact craters.

"That's Gaul?" I asked.

"It is," Usk said. "An ancient world in a dying system. The star went nova centuries ago and is now burning itself out."

"I read about that," I said.

"Gaul was devastated by the process, but the intense heat and solar radiation that destroyed the planet's atmosphere and left a barren world on the surface also created the crystals we need to communicate with Master Gotha and other members of the Fray."

"There are others?" I asked.

"Many that follow the golden one," Usk said. "The battle with the Scion heretics has waged a long, long time."

That was news to me, but it wasn't vital. I knew that some species lived longer than others. Heterrids on Ferret rarely lived beyond fifty cycles of the seasons. But those on Vespa who didn't die in the arena appeared to live much longer. How long the Vanj and other wizards had been fighting against the Order of Scion was unknown. And to be honest, I didn't really care. I was so new to the ways of the galaxy, and there was so much new information to think about, that it was all I could do to look after myself.

"And you think there are Scion warriors down there?" I asked.

"It is almost a certainty."

"Will they attempt to stop us?"

"If they can," Usk said. "The mines have dangers of their own. The Scion heretics may not attack at all, they may simply counter our magic and force us to risk mining the crystals without it."

I wasn't a miner, but I had grown up underground. I didn't like being in the dark, dank caverns of Ferret or any other world, but I didn't fear it, either. Nor was I opposed to difficulty or danger. They were the constants in my life. And while I didn't long for mortal peril, I did want to see and fight the Scion heretics. I can't say why. Perhaps it was to challenge myself, or maybe it was the only thing in my life that made me feel like I was accomplishing something of value. Killing the Osians hadn't been difficult. They were vulnerable beings with no magic who relied on their technology. Slaughtering them left me with a distasteful feeling. I needed to remove their carcasses from the ship we occupied as soon as there was enough time. But fighting the Scion heretics was different. They did have magic and skills with the sword. They carried Cidian blades and were our sworn enemies. Killing them made me feel like my life wasn't being wasted, and that the difficulties I had endured on Ferret and Vespa had some kind of purpose.

"I would prefer to fight them," I said.

"If we could kill the enemy, it would make getting a crystal much simpler," Usk agreed.

He began the descent toward Gaul. I watched from the doorway to the command deck, where the heat wasn't so unbearable. It was a smooth planetary entry. I was learning from my experiences, and while I didn't have access to a library of information, I could sense the magic that Usk was using and how he was using it to fly the ship. In my personal time I had been pushing my own senses out to greater ranges and building my ability to control it. Usk was not a hands-on instructor in the magical arts, but understood the need to stay in shape physically, to continue training with my weapons, and most of all, to exercise my magical abilities.

When the ship came to rest it was near a huge crevasse in the dust-covered bedrock. When I stepped outside the ship I was alone and forced to wear an emergency oxygen mask. Fortunately, the Osian equipment, like their clothing, fit me. My face was slender enough that I could put the breather over my mouth and nose. There was no air of any kind on Gaul. I used a magical bubble to hold the air from the ship around me, but I needed the mask in case my powers were nullified by the Scion warriors. We hadn't sensed them, and there were none of their ships anywhere on the planet that we had seen or felt in our perception of the magical power. But Usk was nervous, and that made me skeptical.

Nor was I unaware that I was once again the bait being used to draw our enemies out of hiding. Elaa'zar had used me that way against the Vanj, and now Usk was doing it. He remained on the ship. It was a massive craft, sleek and powerful. There were gun turrets on the upper sections of the V-shaped vessel. The bomb bay doors were sealed, the rows of explosive munitions still in their storage racks, but it looked menacing on the dead planet. Perhaps we had frightened the Scion heretics away, but that didn't mean I was going to lower my defenses.

I was grateful for the opportunity to practice levitating myself and didn't bother climbing down into the crevasse. Once I separated my bubble of magic from the pull of the planet's gravity, I could drift down slowly through the enormous crack. It ran in both directions as far as I could see. The opposite side at the surface was a hundred yards wide, but looking down into the opening, it was clear that it narrowed quickly. There was a waft of warm air rising from the crevasse, but I couldn't feel it inside my protective bubble.

Stepping out into nothing took mental resolve. I felt the minor strain of controlling my bubble with divine magic. It wasn't difficult, but it was enough of a task that I could feel it. Controlling the magic required strength of mind, focus, and physical energy. The why's and how's of magic were outside my realm of understanding. Most of what I learned was from experience. As I drifted down into the crack, I felt my sense of control at work.

The interior of Gaul was as different from the barren surface as night and day. When I drifted down a few yards I started to see colors. There was no air and no vegetation, but the minerals in the crust of the planet were brilliant. Perhaps, like the communication crystals themselves, the minerals were transformed by the system star going nova. It had grown into a red giant that poured heat and radiation onto Gaul, stripping away the liquid water from the surface of the planet, and boiling the atmosphere until it was sucked out into the hard vacuum of space. The vegetation burned, and the ashes left behind burned again. Even the soil was cooked under the intense heat and gravitational fluctuations caused by the star growing so large. Eventually, there was nothing left but bedrock and dust, at least on the surface of the planet. In some ways it reminded me of bread. The outer surface of the dough bakes into a hard, flaky crust, but the inside remains soft and delicious.

I had not studied the various minerals and types of things normally mined. I knew there were rare minerals that had great value. On Ferret, iron was common, but highly prized. More rare was gold and silver, which was used to mint coins and traded for goods. Other than what I had learned about Cidian, that was the extent of my mineral knowledge. But in the giant crack I saw a wide variety of colorful minerals. Some had been melted and rehardened into thick bands that colored the rocky crust. In other places they had dripped from the layers of rock like tears, spearing against the face of the rock.

The crack descended for hundreds of yards, farther than I could see. After twenty or thirty yards the light from the surface became minimal. It reminded me of the caverns on Ferret where light was meager and precious. I stopped descending beside a cluster of milky crystals that were sticking out of the dull rocks around them. They were beautiful in a way. I could see flecks of gold among the white gray of the crystals, but Usk had said the communication crystals were deep blue in color. These weren't the crystals I was seeking, and so I continued my descent, moving slowly, watching and waiting for the enemy to appear.

Eventually, several hundred meters down into the crack where the rocky walls were only fifteen or twenty feet apart, I came to a ledge. Below me I could see a band of deep blue rock formations. I settled on the ledge and peered down at the blue crystals. My goal was within sight, but I knew something was wrong. Call it intuition, or maybe it came from the divine magic giving me warning, but I sensed I was no longer alone.

The crack in the wall of stone was hard to see. It was gloomy in the crevasse, and the uneven rock walls cast shadows. I might have missed a hundred openings in the rock face, mistaking them for nooks and crannies that led nowhere. But the opening along the ledge led somewhere, to someone, that much became obvious.

The creature that stepped out onto the ledge was pale and had the body of a grub worm, only it was bigger than I was. Its upper section was raised, its body moving slowly on short little legs that looked like small protrusions. It had no eyes and no visible ears. Its mouth was small, but it spoke in a surprisingly powerful voice.

"You are not welcome here," the creature said.

I felt a sudden sense of heat all over and couldn't draw in a breath. Fear stabbed at my insides with an icy, sharp sensation until I pulled the Osian air mask over my face. Air filled my lungs once more and I felt the heat causing my skin to sting as sweat popped up all over my body to try to cool me down.

"Is this your home?" I asked.

"It is mine to guard," the worm said. "There is nothing here for you."

"I need those crystals," I said, pointing, even though I was sure the worm couldn't see me. But I could sense the deep cavern and rocky walls with my magic. Surely the worm could do the same. "At least one of them."

"They are not for the taking, young one. Leave now, while you can. I will not thwart your purpose."

"I will leave with a crystal," I said.

"That cannot be allowed."

"Why?"

"I believe you already know. The resources of the Creator were never intended to be used by the Fray. Leave now and live. Or stay and die. Those are the only two choices."

"You are a Scion heresy adherent?"

"I am a ninety-year member, eighth of my kind, last of the Gaul natives. This world was once home to millions of us, but that was long ago."

"I'm sorry about your planet, but I must have the crystals."

"You would plunder a dying world for your own gain," the worm said, moving slowly out of the open and onto the ledge. "You should turn from this path, child."

I drew my swords and stood ready with them. The worm had no weapon, and as far as I could see couldn't hold one if it existed. How it meant to stop me was unclear.

"I cannot," I replied. "Stand aside and let me finish what I started."

"That isn't possible," the worm said. "The last of Gaul's resources are mine to guard."

I stepped forward, raising one of my swords to slash at the worm, but I was suddenly unable to move. There was a tight sense of magic around my body, holding me stiffly in place. I tried to fight it with my own magic, but it was too strong. Fear whispered in my ear, telling me the worm was too powerful. It could crush me where I stood, or send me toppling down into the crevasse, and I was helpless to stop it. Then another sensation reached me. It was a familiar magic. Usk was counteracting the worm's powerful hold on me.

I stepped back, breathing harder than I should have been. It was partly fear and partly from trying to free myself. The second I hesitated was all the worm needed to extend long, pointed claws from each of its round, stubby arms. When I stepped forward again and slashed at the worm, it deflected my blade. The Cidian sword cut through one of the pointed claws, but there were dozens more. The worm rose up onto the rear third of its body, so that it towered above me. There had to be forty of the pointed claws, and each was about a foot long.

"This is not the way," the worm said. "You are misguided, young one. The Creator gifted us with Power and Knowledge to set the universe in order. You have only chaos in your heart, but it is not too late to change."

"I'll not be held in the bondage of your god," I said.

I attacked again, but stayed on my guard. I slashed with only the tip of my swords within reach of the worm. It blocked my blades easily, but didn't counter. Maybe it wasn't aggressive, or maybe it knew I was out of range. It would have to close in within a foot of where I stood to hurt me with its claws, but the worm's body was long enough that it could fall on top of me at any second. I had to be ready to move, only there wasn't much space on the ledge to maneuver. I locked my swords together, giving me even more reach, and began to thrust the weapon at the worm. Each time it blocked my attack, more of its claws broke off. It didn't seem to hurt the worm, but eventually, it wouldn't be able to defend itself.

Sweat was flowing, my breath inside the Osian mask huffed and puffed, but I was making progress.

"You won't defeat me," the worm said. "Already you are running out of air."

I didn't respond, but kept moving and thrusting. The outcome seemed inevitable to me, and I finally drew blood from the creature. It was black and thick. The outer hide of the worm was soft and my blade penetrated it easily, even though I wasn't close enough to thrust it deep into the creature's body. Still, seeing my Cidian draw blood from the worm gave me confidence. I stepped closer, hacking and thrusting in quick, sharp, stabbing motions. When it dropped I nearly got caught beneath it, but jumped away just in time.

There wasn't much room. My shoulder hit the rock wall hard enough to bruise, and the worm raked its claws down my thigh. Fire seemed to erupt inside my wound, and I shouted in pain. The worm had missed on its first attack, but I was still between it and the wall. Realizing the danger I was in, I thrust my spear down as hard as I could. The Cidian blade punched into the rock ledge and stuck fast only a split second before the worm threw itself toward me in an effort to crush me against the rock. I was still pressed back, but not crushed. The Cidian that lined my spear held, and I twisted off the upper section. There was no time to get fancy; I just pulled the upper sword free and chopped down with it. The blade connected with the worm's back and cut deep. Blood gushed, and the worm scurried away. It tried to rear up again, but either the pain was too great, or the weight of its body threatened to tear the wound even deeper. I slashed again with a diagonal cut that ripped open the worm's side. I didn't reach vitals, if the worm even had them, but I did draw blood and cause the fat just beneath its skin to bulge out in a grotesque fashion.

I attacked again, chopping at the worm, but it rolled off the ledge rather than face my blade. Blood flew in all directions as it spun through the air, dropping deep into the shaft. I staggered toward the ledge and looked down. The worm was gone and I could use my magic again. There was no time to lose, my leg was in agony from the cuts. The worm's claws had gouged deep through the muscle to the bone. It hurt terribly and I could barely put my weight on that leg. But my magic was strong enough to break free a crystal that was as wide as both my legs put together and tall enough to reach my waist. It was heavy, too. My mind strained to levitate it up. But once I did and reformed my bubble, the pull of the planet's gravity fell away. I moved myself up as fast as possible, floating upward out of the hot crevasse to reach Usk's ship. Perhaps it was just as much mine as his, but he operated the V-shaped vessel and I thought of it as his spacecraft. Only when I reached the surface, it was gone. I was all alone in this barren world, and the one thing the worm had said that was true was the fact that I was running out of air.

CHAPTER 7

THERE ARE different types of pain. The agony of a wound or injury is different from the pain of being wrong about something you felt sure of. But the worst type of pain is betrayal. When the people we trust most turn against us, no matter what the reason, it wounds us deep in our soul. It is a pain that doesn't ease with time, and one that no medicine can heal.

Reaching the surface of Gaul only to find it empty was devastating to me. I dropped to the ground, which was hard and uncomfortable. Blood was flowing down my leg, staining my pants and filling my boot. I needed to stop it, but I had nothing to use to stanch the flow. I looked up, hoping to see the V-shaped ship in the sky, but it was gone. I reached out with my magical senses. It was the only thing I could do. The world was completely barren. The mountains had crumbled, all the flora and fauna had been burned away. It was completely empty, its only features craters and cracks in the bedrock.

There were no ships, no way off the planet. I was trapped

here, running low on air, and facing my death. Part of me wanted to throw the crystal back into the crevasse. If Usk meant to come back and collect it once I was dead, I didn't want to give him the satisfaction of finding it waiting next to my dead body. My mind was reeling with fury; a dark hatred for the Vanj wizard had surfaced in my heart. Not that I'd ever felt any kind of affection for him. He was my master, and that was all. I trusted that he was teaching me, building me up into a useful partner in the work he hoped to accomplish. As I sat on the surface of Gaul completely alone, I felt the terrible realization of how wrong I had been.

The pain in my body and in my soul was so terrible I thought I might pass out. Laying back, I bumped into the crystal. Instantly, I felt a vibration in my mind. The stone wasn't quivering, but it caused something in me to move. Thunder in a powerful storm on Ferret would sometimes boom so loudly that it was felt as much as heard. The feeling from the crystal was the same way. I reached out and touched it again, feeling the vibration deep inside my mind.

That's when I heard the voice. The rich, melodious voice of G'all Gotha. He was speaking to me. Maybe I would have thought I was hallucinating, but I could feel as well as hear the master's voice as he spoke to me.

"Azree'el," he said. "Azree'el, you must not die."

"I am dying," I said.

"No, you can survive," he said, and I wanted to believe him. Not just because I feared dying, or even because my hatred for Usk was so strong that I wanted to thwart his intentions. Mostly, I wanted to live because I knew G'all Gotha wanted it. I could see the alien's beautiful, golden skin glowing in the darkness as if he were hovering over me.

"I can?"

"Yes," he said confidently. "I have seen it. You will survive, Azree'el. You will become a powerful ally, outliving your master and joining me in our quest to free the universe from the influence of the Scion heresy."

"How do you know?" I asked in a tremulous voice.

"There is greatness in you," he said. "Not just talent or ability, Azree'el. There is much, much more. You were meant to be powerful and to rule many people."

"Rule?"

"Of course," he continued. "We were meant to rule, to be the gods of this age. You will take your place in the pantheon I am building. We will rule as immortals, worshiped by trillions in this galaxy and beyond. But you must believe it. You must hold to that truth so tightly that nothing can dissuade you. Not failure, not pain, not even betrayal. You must look death in the face and refuse to surrender. Do you hear me, Azree'el? You must never surrender to death. Our fate lies in greatness no mortal has dared to dream of. Do not let it go."

"How?" I said, my breathing shallow, my consciousness wavering.

"Focus on something. Let it fill your mind. Do not release it until you can see your way to it."

"The ship," I said.

I don't know why I thought of it. The ship wasn't mine, or even something I had ever imagined before we went to the Osian system and stole it. Yet there was something about a starship that I found to be spectacular. Perhaps it was the safety it delivered to the people inside it, or the unlimited possibilities of a spacecraft that could travel through the galaxy, but I found myself focusing on it. I saw the V-shaped craft, the smooth hull, the powerful armaments, and the massive engines. It was a beacon in my mind, an emblem of what I wanted. Not that I just wanted a transport, but rather that I wanted a home of my own, one that offered me safety and a way to go where no Heterrid had ever dreamed of going before. I wanted to explore the far reaches of the galaxy, to see every system and world, to be filled with the wonder of the universe in all its complex beauty.

"Yes! That's it. Focus on that. See it in your mind," G'all said. "Hold it tight in your heart."

"It's mine," I said weakly.

"Yours," he agreed. "Yes, your ship, your destiny, your path to the future."

I could see the Osian bomber in my mind, every component and feature, inside and out. The cobwebs in my mind cleared as I focused on the ship. My confusion and weakness, even the pain I felt, faded as the ship became more and more real.

And then, as if I had willed it to return to me, the ship was there. It hovered above me, the safety and escape I needed from the barren planet that wanted to kill me. I didn't have to think about creating a bubble of magic around myself and the communication crystal. I didn't have to will myself to sever the bonds holding me down and conjure the power to lift myself up into the air. It just happened. I rose up to the airlock door. It cycled and opened before I reached and I floated inside. The door closed behind me and air flooded the chamber. I ripped off my mask just as the inner door opened.

The bomb bay was empty and maybe I said what I was thinking out loud, or more likely the communication crystal picked up my intention and expressed it to G'all Gotha. I still had my hand on the crystal after all, and when he spoke to me it was in a calm voice that settled me down.

"No, Azree'el, his time is not yet up," the Fray master said. "His death will not be at your hands, but his death shall mark your ascension. Stay with him, learn from him all you can."

"He betrayed me."

"Usk is a selfish fool," G'all said. "Little more than a blunt instrument to be used by those of us with true visionary purpose, but you must not take his life. The time is coming when we will strike down the Scion heresy that restrains us from reaching our true potential. Usk has a role to play in that struggle. Do not rush his end. He has underestimated your strength, Azree'el. He will fear you now, but you must not give in to your desire to repay his disloyalty. You must learn and grow. There is still much for you to attain before you are ready to take hold of your destiny."

"He deserves to die."

"And he is already on that path. Yours lies on a separate course. You know of the Heterrid prophecy, no doubt."

"That one will rise and free us all?"

"Yes, and you are that one, Azree'el. I have seen it. You will rule over your people, and your people will rule over others. They will revere you."

"Me?"

"Yes, only that time has not yet come. We must remove those who would oppose us. I need your help with that, Azree'el. You shall become my champion in due course. Do you believe me?"

"I believe," I said, not really believing it but wanting to. I wanted to believe him so badly it hurt.

"Then trust me. Take the crystal to Usk and tend to your

wounds. A time is coming when the tides of fortune will shift. We must be ready when they do."

I couldn't walk, but that didn't keep me from moving through the ship. I took the communication crystal to Usk. He wasn't happy to see me.

"You survived?"

"No thanks to you," I said.

"A Scion vessel approached. I had no choice but to leave."

"You could have stayed and fought," I said. "But it matters little now. Here is your trinket."

The Vanj hissed. He was clearly not used to his apprentice speaking so reproachfully to him, but I didn't care. I wouldn't attack him, even though I wanted to. Maybe it would have ruined my destiny, or maybe G'all was trying to protect me. Usk was a Vanj after all, and while I had killed them with Elaa'zar on Ferret, it was never an easy task. Even with all my training and the Cidian spear, it would have been difficult to slay Usk. But I wanted to, despite my wounds which would have surely gotten me killed.

I left the communication crystal there on the command deck. He didn't need me to manhandle the heavy crystal into place. The Vanj was a skillful wizard and could easily levitate the object wherever he wanted it to go. There was part of me that didn't want him to have it. I had gone down into the crack of the barren planet to get it. I had risked my life, fought the Scion worm, and shed my blood to retrieve it. Normally, I might not care about it, but G'all Gotha had spoken to me through the crystal, and that made me want to keep it. I couldn't help but wonder when I would get the chance to speak to the golden alien again.

My leg hurt and I was tired. Almost dying does that to a person. I returned to my quarters and went to work on my leg.

There were probably medical supplies on the ship, but I didn't bother to seek them out. The last thing I wanted was alien medicine. There were four cuts on my right thigh. Walking hurt, but so did not walking. I ripped a clean sheet to make bandages and soaked some in the amber colored liquor that was kept in the crystal container. Cleaning the blood away and applying the liquor soaked bandage burned so fiercely that I was breathing hard and sweating a little by the time I got a clean strip of cloth wrapped around the wound and tied off.

My plan had been to lay down and sleep for a while, but I heard Usk moving in the hallway outside my quarters. Perhaps he was coming to apologize, but I doubted it. We still had Osian bodies on board. The monstrous alien was probably after one to feed on. Either way, hearing him outside of his nest on the command deck was enough of a strange occurrence that it drew me to the door of my quarters. I pressed the touch pad to open the door and stuck my head out. The corridor appeared empty. I reached out with my magical senses and felt nothing. It wasn't just an empty ship, I literally felt nothing. Something was hindering my magical senses.

Every alarm in my mind went off at once. I swayed back into my room and closed the door. It only took a few seconds to reach my swords, but that seemed too long. Part of me said I was safe in my quarters, that maybe I should just stay there and wait. But something was on the ship, something that didn't want me using magic.

It occurred to me that Usk might be neutralizing my magical senses in order to attack me. The Vanj wizard obviously didn't care if I lived or died. All Usk cared about was his own safety, but I didn't think he would try to kill me. At least not in a direct way, and not while I was still useful to him. So what alternative did that leave? There were no Osians on the ship left alive, I was certain of that. But whoever was there had magical power. That meant Usk wasn't lying when he said someone attacked the ship. Only the attack was obviously a distraction so that someone could get on board.

I put my swords together and locked them into the double ended spear. My leg was still throbbing; the cuts felt like they were on fire. Every step I took sent pain shooting up my hip and down my leg. Putting weight on it for very long was agonizing, but I didn't want to die in my bed. In fact, I didn't want to die at all. G'all Gotha had said I had a destiny, to rule with him. I couldn't do that if I was dead.

I returned to the hall and limped back up the stairway to the command level of the ship. Still, I saw no one. Part of me felt foolish. Maybe I was imagining that someone was on board. If I went to Usk and warned him of a danger that didn't exist, he might decide I wasn't worth keeping around. But the door to the command center was open, and I knew I had closed it when I left. I wanted barriers between me and the Vanj wizard, at least for a while. G'all Gotha had warned me not to fight him, but I didn't want to see him or think about him either. He may have been doing the prudent thing by taking off when he did, but being left behind had jaded me. I didn't think I could ever trust the Vanj wizard again.

Limping toward the command center, I peered into the room but kept some distance between myself and the doorway. Nothing seemed strange or out of place. I stepped forward and leaned on the door frame. Usk was in his nest, not moving at all, just staring forward. Glancing around, the room seemed empty, but instinct told me to wait. I remembered kneeling in the tall grass with Elaa'zar, the older man telling me to watch for movement. The Vanj had camouflage that made them nearly invisible when they were still, but when they moved they became visible.

I watched, barely breathing, waiting to see something, and all the time thinking I was going crazy. But then it happened. Movement, almost to Usk in his steamy nest in the center of the room. Something moved. I couldn't say what it was. It didn't make a big movement, nor was it fast. But something was slowly creeping toward my master, and even though I was hurt physically as well as by his betrayal, the sight of the invisible thing sneaking up on Usk propelled me into action.

Lowering my spear, I rushed forward. Maybe rushed wasn't the right word. I lumbered toward the invisible intruder. With my wounded leg I wasn't fast or graceful, but I had removed my boots and my bare feet were almost silent on the highly polished floor.

Usk saw me, his gigantic head snapping around and his terrible face snarling in hatred. He thought I was attacking him, and it probably looked like I was. The invisible intruder was between us, and I might have struck the invader down if Usk hadn't given away my presence on the command deck.

With a swirl that appeared to make the room twist suddenly, the intruder's camouflage disappeared, and I found myself charging a tall, shaggy alien with gray fur. It carried a very thin dagger with a Cidian blade in one hand. The small weapon was no match for my double-ended spear, but the stranger was very fast. At the last second, with my weapon just about to punch into his chest, the hairy alien spun out of the way. I saw the Cidian dagger flashing toward my head and ducked. Then a fist that felt like it was made of metal hit me in the face and sent me sprawling onto the floor.

Usk leaped over me and nearly landed on the intruder, but the hairy alien saw him coming and slid back out of the way. At the same time, he drew a sword with a curved Cidian blade that was much more substantial than the dagger.

"Your apprentice is sharp, I'll give you that," the stranger said, his voice deep and his words almost a bark.

"Die, Scion coward," Usk said, once more launching himself at the stranger.

But to my surprise the alien caught Usk's hands with his blades, severing three of the Vanj's talons in the process and hurling the big alien away. He was faster and stronger than Usk, which, to be honest, frightened me. I was not myself, not with my leg still bleeding from the four gashes made by the Scion worm. Still, I got to my feet. My highest priority, according to my Master, who had in all fairness stolen me from my home and slaughtered my friends, was to protect him. Part of me wanted Usk to die, but if the Vanj wizard was going to perish, it would be on my blade, not someone else's. Certainly not a Scion blade. Besides, I couldn't fly the ship, and if Usk was killed I would have been stuck on Gaul.

I limped forward and slashed my spear at the stranger's legs. He must have heard me coming. He dodged to the side and batted my spear away with his sword. I'll admit, mine was a weak attack. I didn't want to get too close to the shaggy alien. He was fast and strong, while I felt slow and weak. It was frightening to me, and difficult to see how I might attack him successfully. Fortunately, I wasn't alone. Usk was hurt too, but filled with rage. He attacked the alien with a roar of outrage so loud it vibrated everything in the room.

The stranger slashed at Usk with his sword to keep the Usk wizard at bay. I saw my opportunity and took action. My second thrust with the double-ended spear was more balanced, and better timed. To my surprise the alien blocked my thrust with the little dagger, which was surprisingly stronger than I anticipated. It parried my blade, but not enough. The tip of my spear gouged into the alien's side, severing the fur and cutting a furrow along his stomach. The shaggy intruder roared in pain, spinning around to get away from my spear, and simultaneously lashing out with his sword in a level slash that would have lopped my head from my shoulders. I wasn't all that fast on my feet, but I saw the attack coming and ducked while simultaneously chopping down with my spear, nearly landing another blow.

The intruder was the most skilled and agile fighter I had ever seen. Even while missing with his attack, he hopped back to avoid my counter at his feet, then ducked when Usk leaped at him again. The intruder went down to his knees, almost bowing as Usk sailed over him. I saw his legs coiling in that split second and knew he would leap up after my master. I might have landed a blow against the alien, but he would certainly have hurt Usk. So, I jabbed my spear at the alien's head instead, knowing all the while that it wouldn't find the target. It did, however, keep the shaggy alien from following Usk.

"Tenacious," the alien said, rising back up to his feet and bringing his sword around so that it was between us. "You have solid instincts. It's a pity you wasted your talent with the Fray."

I wasn't there to talk, and I certainly wasn't going to lower my defenses. The alien slashed at me with his sword and stepped closer. I knew he wanted to get near enough to me that he could use his dagger. I raised my spear as if to block his sword, but then jumped backward out of range and spun the weapon around my head. The alien kept coming, completely unfazed by my demonstration of skill with the spear. He slashed at me again. I blocked his weapon with my own and then twisted the handles apart. I had just enough time to block his dagger with the sword in my left hand. Then I threw my shoulder into him. It probably wouldn't have hurt the shaggy alien, except I had cut him earlier. My shoulder hit right where the blood from his gash had matted his fur.

The intruder grunted with pain. I was already turning. My goal was to spin around him and strike at him from the side, only my injured leg gave out and I fell. It was a fortunate accident, for just as I hit the deck I heard the swish of the stranger's blade above and behind me. I used the momentum of my fall to roll onto my side and kick with my good leg. My foot caught the alien's shaggy leg just above the ankle and made him slip on the polished deck. He staggered, and I slashed at him with one sword. The tip of my blade severed some hair, but didn't connect with flesh. With a snarl the alien started for me, but had to alter course as Usk waded back into the fight. The Vanj wizard jumped at him again, and the stranger used the flat of his blade to block the attack. He managed to push Usk backward, but he didn't have the right leverage to send Usk sprawling. They were locked together for a moment...just long enough that I could lunge forward and stab the stranger in the back of his thigh, just above the knee.

There are times in a fight when your opponent does something so unexpected it nearly leaves you breathless. The alien dropped suddenly after my attack, falling and twisting in such a way that he flung Usk over the top of him. I had to dive to the side to keep the bony Vanj body from crashing into me with devastating effect. When I regained my footing, the stranger was back up too, only I wasn't the only one limping.

The stranger's body was covered in shaggy fur. The only clothing he wore was a belt with several alien objects on it, including the sheath for his dagger and the scabbard for his sword. His face was prominent but covered with a long beard. All I could really see were his eyes. The skin around them was dark brown, but the eyes were open wide enough that I could see the whites around his irises. They shifted toward the door. It was a glance, nothing more, but it was the first indication that he wasn't as sure of himself as he seemed.

I feinted to my right, then lunged to my left. It should have been an obvious ploy. My right leg was weak. I had cut off the leg of the stretchy pants and my bandage was obvious. The alien should have realized I wasn't going to lunge to my right, but in a fight little mistakes can carry a heavy toll. And the problem was that his own right leg was wounded. He would have easily recovered in time to block my slash with the sword in my left hand, only when he shifted his weight to meet the attack, his leg gave out beneath him. Somehow he still managed to block my initial cut, but I immediately followed with my right hand. He was on his side, and got his little dagger up to parry my chop, but I was able to divert the sword just enough that it cut into his hand. The little dagger flew from his ruined grasp, and when I pulled my sword back it completed the cut. Half the shaggy alien's left hand dropped to the floor. Blood fountained between us, and I moved back.

"You are good," the alien shouted, before somehow finding the strength to leap toward the doorway.

I didn't follow initially. To be honest, I was amazed to still be alive. Usk followed, his body moving with surprising speed. The intruder slashed at my master as he slipped through the door. He was tall enough that he had to duck, as did Usk, who turned his head down when he saw the blade coming. The tip of the sword struck Usk's thick skull. It sliced the leathery skin and cut a gouge from the bone. Usk spun to the ground and I jumped to defend him, but the intruder didn't stick around. I followed him into the passageway outside the command center. He was limping down the corridor. The previously pristine deck and wall were marred with his blood. Even wounded, he moved faster than I could follow, but I pursued him through the passageways and corridors. He was breathing hard, obviously in a lot of pain. My wounds hurt too, but the thrill of the chase dampened my awareness. I chased the alien to the airlock.

"You would have made a great Scion champion," he said when he reached the hatch.

"I would never live in bondage to your god."

"Look around you," he said in his barking voice. "You are a slave to your own ambitions. But you're a great fighter, I'll give you that." He held up his bloody hand. The fingers were missing, and only his thumb remained, but somehow the shaggy fur was matting down the wound, staunching the flow of blood. "I'll have this to remember you by," he proclaimed, as if it were a badge of honor. "Until we meet again."

I flung my sword at him. It flew end over end in a dramatic whirl, but I knew the moment I threw it that I had waited too long.

The airlock door closed and the blade of the sword lodged in the thick steel. There was a narrow window in the airlock. I saw the flash of light as the outer door opened and the stranger escaped. I could feel Usk's magic pulling the ship up off the ground. I instantly did a full search of the ship with my magical senses. There was no one else on board, just me and the Vanj wizard. There were no voids in my sense of the vessel, nothing I couldn't scour with my magical abilities to ensure we were safe. At least inside the ship.

By the time I reached the command center we were nearly in orbit, and there was another ship behind us.

"Is that the Scion heretics?" I asked.

"The same vessel that chased me away," Usk said. "It must have been a distraction to get their assassin on board."

"He escaped," I admitted. "With my leg injured I couldn't catch up."

"You did your job," Usk said. He didn't sound appreciative, or proud of my achievement. He didn't even sound relieved to still be alive. If anything, he sounded angry, but I realized it was his own failure to recognize the intruder was there, and the fear of almost dying, that was making him cross.

"Where do we go now?" I asked, noticing for the first time that the communication crystal was set up next to Usk's nest. The climbing vines had already begun to encircle the base of it.

"Master Gotha ordered us to the Kree system. He has secured the services of Salamandian mercenaries. We will have a few days to recover from the fight before the aliens board our ship."

I thought of the blood trail, and of the Osian bodies that needed to be removed. Not to mention my own wounds, which were throbbing again, and I felt a sense of gratitude for the opportunity to rest.

"All right," I said, unable to keep the weariness from my voice. "Do you need medical care?"

"No," Usk growled.

It felt like a dismissal, and I turned to leave. I made it all the way to the door before Usk spoke again.

"You proved yourself," he said gruffly. "I will hold nothing back from you, Azree'el."

I didn't know what to say. I just turned, gave a little bow and limped away. It took a moment to realize I didn't have to walk on my injured leg. I summoned the divine magic and pulled it around me like a cloak. Severing the invisible bonds that gave my body weight and held me to the deck of the ship, I drifted upward. The relief to my injured leg was instantaneous. And it occurred to me that maybe I could use the divine magic to help the wounds heal. It would be a test of my abilities. The magic could reach far and wide, move heavy objects, even open portals in space, but it could also work in a much more delicate way. I had focused down to the very atoms of the Cidian ore on Fierocite. With a little concentration I was able to draw the muscle and severed tissue together, sealing up my wounds. It required me to keep the bonds held fast, but I found that an easy enough chore.

As I returned to my quarters I thought about what G'all had said, and about the Heterrid prophecy. As a slave in the stables on Vespa, the thought of leading a rebellion to free my people from the Vanj and return us to the stars seemed impossible. But on Usk's ship, racing through the galaxy with alien blood still on the blades of my Cidian swords, anything seemed possible. But there was no hurry, and there was so much to learn. In time, I would come into my own power. Until then, I would serve my master. Not Usk, but G'all Gotha, the golden alien who predicted my destiny as a divine ruler of the galaxy.

AUTHOR'S NOTE

This novel wasn't planned. In fact, I was in the middle of writing *Supernova* (Order of Scion book 4) when Azree'el popped into the story. I was so inspired by her that I had to stop the book I was writing and craft her origin story.

The good news is she appears in *Supernova* and the Scion books that follow. If you haven't read the Order of Scion books, or the Scion Heresy as Azree'el would call it, keep reading for a sample from book one *Latent Prowess*.

LATENT PROWESS CHAPTER 1

Everyone has bad days, but Mitch Murphy hit the trifecta. It started out like any normal day. He woke up at six in the morning, his alarm clock blaring.

"Shut it off," his wife growled, poking him in the side.

He was already starting to reach over to hit the alarm clock but knocked over his glass of water in the process, and his nightstand drawer was open.

"Dang it!" He snapped.

The accident forced him fully awake. He grabbed a towel and began soaking up the water. His wife groaned angrily, even though he was trying to be quiet. A few minutes later, after cleaning up the spill, Mitch went to start some coffee. His job was in the business district, which required a ninety-minute train ride to reach. He normally prepared one cup of coffee in the morning to give him the jolt he needed to shake off sleep. Only that day there was no coffee in the empty container. It was a shocking disappointment.

By that point, it crossed his mind to just get back into bed. And as nice as that might have been in the moment, he had bills to pay. Not to mention that his wife would be furious if he skipped work. She didn't like surprises and claimed that she needed peace and solitude in the mornings. He quietly stepped into the tiny bathroom and shut the door before turning on the light. Once he got the shower running, he had to wait for the water to warm. He tapped the mail icon on the bathroom mirror and several urgent messages appeared. He was behind on his mortgage and several credit cards. It had cost all of their savings to buy the little apartment. Three tiny rooms on the backside of a semi-respectable building cost nearly half his salary each month. They could just get by, but then the Homeowners Association doubled their monthly fees, and there was a significant property tax increase that left Mitch scrambling to pay the bills. Every day he got notifications that left a burning sensation in the pit of his stomach. They would need to sell the apartment and move, but his wife wouldn't like that. And the market was down, which meant they would be lucky to get out from under the place.

When he finally got out the door, he was on the edge of despair. The only good thing that happened that morning was finding a seat on the train that wasn't next to a homeless person. The commuter trains that brought workers from the suburbs into the city proper had become a haven for transient people down on their luck. The police ignored them, and the riders as they were known, could be dangerous. Mitch breathed a sigh of relief and sank into the hard plastic seat he found unoccupied and clutched his satchel close to his chest.

Every day the people on the commuter trains were subjected to advertisements on display screens. The audio was hard to hear over the rumble of the train cars and the hubbub of voices, but there were no windows to look out of and no one wanted to stare at the other passengers. So, they watched the advertisements and tried not to garner the attention of the transient riders.

Mitch was sitting beside two older men who knew each other. He couldn't help but hear their conversation. It was the usual back and forth until the advertisement for the new Latent Tech. The video was a montage of young, fit people, and doctors in lab coats.

"Now, that's crazy," one of the men beside Mitch said.

"Gotta be off your rocker to sign up for that," the other said.

Mitch was familiar with the advertisement. People called it the Escape Plan, but it was actually for a company that had developed bio-enhancement techniques. Latent Tech was the research and development arm of the Colonial Marine Corps. And they were desperate for people to join their mission to help protect New Terra. For half a century, humans had been trying to gain a foothold on the new planet. Space travel had been limited to the solar system. The very best engineers still couldn't design a ship that could survive interstellar travel, or engines that could even approach the speed of light. But explorers had found a wormhole, some people called it a portal through dimensional space. It was essentially a door to another star system. New Terra was a planet with a thin atmosphere that barely supported life. Most of its water was frozen, and much of the land in the warmer climates was still barren. That didn't keep humanity from jumping at the chance to colonize the world, but there were a host of obstacles, from wildlife that hunted humans, to other intelligent races who had shown up in the system shortly after humans did. New Terra was a battleground.

There had been a lot of fanfare about Latent Tech, with claims of amazing technological breakthroughs in human physiology enhancement, but like most government programs, there were just as many conspiracy theories. It didn't help that the therapies they offered were only for people willing to join the Colonial Marine Corps. And those individuals were shipped out on one-way trips to New Terra.

"You'd have to be a fool to fall for that load of crap," the man sitting next to Mitch said.

"It's a death sentence," the other man added. "I know a guy in government. They say the supper serum has a fifty percent failure rate."

"Failure?" the first man asked.

"The lucky ones never wake up," his companion said. "Those that do aren't always better."

"Why would anyone risk that? You'd have to be pretty pathetic to sign on with Latent Tech."

Mitch didn't disagree. He was ten years out of university, still paying off his student loans. Married, with a mortgage and a job in finance. Things weren't good, but people ran into speed bumps in life. Despite his terrible morning, he still felt like things would turn around.

When the commuter train finally reached his stop, Mitch disembarked into a crowd of people. They were all moving in one direction, into the city, toward the towering buildings where millions worked ten hours a day and couldn't afford to live in the ritzy condos on the edges of the business district. Mitch entered the drab building where Sterling Investment Corporation had its Western Offices. Ten years in, Mitch was still an assistant buyer. It was an entry-level job, but everyone paid their dues. His peers had moved up or moved on to better jobs, but Mitch felt loyal to the company that had taken him on right out of college. And the job market was very competitive; his window for finding something better had closed. Employers would want to know why he hadn't been promoted in ten years. He had no good reason to tell them. He was a good worker, but he wasn't aggressive or very confident for that matter. Sure he had hopes and dreams, but things hadn't broken in his favor, and he had sunk to the murky middle where he learned to keep his head down and not attract attention.

His workspace was a narrow desk with a computer in a cubicle that was identical to fifty-nine other cubicles on the thirteenth floor. He dropped into his chair and woke up his computer to log in for the day. He was on salary, but still required to log into the system and account for every hour. Only when he put in his password, the computer informed him that it was no longer valid.

"Are you kidding me?" he snapped, typing in the password again, and a third type after that.

"Problem?" Lois Burman, the frumpy woman who occupied the cubicle next to his asked.

"I can't log into the system?" Mitch complained.

The only response was silence. Mitch stood up and looked over the cubicle wall. Lois was frowning.

"What is it?" he asked.

"Nothing," she lied.

"What?"

"I just heard a rumor, that's all."

"What about?"

"Downsizing," she said softly, looking down at her desk, refusing to meet Mitch's gaze.

He dropped back down into his seat, his heart suddenly beating at twice the normal pace. He felt tired and scared. The hair on the back of his neck stood out, and his hands were suddenly ice cold.

"Murphy!" a gruff voice called. "I need to see you in my office."

It was impossible to ignore the looks from the other assistant buyers and market analysts as he walked down the aisle between the rows of cubicles toward the manager's office. The gruff voice belonged to Stuart Bellamy, who was in his late fifties with only a ring of gray hair left on his head, and a bulging stomach that strained the buttons on his shirt. He was never in a good mood, and always complaining about something. A trip to his office was bad and Mitch felt a strange numbness as he entered the glass walls of the tiny space. Stuart Bellamy's desk was slightly larger than the others, but not by much. He wasn't in a cubicle, but the glass-walled office was barely large enough for the overweight manager to squeeze around his desk.

"Close the door," Stuart ordered.

Mitch pulled the glass door closed and looked at his superior. The man's face had no compassion.

"Orders just came down from the twentieth floor," Stuart said, his voice a grumbling monotone with no real emotion. "They're trimming the fat, so to speak. You'll have an official letter of termination in your inbox by now. The severance package is pretty generous. It's been nice working with you."

"I'm being laid off?" Mitch asked.

"No, you're being fired," Stuart said. "The company won't be bringing you back on."

"But I..." Mitch started to argue, which was unusual for him. But he realized he had nothing to say.

"You've got two weeks of pay in that severance package. A full month of medical covered," the manager said. "That's plenty of time to find a new job. You'll need to gather your things and leave the building, Murphy. Is that going to be an issue? Do I need to get security involved, because if I do, I'll have to put a report in your personnel file, and that will follow you into every interview you take."

"No," Mitch said.

"Good," Stuart said, standing up. "Good luck, Murphy. Send Jennings in here, would you?"

"She's pregnant," Mitch said.

"Hey, I don't make policy. I just carry out the orders they send down."

Mitch opened the glass door and looked out at the dozens of his former co-workers. No one was looking at him. They were suddenly all very, very busy with important work that couldn't wait. Mitch shuffled out of the office and down the row of cubicles. He slowed at Kimberly Jennings's cubicle. She was three months pregnant, and not yet showing. There were rumors that she was faking the pregnancy. It was idle water cooler talk, and Mitch had never joined in, but he saw the framed ultrasound photo on her narrow desk.

"Bellamy wants to see you, Kim," Mitch said.

She was crying before she even got to her feet. Mitch felt hollow inside. The storm clouds that had been hanging over his head for days were brewing. His life had been shattered.

"You okay?" Lois asked as he picked up his satchel and jacket from his cubicle.

"Terminated," he said.

"So the rumors are true. I'm sorry Mitch."

"Ten years," he said. "I've been here ten years."

"You'll land on your feet."

That thought made him almost laugh out loud. He had worked feverishly to get through college, and he had done so with middling grades. Still, he had a degree and nearly two hundred thousand dollars in debt. Everyone told him that it was okay, that he would get on his feet soon. But he had never quite managed to achieve any real stability. His job at Sterling Investment had seemed amazing at first, but he soon found the work to be incredibly boring.

His marriage had been a bright spot. Megan Aubry was two years behind him at the university, and pretty. She wanted nice things, and he had gone into more debt to get them, always believing that soon he would get on his feet. Somehow, he had never managed to get ahead. Ten years into his career and he was still living paycheck to paycheck, with mounting debts he had no way to pay off. She would be furious that he had lost his job, he realized. They had agreed that she would stop working and concentrate on getting pregnant. The idea of having a child terrified Mitch, but he wanted to make Megan happy, so he agreed. She had seemed more like the girl he had known in college for a while, but had not been happy for long, and no matter what he did for her, it was never enough. For some reason he couldn't quite explain, he loved her, at least he thought he did. And that was what mattered, he told himself, not quite believing it.

Normally, the commuter train ride seemed to take forever, but lost in his thoughts Mitch reached his stop in what seemed like record time. He considered stopping for coffee and pastries but decided against it as he shuffled toward his building. They were going to have to make changes, that was all. Megan would need to go back to work, and they would have to sell their apartment. Which also meant they would have to wait to get pregnant, but he couldn't help it. The real difficulty was going to be finding a job that paid anywhere close to what he had been making at Sterling. He had a college degree and a solid work history, but no real achievements to speak of. Still, Mitch tried to think that maybe he could find an occupation that he actually enjoyed. He had worked himself up into believing that maybe losing his job was a good thing. Perhaps, he thought, it was the catalyst he needed to finally do something different and get ahead in life. His student loans could be deferred for a while, and they would probably have to move out of the city, but he was starting to think shaking things up was exactly what they needed. But what he found at home dashed all that to pieces.

LATENT PROWESS CHAPTER 2

He opened the door and stepped into the tiny living room. Music was playing from the bedroom, but that wasn't unusual. Megan liked music and listened to it while she showered. He could also hear the water running. Mitch dropped his satchel, which had his generic reading device, and his sack lunch. He laid his jacket on a chair and walked to the bedroom. There was no door between the small bedroom and the only bathroom. Megan wasn't fastidious about keeping the apartment clean, but she didn't like him leaving his clothes on the floor. And at first, Mitch thought that what he saw was his own clothing. He had an impulse to pick it all up and stow it in the dirty hamper, but then he realized he didn't wear the name-brand jogging pants or the expensive sneakers.

He was dumbfounded, standing at the foot of his bed, looking at the trail of clothing that led to the bathroom. There was a loud ringing in his ears, and he could somehow hear his heart beating at the same time. Laughter broke through his befuddlement.

There was someone in the apartment.

At first, Mitch desperately wanted to believe an intruder had broken in, but he was too smart to accept it. He walked slowly toward the bathroom. The shower was tucked behind a wall, the semi-clear door completely fogged over from the steam, but Mitch didn't need to see what was happening. He could hear the voices and other things. Pain broke through the fog in his mind. His wife was cheating on him. She was laughing in a way he had never heard, or at least, hadn't heard in years. That made him feel like someone had stabbed him through the chest with a sharp object.

The water stopped and shook Mitch out of his daze. He suddenly realized that he didn't want to see who his wife was cheating on him with. Nor did he want to face her anger at being caught. He stumbled out of the bedroom and through the living room. He managed to pick up his satchel, but not his jacket. Megan called out as he opened the front door.

"Is someone there?" her voice reached him just before he closed the door and hurried away.

An hour later he was in a bar. He didn't remember getting there, or even realize where he was. There was a drink in front of him. Whiskey from the looks of it, with ice melting into the brown liquid. Mitch wasn't a heavy drinker, but he needed something to ease the pain. He was lost, not that he couldn't find a way back to his apartment, but it no longer felt like home. The future was bleak. He had no job, very little prospects, a mountain of debt, and a marriage he couldn't face.

"You okay, pal," the bartender asked.

"My wife's cheating," Mitch confessed. He didn't know the man, and the bartender didn't know him. Most places had replaced humans with android servers, but for some reason, people still liked human bartenders. Perhaps it was because most people drank to avoid their problems and there was something about a stranger willing to listen that people enjoyed. Mitch didn't enjoy revealing his failings, but he couldn't hold them back any longer.

"That's horrible," the bartender said as he dried a glass with a clean, white towel. "You just find out?"

"Yeah," Mitch said, swirling the ice in his whiskey, but not drinking it.

"Someone you know?"

Mitch shook his head.

"Been going on long?"

"I didn't stick around to get the details," Mitch said. "I just ran away."

"Nothing wrong with that," the bartender said. "It's better than killing the guy, and I'm guessing you'd have wanted to do that if you stayed."

Mitch looked at his drink and wondered what he had become. He had been in his share of fights growing up. He played ball in school and was athletic, but somewhere along the way he had lost all of that. His instincts were gone, beaten down with fear of upsetting his wife, and the pressure of his mounting debts. That wasn't the way life was supposed to turn out. He had plans but he couldn't remember what they were exactly. His friends had all drifted away. All he ever wanted to do anymore was eat and sleep. When he got home from work on most days, he watched television and tried to avoid the fight with Megan that never seemed to end. On the weekends, he could hardly get out of bed. He told himself it was a phase, just a minor case of depression brought on by the debts he was laboring under. But as he stared at the ice melting into the whiskey, he realized that he had lost himself. Worse still, he had to admit that he and Megan would be better off if he was dead.

"How much do I owe you?" Mitch asked the bartender.

"This one's on me, pal. You deserve it."

"Thanks," Mitch said.

He took a drink. It was foul and burned his throat, but the heat that spread through him felt nice. Still, he didn't want to get drunk. He pushed the glass across the bar, stood up, and nodded to the bartender who returned the gesture. Leaving the bar, he knew he had to do something. He stopped at a bench long enough to eat the sandwich in his satchel. There was plenty of traffic on the street, people walking, hover cars humming by city aircraft gliding above him. Everywhere he looked there was life, but he felt dead inside. It wasn't until he was halfway through his sandwich that he noticed the Colonial Marine Corps recruiting office across the street. It was colorful, with the same advertisement he had seen on the train that morning playing soundlessly on one of the window displays.

Through the traffic, he read the colorful slogans on the recruiting office windows:

Ready for a new life?

Wish you could do the things you did when you were younger?

Are you looking for exhilaration and excitement?

Join the CMC and discover a galaxy of adventure.

Mitch didn't make a conscious decision. There was no reasoning, or rational in his mind. But he remembered what the two strangers on the train had said about the program. People died from taking the super serum that was advertised as being a way to bring out a person's strength and vitality. And Mitch wanted to die. He had been contemplating the many ways he might do the deed. What he didn't want was to be considered a coward. He was tired of being invisible and settling. He wanted to do something bold, something that would show people that he had taken control of his life. Suddenly, he was on his feet, his sandwich forgotten on the bench, as he strode purposely through the traffic and pushed open the door to the recruiting office.

There was a man in military uniform sitting at a desk. He looked up at Mitch and smiled.

"Welcome to CMC recruiting. Can I help you, sir?"

"Yes," Mitch said. "What do I have to do to join?"

"That's the right attitude," the recruiter said. "We'll have to do a few tests and see if you're compatible."

"Compatible with what?"

"The Latent Enhancement Protocols," the recruiter said. "It's not for everyone."

"And if I am compatible?"

"Then we've got a lot to talk about Mr..."

"Murphy. I'm Mitch Murphy."

"It's nice to meet you. I'm Sergeant Lopez. Come with me and we'll get started."

Mitch followed the recruiter into a small room with a bench against one wall and a medical scanner against the other.

"Strip down, get inside, and the system will start all by itself," Lopez said.

"What is it, exactly?" Mitch asked.

"It's a scanner. One pass to make sure you don't have any unexpected disease, then another to see if you're compatible."

"How long does it take?"

"Not long. Once it's done, the door will open. You can get dressed and come on out. I'll be looking over your results."

"Okay," Mitch said, realizing the sergeant was younger than he was.

The hopeless feeling was back. And Sergeant Lopez didn't seem too optimistic either. In fact, he didn't seem to be very good at recruiting. So far, he hadn't done anything to make Mitch feel wanted. But that wasn't surprising. Mitch shut the door and pulled off his shirt. He was pale and on the cusp of chubby. Ten years of sitting at a desk was not a recipe for physical fitness. Megan had insisted that they get a gym membership, but by the time Mitch got home from work he was too exhausted to exercise. He felt a surge of emotions that nearly wrecked him. Looking at himself in the mirror he felt worthless, and instead of fury at Megan's betrayal, he wondered how she had stayed with him so long.

The scanner door was open, and he stepped inside. It sensed his presence. The door closed and a series of instructions flashed on the display. He stood still while the scanner ran up and down the chamber. It was a lot like the tanning booths at Megan's gym. Most doctors used handheld scanners, and the automated medical booths seemed clunky in comparison. The first scan took ninety seconds, the second was longer. But the entire process lasted less than five minutes.

By the time he got his clothes back on, Mitch was ready to find out the bad news. He was in the middle of the worst day of his life, and if the Sergeant told him he had a terrible disease, it wouldn't have surprised him. But the smile on Lopez's face when he opened the door was unexpected.

"Mr. Murphy, the results of your scan were excellent," Lopez said.

"They were?" he asked, feeling nervous.

"That's right. Come with me and we can discuss your options."

LATENT PROWESS CHAPTER 3

They didn't return to the reception room where he had walked in off the street. Instead, Sergeant Lopez took Mitch into a room with reclining theater seats and a massive video display screen.

"Have a seat," Lopez said. "It's a little quicker if you watch the recruiting video. Then I'll answer your questions."

"Okay," Mitch said.

He sat down in the plush, faux leather seat which automatically reclined. The video display screen lit up and Mitch saw the Latent Tech logo rotating slowly as Sergeant Lopez sat in the other recliner.

Suddenly, a man in a lab coat appeared on the screen. "Hello, I'm Doctor Theodore Packerman, head of the Latent Enhancement program. Several years ago, the CMC enlisted us to produce a series of protocols meant to enhance the latent skills and abilities of the average person. Building on the work of Lewis Musthaven and breakthroughs in DNA research, we have created a formula, part serum-based injections, part environmental optimization, that can bring out the latent abilities inside a person. What does that mean? Let me show you."

The video changed from the man in the lab coat to an animated child, but the voice of Theodore Packerman continued speaking.

"This is Teddy. He was born with a wide spectrum of natural talents, but like most people, many of those talents went unrecognized."

In front of the child, a road appeared, and then it split into several more, and each of those roads split into even more.

"Life is a series of choices," the voice of Doctor Packerman continued. "Some lead to wonderful opportunities, but they are also limited in scope. Some natural skills and talents fail to be recognized or encouraged to grow and develop."

The animation of the boy began to change. He grew taller, passing through the teenage years and into adulthood.

"In most cases, the needs of life such as working and family, continue to limit a person's opportunity to hone and develop their talents and abilities. Those innate, but unused talents are considered to be latent. Teddy could have been an outstanding football player, but his mother didn't like the idea of him playing contact sports and his father was too busy to encourage his son's athletic abilities. Instead, Teddy's enjoyment of computer games led him to focus on mental disciplines that eventually coalesced into a job as a computer programmer for a major corporation. But buried deep inside of Teddy is the ability to gain strength and develop agility."

The animation of adult Teddy looked a lot like Mitch. He was pudgy, with poor posture, thinning hair, and a look of defeat. But then the image of Teddy walked into a room where several men in lab coats were waiting. They sat Teddy down and began a series of injections.

"The Latent Enhancement Protocols will not just reactivate Teddy's dormant natural abilities, but they will give his body the chance to recover from a lifetime of poor choices," the voice of Doctor Packerman continued, while the animated Teddy laid down in a strange-looking cylindric chamber. It looked a lot like the medical scanner that Mitch had been in, only it was vertical instead of horizontal. The lid closed and a clock appeared with hands that spun much faster than normal. When the lid opened, Teddy sat up and then jumped out of the machine. He was taller, his hair thick and wavy. His chest was broad, his shoulders wide, his arms bulging with muscles while his waist was thin. And instead of the look of depression he had before, Teddy was smiling and bright-eyed.

"The LE protocols aren't magic, and not every individual has the same latent abilities, but if you're watching this video, it means that you have scored high enough in the DNA scanning procedure to be a top-tier candidate for the LE program."

The video animation dissolved and Doctor Packerman reappeared on screen. "This is your chance," he said, "to discover all that you could have been and make a difference. LE participants will undergo a series of procedures at our private facilities and then proceed via starship to New Terra. As you can imagine, accessing the full range of a person's latent abilities would make them far superior to the average person here on earth, and laws were passed long ago that forbids the use of DNA enhancement. But on New Terra, there are no such laws. You'll be entering a world full of opportunity, with a chance to make history. You can say goodbye to the troubles and disappointments in your life, and yes to a whole new you. The best part is that it's absolutely free to you. In fact, your recruiter will walk you through the many benefits we offer to LE candidates. Once your affairs are settled, you'll be taken to our laboratory on Space Station Epsilon in orbit around Venus where you'll be taken through the protocols to bring out the very best latent skills and abilities you never knew that you possessed. I encourage you to take part in this exciting program and discover all that you can become."

The video ended, and Mitch's chair returned to the normal sitting position. He looked over at Sergeant Lopez who smiled invitingly, as if he had just offered Mitch a billion dollars.

"What did you think?" he asked.

"I think it sounds too good to be true," Mitch said. "What's the catch?"

"No catch," the sergeant replied. "In exchange for the LE protocols, you must agree to a standard CMC enlistment. But with your background, you'll probably qualify for officer training shortly after you complete the basic training program on New Terra."

"Military service?" Mitch asked. He wasn't opposed to the idea or even the danger he knew that was inherent to joining the Colonial Marines, but he didn't like the idea of being locked into a career for several years.

"Trust me," Lopez said, "if the protocols take, you'll want to do something physically challenging. They don't call it super serum for nothing, if you know what I mean."

"What do you mean *if* they take? I've heard that some people die."

"The protocols can be intense," Lopez said. "No pain, no gain, my friend. But the results are spectacular."

"What other benefits are there?"

"We want you to leave Earth with no debts. We'll pay them off for you, up to half a million dollars, with the remainder held in escrow for you."

"Debts?" Mitch asked. "I have a mortgage."

"You're married," Lopez said. "I ran your financials already. We'll pay off the credit cards, and get your mortgage caught up. After that, you can decide how much to leave your wife, if anything at all."

"When would I leave?" Mitch asked.

"I can have you on a shuttle to Epsilon Station tomorrow," Lopez said. "Unless you want more time. The payments to your creditors go out when you report here for enlistment."

"Tomorrow works," Mitch said. "Where do I sign?"

"Follow me, Mr. Murphy. We'll do the paperwork and have you on your way."

He signed no less than forty electronic disclosures. And didn't bother reading any of them. It was as if someone had given him a get-out-of-jail-free card. Yes, he had lost his job. Yes, his wife was cheating on him. But in one fail swoop, the CMC was removing him from those painful realities and giving him a new shot at life. Mitch didn't care if the LE protocols failed. He could die knowing that he wasn't a burden to Megan.

It was late afternoon when he got home, but much earlier than he normally arrived. There was no evidence in the apartment of the man Megan was cheating on him with. And Mitch really didn't want to know who it was. All he cared about was saying his goodbyes. He sent his parents an email. Perhaps they would miss him, and regret his decision, but Mitch hadn't been close with them since marrying Megan. They hadn't approved of her and weren't supportive of him moving to the city. Over the years, their relationship had become perfunctory, just a card on his birthday, an email at Christmas.

It was almost dark when Megan arrived home. By that point, Mitch had already packed his bags. He wouldn't need much once he reached Epsilon Station, but he didn't want to leave Megan burdened with his belongings. He had a change of clothes and a few keepsakes in his satchel. Everything else had already been taken to goodwill. When Megan got home the disappointment on her face was obvious, but Mitch didn't care. He hopped up and gave her a hug. She was stiff and eager to pull away.

"Let's go to dinner," he said.

"What?"

"Dinner," Mitch said. "I'm hungry."

He had already checked his bank account. The severance pay had gone through the banking system. It wasn't much, but it was more than enough to keep Megan going for a while. Mitch had decided to use some of the half-a-million bonus to pay their mortgage for six months. That would be enough time for Megan to get it sold. The money in their joint checking from his severance package would be enough to buy food and pay the utilities for a few months. After that, she was on her own, but he decided that it was more than enough considering Megan's behavior.

"What are you doing home, Mitch?" Megan asked.

"I have good news. Let's go celebrate."

"What?" she asked suspiciously.

Maybe she was being paranoid, or maybe she was suspicious because she felt guilty about her illicit behavior. Mitch knew she wouldn't be happy about him leaving her, and he didn't want to endure an ugly fight, hence the idea of going out for dinner. She had never liked making a scene in public, and he had every intention of using that weakness to his advantage.

"I'll tell you over drinks at La Trattoria," he said. "I've already called ahead. Let's go."

"I don't know, Mitch, I've had a long day," she said.

He was prepared for her to resist and wasn't above simply emailing her the news that he had left the planet. But he wanted to see her face when he told her he was leaving.

"I understand," he replied. "But you can't deny that going out with me would be better than cooking something here. The fridge is nearly empty anyway. Come on, let's go. We don't have to stay out late."

"Fine," she relented. "Just let me get a shower first."

"Can't," Mitch said, knowing that if she saw the tiny space in their shared closet where his clothes had been she would know something was wrong. "I called ahead, remember? They're already expecting us. Let's just go."

She wasn't happy but didn't resist when he took her hand and led her toward the door of their apartment. He locked it for the last time but didn't bother looking at the small abode before leaving. There were so few good memories in the home, which had been a financial weight around his neck from the moment they had bought it. Instead, he walked away feeling light, as if that weight of being behind on his payments was finally gone. For the first time in a really, really long time, he felt a spring in his step.

"What's your news?" Megan asked as they rode the elevator down to the lobby of their building.

"It's a surprise," he said.

"I don't like surprises," she snapped. "You know that."

"It's good news, I promise," he assured her.

La Trattoria was only a few blocks away. They walked. She didn't cling to him the way some couples did. And they didn't talk about anything important along the way. He did ask what she had been up to. She gave him a list of things, half of which weren't true. He knew she hadn't gone shopping that morning since he had been at home and seen exactly what she was up to.

At the restaurant they ordered drinks. She had a glass of white wine, he had a rum and soda. Normally, he hated buying cocktails at restaurants. The drinks were ridiculously overpriced, but he made no comment and even ordered an appetizer of roasted Brussel sprout chips with a fancy sauce drizzle. For dinner, he was having lobster risotto with beef tenderloin medallions and a side of steamed vegetables.

"Seriously?" Megan asked when he tapped the order into the tabletop touchscreen ordering system.

"Yes," he said. "I'm hungry."

"That's one of the priciest things on the menu," she whispered. "I thought we were behind on the bills."

"We were," he said. "But we're not anymore. Get whatever you want."

She ordered a salad, probably just to be obstinate. Mitch didn't care. With every passing moment, he felt better, lighter, freer, and happier. Not that he wouldn't miss Megan or grieve that she had cheated on him. There was pain coming, but he was focused only on the freedom of the moment. For the first time that he could remember, he had found a way out from under the crushing pressure of life. And the relief was so great he was almost giddy.

"What is going on?" she asked quietly.

Megan didn't want to be overheard. She worked hard to maintain the illusion that she had her life all together. But Mitch knew better. He saw her without makeup and knew she sometimes wore a tight-fitting body suit under her clothes to help hold in her stomach. He also knew that the marriage she had pushed so hard for in college was just another false front, a façade to hide her infidelity.

"I got a promotion," he said simply.

"What? You got a promotion at work?"

"Sort of," he said. "They let me go."

Megan stiffened, her face turning slightly red. "You got... fired?" she demanded.

"Yep," Mitch said. "It was terrifying at first. But then I came home."

Her eyes narrowed, and the red flush intensified on her face. She leaned toward him.

"Not here," she said.

"I have nothing to say, Megan," he told her. "But I did have a revelation."

"I won't discuss it."

"Good, just listen," he told her as a short droid delivered their appetizer.

Mitch snatched one of the chips from the bowl. It was drizzled with a sweet glaze, while the crunchy Brussels sprout leaves were covered with salt. He popped it into his mouth and enjoyed the delicious contrast of flavors.

"I don't know what you think you know," Megan said, "but you need to rein yourself in."

"I was there," Mitch said. "I saw it all. But that's not what we're celebrating."

"You're losing it."

"Actually, I'm in control for once," he assured her. "Things are going to get better for both of us."

"No," she said in a furious whisper. "You don't get to decide that for the both of us."

"It's already done. I joined the CMC today. I'm leaving tomorrow."

"You're leaving?" she said, louder than she meant to. Her voice was strained, and she leaned forward, her hands gripping the sides of the table. "You're leaving me? Why? What do you think I did?"

"I think you're cheating on me," he told her. "I saw you in our shower with him, Megan. But I'm not mad at you. I know I'm not the man I was in college. Life has beaten me down and I quit being the man you needed a long time ago. For that, I'm very, very sorry."

"So, you're just running away? You can't do that, Mitch. We have obligations."

"Which I have taken care of. Tomorrow at nine a.m. the mortgage will be caught up, and the credit card bills will be paid off."

"What?"

"Part of the incentive program," Mitch explained. "I'm also making sure the mortgage is paid for the next six months. There's money in our account for you too. Enough to get by for the next couple of months. That's plenty of time to get the apartment on the market and maybe get yourself a job. I've already signed a release, so the house is all yours. Whatever you want to do, you can do it."

"I don't understand what you're telling me. You joined the CMC? That's Colonial Marines, right?"

"That's right."

"You're really leaving the planet?"

"Tomorrow."

"And they paid you, Mitch. They paid you."

"I'm going into the Latent Tech's enhancement program. You've seen the commercials."

Her eyes got big and she shook her head. "No. No that's not okay, Mitch. You know what they do to people. Are you crazy?"

"I don't really have anything left to lose," he said. "You don't love me anymore, Megan. I don't have a job, and I don't have prospects. We're behind the eight ball here. Even if I could get another job, we can't keep the house. Either way, you've got to find a job. At least we didn't have children."

"No, I don't want you to leave, Mitch," she argued quietly. "I know things have been off, but we can come back from this."

"I don't want to," he said. "This is it. The final meal. Let's go out on a high note."

She sat back and there were tears in her eyes. The serving droid returned with their food. She didn't touch the salad, but Mitch ate his dinner with gusto.

"This is delicious. You want a bite?" he asked.

She shook her head. "I can't believe you're leaving me."

"I'm not leaving you alone," he said.

"That hurts," she responded.

"I know it, and I'm sorry. But we both know this is the best thing."

"I don't know anything of the kind."

"You're going to be fine. I've seen to that. As soon as I arrive at the recruiting station tomorrow it's all official. It'll be the same as if I died. Our marriage will be dissolved and you can move on with your life. No more sneaking around. No more fighting. Find someone who makes you happy, Megan. That's all I ever wanted for you."

He pulled his wedding band from his finger. It wasn't worth much, but the gold had some value. He slid it across the tabletop toward Megan. She looked at it for a moment, not moving. Suddenly, he pushed back from the table. Her demeanor changed without warning.

"I hate you," she snapped.

"What?"

"I hate you for doing this to me."

"Okay," Mitch said, not sure how else to respond.

"I wasted ten good years of my life on you. I dropped out of college so we could get married."

"That was your idea," he told her. "I promised you I would wait."

"And we both know that you wouldn't have," she snapped. "Now, I have to find a job and some way to support myself. That's the coward's way out of a relationship, Mitch."

"I thought it was the chivalrous thing to do," he replied, feeling a rising sense of anger. "I'm not holding anything against you."

"You made every decision without me. Then you brought me here so I couldn't fight for my marriage."

It was Mitch's turn to lean close and speak softly. "You had another man in our home, Megan. I think you quit fighting for our marriage the moment you agreed to cheat on me."

"Bastard," she snarled.

In an uncharacteristic move, she stood up so fast her chair toppled over, and everyone looked at her. She threw her napkin onto her untouched food and stormed away. Mitch was shocked, but he noticed that she had taken the ring. Soon, the other diners returned to eating their meals as if nothing had ever happened. And Mitch finished his meal, although he didn't taste it. When he finished, he paid the tab and left the restaurant. Megan was gone, and he didn't try to find her. It was clear what she thought of him. And while he felt like he had done right by her, despite her infidelity, he still felt guilty. Worst of all, he knew he would never see her again. The life he had lived for thirty-three years was over. There was no looking back. It was time to train his eyes on what lay ahead, whether for good or for ill.

ALSO BY TOBY NEIGHBORS

End Times

The Four Horsemen

Surviving Wormwood

Wizard Rising

Magic Awakening

Hidden Fire

Crying Havoc

Fierce Loyalty

Evil Tide

Wizard Falling

Chaos Descending

Into Chaos

Chaos Reigning

Chaos Raging

Controlling Chaos

Killing Chaos

Elder Wizard

Lorik

Lorik the Protector

Lorik the Defender

We Are The Wolf

Total Allegiance

Kestrel Class

Jump Point

Gravity Flux

Modulus Echo

Zero Friction

Planet Fall

Charter

Jack & Roxie

My Lady Sorceress

The Man With No Hands

ARC Angel

Battle ARC

Broken Crucible

Hidden Kingdom

War INC

Carthage Prime

Cronus Team

Skandia Seven

Mercurial

Magnificus Prime

Incursio

Merlin Appears

Runners

Survivors

Evolving Threat

Lingering Threat

Latent Prowess

Gravity Masters

Gravity Storm

With Pete Garcia

Apocalypse One Percenters

www.ingramcontent.com/pod-product-compliance
Lightning Source LLC
LaVergne TN
LVHW091120080826
845145LV00008B/1985

* 9 7 8 1 9 5 2 2 6 0 8 0 3 *